William Nicholson is thay *Shadowlands*, wb . . . . . .ng Anthony Hopkins, i . wi . . . . . y. He has been the screenwr . . . . .ong them *Gladiator*. He is also . . . . . . .ining author of the bestselling trilogy of novels for children, *The Wind on Fire*. His new novel, *The Trial of True Love*, is now available from Doubleday.

William Nicholson lives in Sussex. Visit the author's website on <u>www.williamnicholson.com</u>

Acclaim for *The Society of Others*

'This extraordinary book, a sort of wild combination of Kafka and *The Catcher in the Rye* whirls its catatonically dysfunctional hero into a maelstrom of violence and danger to learn from oppressed strangers what really matters in a human life, and to face the most terrifying of interrogators, the self. The reader will not escape unchanged'
Jill Paton Walsh

'Exciting, funny, wise and beautifully written . . . Nicholson writes with such panache that *The Society of Others* transcends genres: it entertains us while it reflects with great profundity on the human condition – [Nicholson] has to my mind established himself with this first work of adult fiction as one of the best novelists around'
Piers Paul Read, *Spectator*

'Part philosophical treatise, part spy story, part reflection on loyalty and statehood . . . There are echoes of Albert Camus in Nicholson's wonderfully perceptive story . . . displays the full range of the exceptional talents of the creator of *Shadowlands* . . . It is thrilling in every sense, but also hypnotic, fast-moving and intellectually challenging and, as

it twists and turns, leaves you confused, uncertain, even uncomfortable and yet utterly hooked. A philosophical masterclass, it is quite staggeringly good'
Geoffrey Wansell, *Daily Mail*

'An intriguing story, a suburban drama that quickly unfolds into a surreal tale with big ideas and meaning . . . thought-provoking' *Daily Mirror*

'*The Society of Others* is a novel that demands attention. William Nicholson is someone we are going to hear a good deal more about' *Catholic Herald*

'A baffling, staggering, grandly ambitious work . . . quite remarkable. It should be cliché-ridden, and yet it's enlightening; it should be laughable, and yet it's chilling. And boy, does he nag us with some big questions . . . a vision that highlights the intellectual vacuum we may be heading towards now' *Time Out*

'Nicholson describes it as "a thriller about the meaning of life", and that's pretty accurate . . . A genuinely thought-provoking read' *Mail on Sunday*

'Urgent, spontaneous and exhilarating' *Sunday Telegraph*

'Thought-provoking and multi-layered . . . a modern day fable, written in the style of a fast-paced thriller' *Yorkshire Evening Post*

By the same author

THE WIND ON FIRE TRILOGY:
THE WIND SINGER
SLAVES OF THE MASTERY
FIRESONG
THE TRIAL OF TRUE LOVE

THE SOCIETY OF OTHERS

William Nicholson

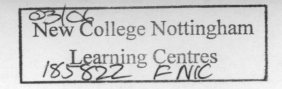
THE SOCIETY OF OTHERS
A BLACK SWAN BOOK : 0 552 77202 X

Originally published in Great Britain by Doubleday,
a division of Transworld Publishers

PRINTING HISTORY
Doubleday edition published 2004
Black Swan edition published 2005

1 3 5 7 9 10 8 6 4 2

Set in 11/15pt Melior by
Falcon Oast Graphic Art Ltd.

Black Swan Books are published by Transworld Publishers,
61–63 Uxbridge Road, London W5 5SA,
a division of The Random House Group Ltd,
in Australia by Random House Australia (Pty) Ltd,
20 Alfred Street, Milsons Point, Sydney, NSW 2061, Australia,
in New Zealand by Random House New Zealand Ltd,
18 Poland Road, Glenfield, Auckland 10, New Zealand
and in South Africa by Random House (Pty) Ltd,
Endulini, 5a Jubilee Road, Parktown 2193, South Africa.

Printed and bound in Great Britain by
Cox & Wyman Ltd, Reading, Berkshire.

Papers used by Transworld Publishers are natural, recyclable
products made from wood grown in sustainable forests. The
manufacturing processes conform to the environmental
regulations of the country of origin.

THE SOCIETY OF OTHERS

1

I'm writing this by the light of a new day, with a pen on paper, the old way. No seamless corrections possible here. I want to see my first thoughts, and the words I cross out, and the words I choose to replace them. First thoughts are usually lies. Vicino says, Write something about yourself, then write the opposite. Then open your mind to the possibility that the second statement is true.

I'm not a bad person. I'm a bad person.

I didn't mean to kill the man in the reading room. I did mean to kill the man in the reading room.

What happened afterwards wasn't my fault, don't blame me. It was my fault. Blame me.

So this is the story of how everything changed. I'm not going to tell you my name. If you want a name, use your own.

Begin with a day picked at random, recalled without

hindsight. I must do my best to make you understand what I was, because only then will you understand what I have become. The operation has been a complete success, but, as they say, the patient died.

On this random day from all that time ago, longer ago than yesterday, I'm sitting alone in my room, the blind down over the window and the door locked. There's music playing to which I am not listening. The television is on, with no sound. I'm not watching. It's just there like the crack of light on the windowsill and the pressure in my bladder that tells me I need to piss. Maybe I'll go soon. I'm doing nothing in particular. I do nothing most days. You could say it's what I do, like it's my occupation. This is not a problem. I don't want anything. I have the animal needs like you do, to eat and excrete, to mate and to sleep, but as soon as the needs are met they go away, and everything's the way it was before. That stuff is necessary. We're not talking desire.

I don't even want money. What's the point? You see something you want to buy, you get excited about having it, you buy it, the excitement fades. Everything's the way it was before. I've seen through that game. They make you want things so they get your money. Then they take your money and then they've got it, and what do they do? They use it to buy things someone else has made them want. For a few moments they think they're happy, and then it all fades and everything's the way it was before. How stupid can you get? It's like fish. Fish swim about all day finding food to give them energy to swim about all day. It makes me laugh. These people who hurry about all day making money to sell each other things. Anyone with eyes to see could tell them their lives are meaningless and they aren't getting any happier.

My life is meaningless. I'm not getting any happier.

My late father says, 'Your mother tells me you spend all day shut up in your room.'

I say, 'She does not lie.'

He says, 'There's a big wide world out there. You're not going anywhere so long as you stay shut up in your room.'

I say, 'There's nowhere to go.'

He hates that. My negative attitude. I could tell him he's not going anywhere either. But why pop his balloon?

I like my room. I said before I don't want anything, but this isn't entirely true. I want my own room. I don't much care what's in it so long as it has a door I can shut and lock so people don't come asking me to do things. I expect maybe I'll spend the rest of my life in my room, and at the end I'll just die here and no one will find me and that's just fine with me.

This big wide world: first of all, it's not so big and wide. Really the world is only as big as your experience of it, which is not big at all. And what sort of world is it? I would characterise it as remote, uninterested, unpredictable, dangerous, and unjust.

When I was small I thought the world was like my parents, only bigger. I thought it watched me and clapped when I danced. This is not so. The world is not watching and will never clap. My father doesn't get this, he's still dancing. It makes me quite sad to see him.

Cat says my world view lacks depth and is merely bitterness. I dispute this. I feel no bitterness. I see things as they are. Nature is selfish. All creatures kill to survive. Love is a mechanism to propagate the species. Beauty is a trick that fades. Friendship is an arrangement for mutual advantage. Goodness is not rewarded, and evil is not punished. Religion is superstition. Death is annihilation. And as for God, if he exists at all he stopped caring for humankind centuries ago. Wouldn't you?

So why leave my room?

My education, such as it was, has ended. I have graduated. I'm supposed to be excited about this. My late father has put aside some money for me, quite a lot, a thousand pounds, so that I can have one last great adventure before real life begins. What kind of sales pitch is that? I mean, real life, *bonjour tristesse*. Appreciate the gesture, but truthfully there's nowhere I want to go and nothing I want to do.

For as long as I can remember I've been at some kind of school. I don't believe I learned anything at all. It was like half-listening to the safety announcement, the kind they give you on planes before take-off. The voice says this is really important, and to please listen carefully, but you still don't listen because it's not going to happen, and if it does you're dead anyway. However I admit now when I look back that the class system gave life a shape. One year followed the next, and without any decisions having to be made on my part I moved up from one class to the next, as if I was climbing a giant staircase. Now here I am at the top, and before me lies what is laughingly called the real world.

I am in the process of not applying for jobs. I'm thinking of becoming a journalist, or possibly a film director. It's hard to decide. Journalists meet a lot of interesting people and get to travel and do their work in short bursts, which means they don't get bored. Film directors spend years on one project and have a seriously bad time if it fails but they get to meet attractive young women and eat location catering. So it's hard to decide.

I'm joking of course. I have a not impressive degree from a not famous college in a not useful subject which I have already entirely forgotten.

'There are any number of jobs out there you could do,' says my father, looking at me with faux-sprightly eyes. Despite or perhaps because of the fact that he left us, he knows it's vital that he does nothing to undermine my self-confidence. If you believe in yourself you can do anything. That's what my father believes. It's the post-Christian faith that has replaced faith in the resurrection. Now each of us is supplied with our own personal resurrection. We get to pump ourselves up out of the tomb.

I don't disagree with this. I just ask: why bother?

Anyway my father points out to me all the great opportunities there are out there for me, but neglects to name them. I fill in the gaps. I could join a corporation and sell things I don't want to have myself to people who don't need them. I could be a teacher and tell things I don't want to know to people who don't want to hear. I could be a soldier and kill people. That would be alright if it weren't dangerous.

My friend Mac is going to be an aid worker in Nepal. This is hilarious because all the aid they need in Nepal is getting out from under all the people like Mac who've gone there to find meaning in their lives. They've sucked all the available meaning up and now there's none left for the Nepalese, who have nothing to do except carry explorers' bags up mountains and sell them drugs. Mac says he doesn't care, at least he'll see the mountains. I tell him the thing about a mountain is when you're on it you don't see it. You need to be far away to see a mountain. Like at home, looking at a postcard. Mac says you stand on one mountain and look at the next mountain. I say, Then what? Mac says, You're a real wanker, you know that? Yes, Mac, I'm a real wanker. The genuine article. A simple pleasure that does no harm to man or beast. Be grateful.

So here I am in the process of not applying for jobs

because the only jobs that would take me are the jobs I do not wish to take. It's exactly like sex. The women you really want are the ones who don't really want you. This is not a coincidence. Things that are out of reach are desirable precisely because there's no chance you'll get what you want. Getting what you want is to be avoided at all costs. Ask for the moon.

You may be wondering how I propose to live, given that I have no means of earning my living. I propose to be a parasite. To be precise, I propose to live in symbiotic parasitism. My host and provider is of course my father. My father makes a lot of money, he can afford it. I'm not expensive to run. And if you're thinking, Why should he keep you? I reply, Because he asked.

Think about it. I wouldn't be at this party if he and my mother hadn't invited me. Between them they hauled me off some cloud where I was peacefully bothering nobody, and fixed me up with a helpless needy baby body, and made me dependent on them. They never said, Here's the deal, we look after you till you're not cute any more, then you're on your own. If they had I would have said thanks but no thanks. I'll stay incorporeal on my cloud. It was all their idea. So now they've got me.

Don't get me wrong, this isn't about what happened between the two of them. That's their business. My mother's totally cool about it apart from calling my father 'the late' which is relatively modest in the retaliation stakes. You won't hear me sadding on about broken homes either because absolutely nothing is broken and everyone's good friends with everyone and my mother and Gemma are like sisters, particularly now that Gemma is pregnant, though with a considerable age gap. So I come from an expanded home. I like Gemma too, despite not knowing what relation she is to me, maybe step-partner? Also I admit it kind of throws me that she's so attractive, especially when I catch myself looking longer than is strictly polite at her mouth.

My father of course is guilty which is not my problem, and if it makes him more inclined to go on supporting me, why should I complain? It's not such a bad deal for him. A small financial outlay buys him the comforting sense that he's doing his duty. So don't give me a hard time about not getting a job.

This morning, on the day before it begins, I have a premonition. This is not as significant as it sounds. I'm always having premonitions. Like when I see a nice-looking girl coming up an escalator towards me, say, I'll have this premonition that she'll smile at me and I'll get off at the bottom and go up her side and she'll be waiting. Or I get a message to ring home and I have this premonition that a jumbo jet has crashed on our house and all my family are dead and I'm alone in the world and a homeless wanderer. None of these things ever happen but the premonition happens, so maybe the wonders and disasters are still to come, stacked up somewhere in my future. Maybe some time soon they'll all happen at once, in a sequence of rapid-fire explosions like a firework.

This particular premonition is that someone is calling me. I listen, and hear nothing. So then it seems to me not that someone is calling me, but that someone is wanting me. I think about it some more, and realise there isn't a someone, only the wanting. So this is my premonition: I am wanted. This is a new one on me. There's nothing to get excited about in it, so I forget about it. But it doesn't forget about me. It comes back, from time to time, like something I'm supposed to do but have forgotten. It annoys me.

My mother's upset because I don't come down for meals any more. It's not the food I mind, it's her face watching me as if it hurts her just to see me eat. Or not eat. I'm not much of an eater. I prefer to sort it out for myself, without all the fuss and conversation. So long as there's bread and cheese or a bowl of cereal I'm okay. It turns out to be easier to eat at night, when they're all asleep. I don't even switch on the kitchen lights. I just leave the fridge door open and eat by the light that comes out from behind the eggs.

Cat found me eating like this the other night. She was out late with her boyfriend doing I hate to think what and she came creeping in and saw me and said, 'You are so sad.' I just looked at her and went on eating. I could have said, Oh yes, and you're having such a great life? I know that so-called boyfriend of hers. He's famous for going out with plain girls because they fuck on the first date. He's an animal. Cat says she doesn't care and anyway all men are the same including me. This is true. I have a so-called girlfriend who I only want to see for sex, though I go along with the rest of it for the sake of appearances. She doesn't know this. That is, she knows it very well, but I never say it and she never asks and I suppose she must be getting something out of it or she wouldn't go on seeing me. Her name is Am. I think she's disappointed in me.

Actually I'm a disappointment to everyone who cares about me. Both my parents are disappointed in me. My grandfather is disappointed in me. My godmother Sheila who never forgets my birthday and keeps photographs of me as a baby is disappointed in me. They used to want me to have hobbies and ambitions and a great object in life. Now they just want me to get a job. What can I say? It hasn't happened. I quite liked films for a while, and they all thought this would give me a direction in life. But my interest waned.

My mother says, 'All I want is for you to be happy. I can't believe you're happy living like this.'

What I want to say to her, and to my father and my grandfather and Sheila, is: Why must I be happy for you? It's like a weight they've tied onto my back, this requirement that I be happy. It's not for me, it's for

16

them. They want to stop feeling they've failed with me.

What I actually say is, 'I'm alright.'

They have failed with me. Looking at me in that wounded worried way won't change anything. It just makes me not want to make eye contact. I'm so tired of being a disappointment to everybody. Why can't they all go and care about someone else, and leave me alone?

So now you hate me. That's alright with me. Only, ask yourself, what do you care? I mean, think about it. You don't hate me really, you're just afraid you'll turn out like me. Maybe you have already.

Actually I could be worse. I'm not aggressive or rude. I spend very little money. I keep myself clean. I'm polite to my mother's friends. I don't come home drunk, or take hard drugs, or smoke cigarettes. Naturally I smoke a little dope from time to time, but not as much as you might think. My inertia is nothing to do with drugs. It springs from the true source, the mother lode, a clear-eyed awareness of the nature of existence.

Life is hard and then you die.

I sprayed it on the glass of my window using a spray can. Like graffiti. I used to lie on my bed looking at the wobbly letters dark against the dull white sky thinking, That's just about it. That's how it is. That won't change. This is the closest I get to satisfaction.

The thing about the thousand pounds is my father has given it to me in cash. Fifty-pound notes and twenty-pound notes. There's nothing I want to spend it on but I like having it.

'Don't do something sensible with it,' he said, giving me that crinkly smile he does. 'Do something crazy. Something magnificent and crazy.'

I get a pack of Blu-Tack and stick the notes onto the walls of my room like a frieze. He'll never know. He never comes into my room even when he's round here. This is supposed to be giving me respect and my own space and so forth but really it's about not seeing how he's failed me. When Am sees the row of fifty-pound notes she's impressed. She says I'm not like anyone else she knows and this is why she's attracted to me. She says I'm strange and moody and she's sure I'll be famous some day. I say I don't want to be famous, I just want to be real. That impresses her too. So I say why not do it now, but she says it's the wrong time for her and we can always just talk. So she talks and I look out of the window where there are pigeons fooling about and then it turns out she's crying.

'What's the matter?' I say.

'I feel like I can't reach you,' she says.

'No one can reach anyone,' I say.

So she kisses me really passionately and then says, 'Did I reach you?'

What can I say? Everyone lies, out of kindness and pity and cowardice.

'Sure.'

She looks at me with her big blue eyes all wet round the edges for what seems like several hours.

'What would you say if I told you I wanted to end it?'

'End what?'

'Us.'

'Do you?'

'What would you say if I did?'

These stupid conversations.

'I am what I am, Am.'

'Yes.' Long sigh. 'I know it.' Longer sigh. 'I should get out, but I can't.'

If we're not going to do it, I'm thinking, you might as well go. I don't say it. People never say those things. They should.

I say, 'I'm kind of tired, Am.'

'You're always tired. What is it you do that makes you always tired?'

'Nothing. I'm tired by nothing. Nothing exhausts me.'

She thinks it's a joke but it isn't.

Then as she's looking at me she slips into this parallel universe or something because for a moment she seems quite different. It's like seeing a small child hiding in her face, peeping out, not knowing I can see her. This small child is so lovely and so unaware that

19

the sight of her makes me catch my breath in surprise. I've forgotten that people can be so without guile. She's so fragile, so bound to be hurt. I almost cry out loud.

'What?' says Am.

'You,' I say.

'What about me?'

'You're beautiful.'

For me beauty isn't just a look, it's a feel. I expect it's like that for everybody. Marilyn Monroe isn't the most beautiful woman ever, actually she's got quite a pudgy face if you look at unposed photographs, but she's got this feel to her that says, I want to please you more than anything. That's what does it. And actually I personally believe that's the lost child in her reaching out to be hugged, but because she's a grown woman it comes out as sex. But then I have a thing about lost children. There was a documentary once on TV about state orphanages in China where tiny children are abandoned to die. I only watched about five minutes of it and then switched over to the news, where people were being blown up in some faraway war. I can handle adults destroying each other. But those babies in unvisited cots.

Am is crying again.

'What now?'

'It's not fair,' she says. 'I'd just decided not to love you.'

2

So it turns out Gemma's had her baby and it's a boy and everyone's doing fine and he's called Joey. This happens to be what you call baby kangaroos but it takes all sorts. Joey is coming round to our place to meet us on this day that coincides with my grandfather's birthday so the plan is the one celebration will do for both. This may sound cheap but is actually good thinking because everyone will be there, except possibly myself. I don't do family gatherings.

'You have to come down,' says my mother. 'Your father would be so hurt.'

That's my mother for you, protecting the man who dumped her for a younger prettier woman, and now there's even a cuckoo baby to fatten on the love that should be hers. Why doesn't she hate him? Actually I know perfectly well. You can't hate my father, he's one of the world's few good men. What do you do with a good man who hurts you but doesn't mean to? You hurt but you don't hate.

So I come down to the party making sure to be late only to find that Joey and Gemma and my father haven't showed yet because Joey hasn't woken up. This is terrific. I'll try that one myself. Sorry I'm late, folks, but my sleep is more important than your party.

'Hail, holy light, offspring of heaven's first-born!' says my grandfather, holding up both hands like a priest giving a blessing. This is his jokey manner. I don't know why he has to talk in quotations the whole time, maybe he can't think of any words of his own.

'Happy birthday, grandpa.'

It's his birthday, he's seventy or eighty or ninety. I pour myself a tumbler of Bellini, which is the drink my family makes for parties. It's this fizzy dry Italian wine called prosecco mixed with peach juice, two-thirds wine and one-third juice, and is quite excellent.

Bellini, the painter it's named after, is also by way of being a family favourite because he painted this Venetian doge who looks exactly like my grandfather, except my grandfather doesn't wear the wacky hat with the strings and the hump at the back.

My mother comes over with a loaded plate of food.

'Don't just drink, darling. They'll be here soon.'

This is a sequitur?

She's put a whole lot of stuff aside for me on this plate. Little sausages on sticks, chicken drumsticks, carrot sticks, cheese sticks, everything sticks. You eat with your fingers and it saves washing up. There are people who actually think about these things.

My godmother Sheila's here. She's waiting for me to say hello.

'Hello,' I say.

'You get taller all the time,' she says. 'When will it stop?'

'I think it's stopped.'

A lot of people tell me I'm tall as if I should be proud, but it's not like I've been working at it. Sheila is small.

'You look exactly like Salvator Rosa's self-portrait,' she tells me. 'He's wildly dark and handsome and sexy. So that's a compliment.'

'Oh. Okay.'

'*Aut tace aut loquere meliora silentio.* Either be silent or let your speech be better than silence.'

She's quoting the inscription that forms part of the Salvator Rosa self-portrait. As you can tell, we go in for this game. You too can pose for an Old Master. Fun for all the family.

I say, 'Right.'

'There. You see.'

Not much you can add after that.

'So are you excited about having a new baby brother?'

'Palpitating.'

She raises her eyebrows.

'So. What are you doing with yourself these days?'

'Oh. This and that. You know.'

She smiles at me. Her smile is meant to say: I'll never disapprove of you however much of a failure you make of your life. This is what they call unconditional love, and it's supposed to be what young people need. Well I'm here to tell you that what young people need is to be left alone. This unconditional-love act is just another scam. Nothing's free. Nobody butters your toast for the heck of it. The deal is I love you and you turn into this healthy well-balanced individual.

Sheila is the same age as my mother and she's just got this job as professor of history of art at somewhere university, which is a tremendous achievement and everyone's awestruck and impressed except that she's small and unmarried and childless and looks like a man.

'There,' said my mother when she heard. 'Sometimes the good people do come out on top.'

'Great,' I said. 'Good for Sheila.'

'She loves you so much, darling,' said my mother. 'Do drop her a line of congratulations.'

Sheila picked me out to love when I was born. I was too little to have any say in the matter. The general idea is I'll inherit her money when she dies. I don't like to seem ungrateful for the presents she's given me down the years, but this is all her idea not mine.

I'm not the only one who feels this way. My mother acts like she's doing Sheila a favour by lending me to her to love. I don't think she realises this. Things are complicated by the fact that my mother and Sheila joined the National Gallery as lowly researchers in the same year, and here's Sheila a professor and here's my mother still doing picture research for book publishers. That's because she stopped to have children, which means me and Cat, so somehow neither of them have got what they want and I'm supposed to make it up to them.

I meant to write that letter of congratulations but in the end I didn't.

'Well done on the job.'

'Thank you. I'm about to give my first series of lectures since the appointment. I'm terrified everyone will be sitting there thinking, Why her?'

They won't. They'll be thinking about what's for dinner.

My grandfather brings over dear old Emil to talk to me. Dear old Emil is a friend of my grandfather's from the days when they all lived in Prague or Budapest or Bucharest and had real suffering and acquired real wisdom in cafés and internment camps.

'Here is our young man,' says my grandfather. 'What bliss it was in that dawn to be alive, but to be young was very heaven!'

This as addressed to me is of course a criticism, since I come up short in the bliss department. But is it my fault? He grew up under a repressive regime where it was a radical act to look at a copy of *Playboy*. And this was before they started showing pubic hair. Some people have it handed to them on a plate.

Dear old Emil says to me, 'So, young man, what next?'

'I haven't decided, exactly.'

'Of course not! The world lies before you. You have no responsibilities. All is adventure.'

I'm supposed to be happy about this. All I want to do is go back to my room and lock the door.

'Right.'

He puts one arm in mine and leads me off into the hall. He has some dear old wisdom for me.

'Your father worries about you, you know.'

'Right.'

'But I tell him, don't worry. Your son is not you. He follows a different road.'

'Right.'

Emil is some kind of shrink. All those old guys who came out of Eastern Europe thinking *Playboy* was liberating turned themselves into shrinks.

'But may I ask you to do me a favour?'

He's whispering now. I can smell the guacamole dip on his breath.

'When he comes, say to him, six words.'

'Six words.'

'Say to him, dad, I love you, let me go.'

Seven words.

'Will you do that for me?'

'Okay.'

'Thank you.'

He squeezes my arm and we go back to the party. Cat finds me.

'Who rained on your parade?'

Apparently it shows on my face. Dear old Emil pisses me off with his all-you-need-is-love. Look at what happened to John Lennon and run that by me again. I'm not talking about getting shot dead. I'm talking about living in a hotel room and having Yoko Ono call out for hookers.

'Sod off, slag,' I say.

'Oh! Repartee!'

This is why I don't do family gatherings.

Now there's this great clattering in the hall which turns out to be the arrival of the baby-servicing equipment, followed by the baby. My father's head appears round the living-room door to say, 'Just putting on our bonnet.' Cat and I look at each other. This is not promising. This is a man who uses words for a living and he's losing it on the pronouns.

Then they come in. Gemma's holding the baby in what looks like embroidered wrapping paper and my father's coming behind like he's the gift-tag tied on with string. Everyone except me crowds round and looks down the hole in the wrapper and sees I imagine a baby much like any other but they profess astonished admiration. Gemma looks at them looking at her baby like she's a conqueror exacting tribute. She's had her shiny black hair cut short and actually looks terrific, her eyes have got even bigger, ditto her mouth. When my mother's turn comes to worship at the shrine I think how old she looks beside Gemma and how unfair it is, and I try to imagine what my mother's feeling and stop, because it's impossible. Then she comes over to me and takes my hand with this odd little smile and says:

'You will be nice, won't you, darling?'

That's what her mouth says. Her eyes are searching my face like she's counting my pores. Her eyes are saying: you were my little baby once. Where did you go?

My mother used to sing us songs on long car journeys. There's one called Waly Waly that ends:

> But had I wist, before I kissed,
> That love had been so ill to win,
> I had locked my heart in a case of gold
> And pinned it with a silver pin.

We have an unresolved problem, my mother and I. She minds about my happiness too much. She should mind about her own happiness instead. I have this fear that she wants me to be happy because she's not happy herself. This is bad news. Just about the only duty parents have towards their children, it seems to me, is to enjoy their life. After all, there they are in the prime of this life they've given us, and if they don't like it, what hope is there for us? Really if you're a parent you've got to be having a good time. And telling me that having children is the true happiness doesn't cut it at all. That just pushes the problem into the future. Someone somewhere has to be getting the benefit.

My mother loves art. I'm talking old art, Dutch seventeenth century most of all. When we were still too little to resist she took Cat and me to the National Gallery maybe a million times. She made up these games for us, like King Red, where we had to say why the red was where it was in the picture. There was always some red somewhere, only the painters chose very carefully where to put it because it was the king and bullied all the lower colours. Also there was Spot the Lion with St Jerome. There's enough St Jeromes in the National Gallery to sink a boat. They mostly wear red, and they mostly have beards, and they all have lions except one, and maybe that lion's hiding. In my favourite picture, where St Jerome's sitting in a study like on the bridge of a ship, the lion's sloping off to one side, getting the hell out of all those weird arches to run free over the distant green hills. That St Jerome hasn't got a beard, now that I think of it. Funny the things you remember. The hours I've spent pushing at those green ropes, wanting to feel the dark red wallpaper.

Now here's my mother spending all day in gloomy old libraries looking for pictures for books other people have written. I know she wishes she'd written the books herself. So secretly her life is a disappointment to her in several ways. I really hate that. The dwindling away of dreams.

So I pour myself another pint or two of Bellini and my mother goes off to hear what Sheila thinks of the baby and I look round and see my father looking at me. He has this wry smile on his face that says: I don't take myself seriously. Naturally it's a lie. My father's problem is he makes a lot of money doing something entirely invisible, which is writing screenplays. Years ago he wrote a stage play that was the imaginary trial of Judas, it's called *The Mercy Kiss* and it was a success and got made into a film and it's still the only thing he's ever done that anyone's heard of. In the family we call it The Messy Curse to show we're cool about success. People are nice to him and say, Oh yes, *The Mercy Kiss*, I saw that, it was so good, I loved it. But there hasn't been anything else since, only money.

There you go again. The dwindling away of dreams.

'This must all look quite strange to you,' he says.

'Everything looks strange to me,' I reply.

'Your brother. Your half-brother.'

'Half a brother. Bee-zarre.'

He smiles his smile.

'Gem wanted it so much.'

I am dumb. My father's speech is booby-trapped at every word. *Gem* wanted *it*? A baby can't be an it. But maybe he means motherhood, fulfilment, holding hands in the unbroken chain of generations, whatever it is that drives people against every sane self-interest to reproduce. He feels like he has to apologise to me. Mind you, as Cat pointed out to me when we first heard, this new arrival means we both get less money when he dies. Maybe none at all.

The truth is I don't care about that. I don't want his money. Or at least not much of it.

'You'll say hello, won't you? Gem would like it.'

'Yes. Of course.'

We're civilised in our family. Everyone gets on really well with everyone else. It's so much better for the children.

So I go to pay my respects and Gemma gives me this nervous smile which make me like her more.

'How was it?' I say, meaning the birth.

'Fucking agony,' she says. 'Don't do it.'

'Okay. I won't.'

I can see what my father sees in her. Now it's time to peer down the hole and greet the new prince. I'm doing this in an entirely neutral spirit of going with the flow and not rocking the family boat, so it comes as something of a shock to meet those wide-open dark dark eyes staring back up at me and to know without the possibility of any doubt that this baby hates me.

Who knew? I don't claim to be an expert on babies but there's all these plump Jesuses on Madonnas' laps in paintings and sometimes they look a little out of it, but they don't hate. I didn't even know babies could hate. I'd have said that was one of those things you learn later, after you get fucked up and betrayed by life in the customary manner.

'What's the matter?' says Gemma.

'He's frowning,' I say.

She takes a look.

'He does that when he's shitting,' she says. 'Six days old and all he does is eat and shit and sleep.' She looks at him proudly.

'He'll go far,' I say.

I don't tell her how the baby hates me. That's between him and me. Also to tell the truth I'm quite shaken by it. So I drink my Bellini up and leave the room, to go to have a piss and to regroup.

I don't go directly back to the party. I decide to take a short break. So I go to my room and lie down on my bed and look out of the window at the pigeons. These pigeons are forever flying down onto the ledge outside my window and then flying up onto the roof next door and then back to my ledge. What's going on? There's nothing to eat in either place. You'd think they'd stay put and conserve some energy.

Then this one pigeon looks at me through the window. I look at the pigeon and it looks back and I get this creepy feeling that it knows me. I don't go anywhere and the pigeon doesn't go anywhere and we look at each other and I feel that premonition again about being wanted, only this time it's the pigeon. The pigeon is calling me. The pigeon wants me to do something.

32

'What do you want me to do, bird?'

I say it out loud. Why not? There's only me and the pigeon to hear.

The pigeon gets up and flies away. That annoys me. I can see it, sitting on the roof ridge of the house next door, ignoring me. Well, I don't care.

Then it comes back. Only this time instead of flying down onto the window ledge it flies bang into the glass.

Thob! The sound is not as loud as I had been expecting.

How stupid can you get?

I can't help feeling it had intended to come into my room and tell me what it wanted me to do. Only now it's lying stunned in the gutter outside my window. Probably it's dead. I can see it lying there.

Life is hard and then you die.

So I open the window. The air is bitter cold outside. I reach down for the pigeon and take it in my hands. The puffy feathers are unexpectedly soft. I cradle the bird in my hands, and feel a tiny heartbeat. Then it begins to twitch, little involuntary movements, as if it has been dead but life is returning.

'Are you alive after all, bird?'

Suddenly it starts to thrash its wings. Then it bursts out of my hands and up into the white sky.

My empty hands feel cold.

I follow the bird's flight. It zigzags drunkenly over the neighbour's roof, swoops down almost to the gravel of the drive, and then climbs up, up, up, and flies away towards the railway line.

So it hasn't died. And it hasn't told me what it wants me to do. It has got away.

I go back to the party. Gemma's in the kitchen swabbing Joey down with my mother and Sheila and Cat in attendance. My father's talking with dear old Emil and I know from the way Emil looks at me as I come in that he's working this like a Yiddish matchmaker. So he shuffles off to sit with my grandfather and my father heads for me like a heat-seeking missile. Emil will have primed him with six words to say to me. It's a set-up. But it's not going to work because my father's said it all before and I'm not saying my six words.

'Emil's been telling me I'm a possessive father,' he says.

What did I tell you?

'How's that, dad? You're not exactly round much, and when you are, you're always telling me to get out.'

'That's what I thought. But Emil says I'm clinging on to you without realising it.'

'What does he know?'

'He can be very perceptive sometimes. Anyway, I have to let you go.'

'It's okay. I'm going.'

He looks surprised. I feel annoyed. I'd meant to make a bigger moment of this, but here it is trickling out as if it's Emil's idea.

'You're going?'

'Yes.'

'Where?'

'I thought I'd go to Nepal with Mac.'

His face clears. This is the sort of thing people like me are supposed to do when their father gives them a thousand pounds to have an adventure. So all at once he feels I'm normal after all.

'Good idea. Sounds great.'

It's not that great. It's also not true, but he doesn't need to know that. I'm going alright, but not to Nepal, and not with Mac. I made the decision all of five minutes ago, when I saw that pigeon fly off. I decided that was the pigeon's message to me, and it had made this really big effort to deliver the message, so I should do something about it.

The message was: get away.

My big news is round the family in no time, and everyone starts to beam. This is quite offensive in its way. Evidently they all thought I was sick or something and now it turns out I'm alright. Old Emil nods his head. He thinks he managed the whole business.

Sheila says, 'What's this about Nepal?'

'Somewhere different,' I say.

'Will you go overland? Do see Ephesus if you're crossing Turkey.'

'Okay.'

'Send me a postcard.'

'Sure.'

What is this thing about sending postcards? Back in the days before cheap travel I suppose it was quite a thrill to get a postcard with a picture of Vesuvius or something. Nowadays everyone's been there or seen it on TV and anyway the sender of the postcard came home weeks ago and showed you his ten thousand holiday photographs already.

My grandfather says, 'Then felt I like some watcher of the skies, when a new planet swims into his ken—'

Why does he think I want to hear his quotations? I haven't bought a ticket.

'Or like stout Cortez, when with eagle eyes he stared at the Pacific, and all his men—'

Cat comes over and says, 'You're not going to Nepal.'

'Looked at each other with a wild surmise, silent upon a peak in Darien.'

This seems to be it. My grandfather totters off.

'That's just bullshit,' says my sister.

'How would you know?'

'Mac would have told me.'

'I only decided today.'

'And anyway, Mac's already gone.'

'I'm meeting up with him in London.'

Cat stares at me suspiciously. She doesn't believe a word of it.

'Oh? So when do you go?'

'In the morning.'

This is my second surprise. It's even bigger than the first. My family go into meltdown. All this time they've wanted me out of my room and now I'm going they act like I'm about to die. Their idea of going somewhere is talking about it for weeks and making lists and going shopping for stuff and counting down to the day of departure. I hate all that. Even waiting till the morning makes me itchy. Either do it or don't do it.

My mother's having a spasm about inoculations. Apparently I'm going to die in India. What about all those Indians? They don't all die. Also I'm not that agitated about dying, to tell you the truth. I'd rather die now than live on into the dwindling away of dreams.

Only dear old Emil thinks my plan is okay because he thinks he made it all happen. He even gives me this dear old wink that says he knows my secret. I pretend not to see the wink. He doesn't know my secret. Only the pigeon knows.

So I'm going to get away.

I'm not showing it, but I'm actually almost excited. I had thought when my father gave me that money that I could escape the job problem by going somewhere, but I kept on failing to decide where. Every scheme collapsed under the weight of my lack of enthusiasm. Macchu Pichu, Goa, Bali, Kathmandu: how do you choose? Anyway I have a problem with choice. I'm better at having to put up with situations I haven't chosen. Once you choose, it's like if you don't like it, it's your own fault. Even catching a programme on TV is better for me if I'm for example in someone else's house and the TV's on and the other people are watching and I'm looking over their shoulders. Once I turn on my own TV in my own room to watch something I thought I wanted to watch, it's always a disappointment.

The breakthrough was this: I don't have to have a destination. I can get away without going anywhere. The pigeon didn't go anywhere. Just away.

You're thinking, how can you go away and not go somewhere? The answer is, you go, but you don't know where. That way when you do get somewhere, it's not your fault. If you don't like it, that's no big surprise, because why should you like it?

This strikes me as the cleanest, purest, lightest, leanest plan in all existence. No destination. No baggage. No expectation. No arrival. Journey without will. Roll like a pebble, fall like a leaf, sail like a cloud.

Don't ask me your questions. Don't suck me with your sad eyes. Don't burden me with your hopes. Look aside and talk among yourselves. Before you know it I'll be gone.

3

I'm sitting in the service station by the motorway servicing myself with a coffee and a Danish pastry, watching this young mother with two screaming kids and wanting to kill her. There's a boy of maybe six and a girl of maybe four and the mother's got chocolate bars in her bag that they want while she has a cup of tea. They scream for the chocolate bars and she screams back and they cry and she smacks them and they cry louder and she gives them chocolate. They gobble it up and scream for more, and it all happens again. I simply can't believe it. I'm watching small human creatures being systematically wrecked for life. She might as well just shoot them both now. But she's got this limitless supply of fun-size chocolate bars and they know it. They won't stop screaming until they've had them all, by which time they'll be so sick and smacked and weepy and snotty they'll wish they were dead.

Everyone in the place wishes they were dead already. There's a couple of women keep sneaking looks and wagging their heads, and a fat man in a ski jacket eating an all-day breakfast who glares at them, but nobody actually does anything. I'm ready to go and I've paid and everything and I'm actually heading on out when the screaming and smacking starts up again, and my feet turn about and carry me over to the table with the kids.

I squat down so I'm not towering over them and say, 'Hi.'

They're so surprised they stop screaming and stare at me with their big wet eyes. They have chocolate all over their faces as if they've been trying to push the chocolate bars through their pores.

'When I was your age,' I tell them, 'when my mother gave me a chocolate bar, I would first lick off the chocolate on the outside. That takes time. You have to go slow. Then I'd bite the inside part, in big chomping bites. That part goes fast. I loved to do that. Slow and licky, then fast and chompy.'

They're staring at me like I'm a visitor from a distant galaxy.

'You should try it.'

'You leave them alone.' Their mother thinks I'm molesting them.

'Madam,' I tell her. 'You're all they have in the world. You're their sun and their moon. They live for you and they'll die for you. Use your power gently.'

Then I stand up and leave.

I don't hear any more screaming as I go, but I'm not looking back. To tell you the truth I feel quite confused. I'm not at all sure why I did that. I just couldn't take it any more. Those scared chocolatey faces. Children aren't the problem. All they want is for someone to tell them they're doing okay. I've not forgotten that.

Outside it's raining. I pull up the hood of my coat and head past rubbish bins and petrol pumps to the slip road. There's another guy standing here hitching already. He's got no head covering and looks like he's drowning. I go past him with a nod and a grunt and take up a position about twenty metres beyond. That way he gets first shot at any lift. This is correct hitching etiquette since he was here first. However he looks insane with his long hair plastered to his head and I don't give him much chance.

So we stand in the rain, the other hitch-hiker and me, and cars come out of the service station and spray us with their tyres and speed off onto the motorway. The drivers don't look at us. They've seen us, you can tell that from the way they don't look at us. That really focused not-looking is a kind of looking. They're thinking, I don't have the time to pull up, and I'm not going where they want to go, and they're probably mad people anyway, let out of their padded cells to be cared for by the community that doesn't care. I don't mind. It's all true. Time is running out and there are mad people roaming the streets. Be afraid.

I am travelling light. I have a small canvas kit bag over one shoulder which contains a second pair of jeans, a second T-shirt, a second pair of socks, a navy-blue fisherman's jersey, and a wash-bag. No maps, no guide books, no mobile phone. Before leaving home I took my phone and called Am to tell her I was going, and when we were done, without ending the call, I dropped the phone down the lavatory and flushed it. It went down fine. These days phones are about the size of a turd. So I suppose it's working its way through the sewers to the sea, still listening out for Am's last words.

A big truck comes juddering by and I'm looking at its side which says Hilton & Son, the Complete Home Removal Service, and imagining them taking away the house along with the furniture, when I realise it's stopping. The other hitch-hiker comes running past me, because he's first in line, but the truck driver's waving him away and pointing at me.

'But I was here first,' protests the hitch-hiker.

'My cab,' says the driver, 'my rules.'

He beckons me.

'Jump up.'

I give a shrug of apology as I go by the other hiker. He turns away, bitter at the rejection.

'Fucking bum-bandit,' he says.

This is seriously not the right approach to hitching. You have to stay sunny. Let yourself get bitter and the bad vibrations stream out of you in psychic waves and nobody stops for you. However now is not the time to pass on my insight.

The driver has reached across and opened the door for me. It seems a long way up. As I climb into the cab I say, 'Thanks,' and he's the fat guy in the ski jacket from the service station.

'Where do you want to go?' he asks, putting the truck into gear again.

I've planned this moment carefully.

'I have options,' I say. 'Where are you headed?'

He says the name of some place, but at the same time the engine is roaring as he picks up speed on the slip road, and I don't catch it. As it happens this is not a problem.

'That's fine,' I say. 'Drop me off there.'

He throws me a quick look of surprise.

'Long journey,' he says.

'Let me pay something towards the diesel.'

You have to make the offer. They always say no, it's on the company bill, but it makes them feel you're not a total loser.

'I don't want payment in money.'

Ah. Maybe he is a fucking bum-bandit after all. I check him out as discreetly as possible. Not a big guy, but wide. Even so I calculate I can handle him.

'I like to talk,' he says.

I start to un-tense.

'About what?'

'Philosophy.'

Jesus in a jockstrap. I'd almost rather be buggered. Several hours listening to a lonely truck driver searching for the meaning of life is going to give me a serious crick in the neck.

'I don't know anything about philosophy.'

'Then isn't this your lucky day.'

I look round the cab, which is not so much a cab as a home. The part we're in is like the living room, with the windscreen playing the part of the TV. On a box between the front seats there's a small fridge and an electric kettle and a mug that's had tea in it. Behind our seats there's a bunk bed with blue check curtains that draw right across. There are even portraits on the walls, which are actually postcards of people who turn out to be great philosophers: Renée Descartes, Blaise Pascal, Emanuelle Kant. Fun names, fun people. There are books on the floor by my feet. *The Last Days of Socrates. The Social Contract. The World as Will and Idea.*

'These three-day jobs,' he says. 'You need someone to talk to.'

Three days. That means deep into Europe. I try to remember how long it took to drive to Venice that time. We stopped at Neuschwanstein to see the mad castle, which added a day. Truck drivers don't stop to do the sights. I could always ask again where we're going, but the idea of not knowing excites me. I decide there and then not to look out for road signs, not to anticipate any part of the route. When at last we get there I'll say very casually, 'So where are we now?', and he'll stare at me and say, 'You mean you didn't know?' Maybe I won't ask even then. Maybe I'll say, 'Don't tell me. I prefer not to know.'

'My name's Marker,' he says. 'Arnie Marker.'

'Right,' I say, not giving my name back.

This Marker turns out to be an unusual man. Not that he looks it. I've said he's fat, but more accurately he's stocky. His head is stocky too, like a cube, with florid skin and not much hair at all. You'd say he was a pig farmer until you catch the look in his eyes. They're little piggy eyes, but the look in them is something else. Most people don't look at you, they look at their own reflection in your expression. They're wanting to know, does he like me? Is he a threat? How can I use him? They're not looking to see you at all. But Marker's eyes are interested. He's curious, and when he finds things out, he thinks about them. This makes him an unusual man.

We go along the road in the travelling home that is Marker's cab, watching the movie on the screen before us that is the Kent countryside in the rain, though somehow all I register is the place-names on the road signs: Charing, Challock, Chilham. We are going to none of these places so it doesn't matter that I read the names. They are some of the infinite number of destinations that will not be mine. Even Ashford, which I read before I can stop myself, is not our

45

destination. We will pass through Ashford and our windscreen wipers will wipe it away and our journey will barely have begun.

Marker is self-educated. More precisely, he is in the process of self-education. He is doing a correspondence course in Western Philosophy, sent to him in monthly packages by the Cambridge College of Advanced Learning. I don't tell him that this college is probably a single mother in a basement flat with a photocopier. He seems happy with the course.

'I heard what you said to that woman,' he informs me. 'The one with the kids.'

'Oh. Right.'

No good deed goes unpunished.

'That was good. What you said.'

He reaches into his bag and pulls out a notebook while driving over seventy in a high-sided vehicle on a blustery day.

'Wrote it down.'

He tosses me the book. There it is, the most recent entry, written in pencil, in capital letters.

USE YOUR POWER GENTLY.

Right above it, also in capitals, he's written:

GODS ARE MORTAL, HUMANS IMMORTAL, LIVING THEIR LIFE, DYING THEIR DEATH. HERACLITUS.

I ask him what that's supposed to mean, and he says he thinks it means nothing very much but at least it makes you think. I'm inclined to be amazed. I never knew ancient Greek philosophers talked like Bob Dylan. I wouldn't mind thinking about it for a while, only Marker wants to talk. He knows more Heraclitus.

'You can never step twice into the same river. What do you say to that?'

'I don't have a problem with that.'

'It's bollocks. If I step twice into a river, and I've not gone anywhere else, then it's the same fucking river, isn't it? It's not a different fucking river. It's not a bowl of porridge, either. Don't make me laugh.'

Next Marker tells me how Socrates went wrong.

'Socrates has this big idea that if you really know what's the right thing to do, you'll do it. You only do wrong things out of ignorance, because everyone wants to lead a good life and be happy. What do you say to that?'

'Well,' I say, growing more cautious. 'I suppose everyone wants to be happy.'

'What about the fuckers who are plain evil? Come down the Rainbow at the bottom of our road and I'll introduce you to a whole roomful of people who get their jollies by being evil. It's their idea of a good time. Stroll on, Socrates.'

'Right.'

'He killed himself, you know? Drank poison. "The difficulty, my friends, is not to avoid death, but to

47

avoid unrighteousness, for that runs faster than death." So he takes the poison. Now if I'd been there, I'd have said, Avoid unrighteousness, but avoid death too. Don't give me this either-or shit. Stay alive. Make yourself useful.'

After this Marker launches into an attack on Jean-Jacques Rousseau's theory of the general will.

'You want a short laugh on a wet Sunday? Try Rousseau's social contract. The deal here is we give up our freedom so we can be part of the general will. So you ask, what the fuck is the general will? Okay. Rousseau says you find out by taking a vote. So you say, what about the villains and half-brains and comedians who would vote for their own dick if it was standing? No, not them, says Rousseau. Every voter must be educated and fully informed. No two voters must talk about the issues before voting. Each citizen must hold to his own thoughts. So where does Rousseau live? The real world, or fairyland? You tell me.'

I guess fairyland.

'It's not South Croydon, and that's for free. But guess who bets the ranch on Rousseau? Robespierre! Monsieur Terror himself! The God of Reason tells him he can guillotine every poor sod who disagrees with him. The general will, *c'est moi*!'

By the time we reach the Channel Tunnel Marker has demolished Aristotle's theory of happiness, Aquinas's proofs of the existence of God, Kant's categorical imperative, Marx's labour theory of value, and all of Wittgenstein.

'Wittgenstein went to school with Adolf Hitler. Did you know that? The Realschule, in Linz. A whole lot too fucking real for me.'

I tell him how I'm struck by the fact that he, a self-educated truck driver, is so much smarter than all the great thinkers of history. He says it surprised him too at first, but he'd come to the conclusion they couldn't see the wood for the trees.

'All they do all day is read each other's books. They should get out more.'

He does allow that some of them get it right sometimes. He has a grudging respect for Schopenhauer.

'Try this for size. "The gratification of desire is like alms thrown to a beggar. It keeps him alive today, so that his misery may be prolonged till the morrow." Not a barrel of laughs, but true enough as far as it goes.'

Again I'm amazed. I thought I was the only person who'd had that idea.

We have to wait to drive the truck onto the shuttle train that will take us through the Channel Tunnel. Marker stops telling me about the failures of Western philosophy and starts looking round like he's expecting someone to show up. So I look round too and soon wish I hadn't. The shuttle terminal is designed to overwhelm the human spirit and cause it to lie down and weep. Everything is enormous and made of either steel or concrete, and everything is fenced in behind serious prison-style fences. Even the train onto which we load the truck is built like a cage.

There's no driving to do once we're on the shuttle, so Marker opens his fridge and brings out food and drink. The food is cold pork pies, doughnuts and apples. The drink is bottled water.

'Help yourself. Or did you bring something with you, as if I don't know.'

I have no supply of food. My plan is to live off the land. I don't mean nuts and berries, I mean burger bars and pastry shops. I have cash.

'You're not what they call proactive, are you?' says Marker.

He has a jar of extremely hot mustard to go with the cold pork pies. The combination is very successful. The doughnuts have been chilled in the fridge, which is another new experience for me. The train starts to move so quietly at first I don't notice it. It slides quietly into the tunnel. I don't like the feeling. I'm not claustrophobic, it's just that I like to see out.

'What's in the truck?' I ask.

'Well, fuck my uncle with a chunky monkey! Was that a question?'

'I was just wondering.'

'And there I was beginning to doubt you were gifted with the powers of external perception.'

'What do you mean?'

'Let's say you're not exactly curious by nature, and I am.'

50

I start to feel irritated.

'Actually you're not all that curious. You just tell me things. You don't ask me things.'

'Touched a nerve, have I?'

'I'm not complaining.'

As it happens I do get quite quickly pissed off when people tell me I'm passive. Like, how do they know? They're not inside me. Just because I'm not jumping up and down they assume nothing's happening. What I call passive is following the herd and being a sheep. Sheep don't choose to be alone in their room. Sheep don't hitch a ride to nowhere. Enough with passive. I go my own way.

It's only later I realise Marker never answered my question.

4

The Complete Home Removal Service carries me across northern France or Belgium or Germany. You can't tell any more. There aren't any borders and everyone drives the same cars. Then darkness falls and all I can see are the headlights of approaching vehicles and without meaning to I fall asleep.

When I wake the truck isn't moving and Marker isn't there. Then I hear this loud snore from behind the blue check curtains and I realise he's on the bunk, asleep. I look out of the window. We're parked in a service station somewhere in Europe.

I climb down from the cab to stretch my legs and walk across to the main building, in search of toilets. It feels like it's the middle of the night. The windows of the restaurant are brightly lit so I can see inside. There aren't many people about.

The toilet has an automatic flush that knows when I've finished. To be precise it knows when I walk away from the urinal. If I wanted I could stop peeing in the middle, walk away, wait for it to flush, walk right back, and go on peeing. It would never know. But I don't. Instead, I go to the restaurant and get myself a cup of coffee and a roll. I pay with English money and get change in euros, which I don't understand. You could charge me anything and I'd just hand over the money.

The coffee is quite good. It actually has a taste. I can feel my body coming back to life. There's a rack of postcards near me, and I toy with the idea of sending Cat a postcard with a view of Heidelberg and a message on the back saying Greetings from Nepal, but I don't. The other people bent over their cups of coffee all look like truck drivers to me. I think about Marker and wonder where he's going and again I get that zing of excitement that I don't know.

That sets me guessing about Marker. Where does he live? How come he doesn't have a second driver in the cab with him? You don't usually see removal vans with only one man in the cab. One man can't lift all those sofas and washing machines that have to be moved in a complete home removal service. And what has he got in the back of the truck?

Since he's not here for me to ask, I make up a life for him. He lives in South Croydon, in a three-bedroomed house built ten years ago as part of a development called Rainbow Village. The front gardens all join up. He has a wife who works as a receptionist at a beauty salon, and two children who stopped listening to him when they started primary school. He has a shed in the back garden where he keeps his books on philosophy and lives a parallel life in which he duels with the great minds of the past and is victorious.

As I walk back to the truck, I see a brief movement behind it. There's someone walking away, head down, hands in pockets. He's not heading towards the restaurant, he's going down the lines of parked vehicles. Then I lose him in the darkness.

Marker is out of bed.

'Thought I'd lost you,' he says.

'There was someone hanging round your cab.'

He looks up sharply.

'What sort of someone?'

'I couldn't see. A man.'

I can tell this bugs him, but he says nothing more. He pulls out a wash-bag and goes off to the toilets to shave. I look round the cab. At the foot of the bunk there's his bag, where he keeps his notebook. I open the bag to take another look at the notebook, but the first thing I see is his passport. Yesterday when he showed his passport he took it out of a wallet in his coat pocket. And the name on this passport is not Arnie Marker, but Armin Markus.

We drive on. He's not talking philosophy any more.

'When will we get there?'

'We'll be at the border by lunchtime.'

Not quite what I asked.

'You have any plans?' he says at last. 'For after we get there?'

'Not really,' I say. 'Nothing I can't change.'

He nods. He thinks I'm an aimless drifter. That's not a problem with me.

'You want to do me a favour?'

'If I can.'

'In the fridge, in the little ice-making compartment, there's an envelope. You could take it out and put it in your coat pocket until we're the other side of the border.'

This does not sound so cool. I want to help but I don't want to end up in some Eastern European jail.

'What's in it?'

'Nothing of any importance. But these border guards, they can be very stupid.'

'Will they search us?'

'They might.'

'So they'll search me too.'

'You're not the driver. They won't bother with you.'

'What if they do? They'll find it.'

'Then they find it.' I'm rattling him. 'It's not a big deal, okay?'

'So why hide it from them?'

'Christ on a bike! Do you want to do me a fucking favour or don't you?'

'Okay, okay.'

Actually I don't want to do the fucking favour but I

can't see how to get out of it. He's given me this giant ride and shared his food with me and told me his philosophical thoughts and somehow it just feels like I owe him. Plus he's right here sitting beside me and saying no takes more effort of the will than saying yes.

I believe this is how it goes more times than people admit. The theory is we make moral decisions according to what we believe, or what's in our best interests. Like fun. Most times we go for whatever will cause the least grief to the other party. I once knew this girl, I had a thing with her which lasted all of three days, and afterwards she went round saying she'd never been that bothered about me in the first place. So I ran into her somewhere and asked her straight out, if that was true, how come she'd done it with me the night we met? She said, 'Because I couldn't think of a reason not to.'

'So you'll do it?'

'Yes. I'll do it.'

After that he calms down. I look out of the window. We're somewhere where they believe in window-baskets like it's their religion. Or maybe it's the law. Maybe they have teams of enforcers going from house to house, making sure the petunias have been potted out.

So I'm in the truck with a guy who's carrying a false passport and an illegal envelope and this whole thing could go very not funny for me if I'm not careful. On the other hand, what does it mean in this context to be

56

careful? What am I to guard against? I lack information. So really I might as well go with the flow. My
protection is my ignorance, which will carry the ring
of truth, being true.

A few miles before we reach the border Marker tells
me to take the envelope out of the fridge. It's right at
the back of the ice-making compartment, and folded
over and frozen in.

'I can't get it out.'

'You really give up fast, don't you, son?'

I hate being called son. He's not my father. And
anyway, my father never calls me son. Still I keep on
scrabbling at the frost until my fingertips are numb
and I get it out at last. A deep-frozen folded-up brown
envelope. It's not so fat or anything, so I don't see how
it can be drugs, which is a relief.

'You have some kind of inner pocket?'

I put it in the breast pocket of my coat. That's as
inner as my pockets get.

The border is a serious border, not one of these
blink-and-you-miss-it Eurozone borders with a sign
saying *Please drive carefully while passing through
Belgium*. This one is a retro-Cold War frontier complete with razor wire, guard towers, goons with guns,
and striped poles that go up and down. We get into
line for the passport check and I can feel that Marker
is tensing up. I start to wonder what country we're
about to enter, but then remember I've decided not to
ask. Without realising I'm doing it I let my eyes scan a

big notice which is in a language that looks like German but isn't. Underneath is an English translation. I read as far as the part that tells me please on alighting at my destination to register the self with the authorities. I kind of like the picture this creates in my mind. Maybe once I register, the authorities issue the self with a licence that allows me to operate it within designated limits, like on public roads and in places of entertainment.

The line of vehicles moves faster than I'd expected. Most cars get waved on past by the border police. Our truck is pulled out of the line for a more thorough search. Of course.

'Everything's going to be cool,' says Marker, sounding like he's in the process of soiling his underwear.

They check our passports without a word and then sign to Marker to open up the back of the truck. They give us back our passports and go to see what we're carrying. I'm interested myself. Brown cardboard cartons, stacked floor to ceiling, side to side. Another sign from the guards, meaning, Open up one of the cartons. You begin to realise the human race needs much less spoken language than is widely believed. Most times the meaning of what a person says to you can be inferred from the context. My grandmother, who became very deaf before she died, would do this all the time. She would see someone speaking at her with a be-kind-to-dumb-animals smile and she would answer, 'Not so bad after all, considering my age,' or

'Tottering on, a little slower every day.' She once told me her life was like being in a cinema and trying to find the exit in the dark. Behind you there's gaping faces and flashing lights but all you want to do is find the way out and leave without making a fuss. She was fine, my grandmother. I miss her.

Marker reaches up for a carton. No, they gesture at him, not that one. This one. So he pulls down a different carton and opens it in front of them. There's nothing on the outside of the boxes, but inside, very tightly packed in tissue paper, are pairs of Nike trainers. The guards look at them. My guess is they're fakes. Then one of the guards pulls a pair of trainers out, and another pair, and throws them onto the muddy ground, as if he doesn't care how dirty they get. Marker makes no complaint. The guard keeps on pulling out tissue paper and trainers and more tissue paper, and then all at once he gives this fat grunt of satisfaction. Out from the lower half of the carton comes a videotape.

He shows it to his companions. It's called *Nympho Diaries*. Just in case their English isn't so good, the picture on the case shows a mostly naked woman pulling a completely naked man towards her by his enormous erect dick.

Marker is smuggling hard-core pornography. So much for Western philosophy.

I sneak a look at him. He's diving into the box and pulling out more videos. *Stick It Up*. *Dirty Debutantes*.

Big Butt Action. He gives them to the guards like he's handing out sticks of chewing gum. The guards love it. They're grinning and studying the pictures on the cases.

'Keep them,' says Marker. 'For you.'

Suddenly they're all the best of buddies. They slap Marker on the back and help him put the trainers back in the carton. So they're not going to throw us into prison for corrupting the morals of the nation after all. They're going to take their free gifts like Christmas has come and go and do what a man has to do. Now that they know Marker is a sicko pervert peddling rip-off filth they're all smiles. It's a funny old world. Though actually I'm not as moralistic as this may sound. I understand the surge of fellow-feeling that is coursing through the goons' veins. It's not really porno-lust at all. It's plain relief at finding their own secret self mirrored in a stranger.

So we're back in the truck and we're on our way.

'You've done this before,' I say.

'Couple of times.'

'Do they search the truck every time?'

'No,' he says. His eyes are scanning the road ahead, and the warehouse yards on either side.

'So that was a scary moment for you?'

He doesn't answer. I'm only trying to show some fellow feeling. Maybe he's ashamed.

'I am grown up, you know. I've seen that stuff before.'

'Good for you,' he says.

So I stop trying and look out at the road. We're passing through one of those nothing regions between the border and the first proper town, where commercial goods are marshalled as they come and go. Nobody lives in these yards, and nothing grows here, not even the false blooms of advertising hoardings. Long lightless sheds stand in dull deserts of concrete, where immense trucks slouch slowly by. Who designs these places? Do they go to sleep at night proud of their work? Maybe it's all deliberate. Maybe they say to each other, let's take these cocky travellers down a few notches as they come into our country, wipe that smug smile off their faces. Foreign travel's not smart any more, or picturesque, or even different. This could be any border road. This is trade, this is how we all get rich. So as we enter each new country we pay our dues to the machinery of our wealth, and then we avert our eyes and look ahead, to the charming hotel in the recently pedestrianised historic centre of the capital city.

From this, my free-wheeling thoughts turn to the performers who are now to be found in every tourist-frequented car-free plaza. The buskers playing violins, the fire jugglers, the living statues. I saw my first living statue on La Rambla in Barcelona. I don't know what impressed me more: the sheer nerve of the core idea, or the performer's ability to keep still. He was all in white with a white face and stood on a white pillar like a classical Greek statue. Later I realised these living statues were all over the place, and it was a fairly low-energy form of begging, but I still wonder who had the idea first. Like everything in the art game, doing it first is the key. Anyone can call a bottle-rack art, but Marcel Duchamp did it first, so he's the one in the art-history books. If someone else has already done it, forget it. In art, you have to start by being new, then you have to do the same thing over and over again, and then you're made. You've become part of art history. You don't have to do anything else. In fact it only confuses people if you do something else. It spoils the story.

What amazes me is that I can see through all these games and no one else can. Then it strikes me that this is just what Arnie Marker believes about Western philosophy. Or Armin Markus.

'FUCK!'

The brakes are squealing. I lurch forward. A road block has appeared out of nowhere. Men in black nylon bomber jackets are waving guns.

'Hold onto your seat! I'm going to run the blockade!'

'But why—?'

'SHUT THE FUCK UP!'

He sounds completely different: powerful and urgent and deadly serious. I shut the fuck up.

We're slowing down, cruising towards the road block, which is just a line of plastic cones and a couple of vehicles like people carriers. The guys with the guns look like gangsters to me. I understand Marker's thinking. It won't be hard to swing round the cones and get the hell away, only what about the guns? Are they part of his calculation? I mean, hard-core porn videos have their place in the scheme of things, but I'm not planning to die for them.

The men with the guns and the not-cool dress sense are waving us to a stop. Marker barks at me.

'Down!'

I drop down to the floor of the cab. The engine gives a massive roar and we're launched, we're hurtling through the cones. I hear crackling sounds that might be gunfire. Marker's swinging the truck like a lunatic and I'm rolling about in the well, smashing my head on the mini-fridge –

'Got the envelope?' he shouts. 'Got the envelope? Got the envelope?'

'Yes! Yes!'

'Eat it! Burn it! You hear me?'

'I hear you!'

Crackle-crackle-crackle-crackle!   Krang-klungle-klang! The windscreen turns to snow. Marker punches a hole with one fist. Cold air comes blasting in. Frosted glass-flakes clatter round me.

'When I say jump – open the door – jump! You hear me?'

'I hear you!'

'When I say jump – Jump! Run! Hide!'

Bang! That's my head damaging the fridge again. I

try to locate the door handle. Jump, run, hide: sounds good to me. Another vicious swing and I'm spread all over the door. Marker must be slaloming the truck. Now I have the handle. I grip it tight. This is my way out of here.

The strange thing is I'm not scared. I'm too confused to locate the danger, and my mind is on immediate business such as not getting my head banged any more than is necessary. I'm aware of bruises on my head and on my upper arms, but they're going to have to wait their turn.

'JUMP!'

I open the door. Marker wrenches the truck into a tight right turn, and I'm flung out. I hit the dirt and roll. I hurt something. I stop rolling and lie there, feeling the ground, just to get clear about which way is up. I spring to my feet and run.

So I've jumped. I'm running. Next I hide. For all I know I'm running towards the bad guys. However the survival instinct is doing its job. I can hear the sound of gunfire, and without in any way processing the chain of reason my legs are propelling me in the opposite direction.

Now I'm among trees. While we were driving down the road I saw no trees. How is it that when you want somewhere to hide, there's always trees? Not so many trees, maybe twenty or so. I drop to the ground beside one of them.

I've run a long way. My heart is about to explode and

my legs have gone numb and I hurt all over. I've crossed a field of winter cabbage sown in long sad rows. It's hard work plunging across ploughed land but I might as well have flown for all I can remember. In the middle of the field, quite a long way from the road, is Marker's truck. The gangsters are all round it. Not much noise any more. No engines, no guns.

I heave and pant and groan, and slowly my brain remakes its links with my body. Question number one is, how badly am I damaged? You'd think this is an easy one but in fact a bruised muscle can feel much like a broken bone, especially if you've not broken bones on any regular basis. As far as I can tell all my parts still join up, and there's no blood.

I hear a distant scream.

Sound travels well out here. It's a cold day and there's nothing in the way except low-growing cabbages. The men in bomber jackets are clustered round something I can't see, and something I can't see is screaming. It's a sound like I've never heard, but its meaning is entirely and instantly clear: it's the scream of a man in unbearable pain, who sees no hope of the pain ending. Not a plea for mercy or a cry of defiance, just elemental agony.

Now I'm afraid.

What am I supposed to do? There's a whole gang of them and they've got guns, there's no way they're going to stop because I ask them. More likely they'll do what they're doing to Marker to me as well, and then

I'll be making that sound too. So I huddle by my tree and stare across the field and try to understand what's going on.

Now some more of the bad guys are pulling stuff out of the back of the truck. They're tipping out the cartons and because I know what's in them I can make out the top layers of Nike trainers and the porno videos beneath. Then one of the videos flutters open to reveal a flash of white inside, which is not how video cassettes are constructed. As I watch I see that the men are tossing the trainers back into the truck, and also the videos, but they're making a pile on the ground out of the something else, the things they're pulling out from the bottoms of the cartons that flutter white.

The screaming has stopped. The guys round where the screaming was lose interest and join the guys at the back of the truck. I can see them picking out the videos and laughing at the titles. One of them gets out a petrol can and splashes petrol over the pile they're building.

Now they've emptied the last carton and they're getting back into their people carriers. The last one strikes a match and sets light to the petrol-soaked pile. Then they drive off.

The fire smokes for a bit, then a flame jumps up, and then black smoke starts to stream up into the still air. The truck and the people carriers rumble away over the cabbage field back to the road. Nobody has come looking for me.

When all the sound has ended but for the distant

whine of cars passing on the road, I stand up. I review my situation. I'm alone in an unknown country where the inhabitants use extreme violence in broad day-light. I'm in pain and very frightened. I'm willing to do whatever is necessary to save myself, but I have no idea what that is. Meanwhile, I'd very much like a wash, a change of clothes and a meal. None of these amenities are present here by the cabbage field. And I no longer have my kit bag.

This is a bad situation for which I did not ask. Surely of all the sentient beings in the universe I am one of the least demanding. I do not deserve this. Into my mind unbidden come Am's last plaintive words to me, before my Nokia began its adventure holiday to the sea. She said, or rather whispered, like I was going to my doom, 'Look after yourself.' Now here I am right in the heart of my doom and what the fuck am I supposed to do? I mean, how does a person look after himself? It doesn't work that way. Other people look after people.

I wish Am was here right now. Not so she'd look after me, but because she wants me to be happy. Really that's the opposite of this screaming and burning, which is all about wanting people to be unhappy. Am would put her arms round me and look at me with those dopy eyes of hers and if I smiled she'd smile back like I'd given her a present.

Oh Am.

The fire burns on. Nor far from the fire there is

something else among the trampled cabbages, a low dark mound. I know I must get away. I must walk in the opposite direction, so that I don't get involved in this business that included screaming.

I walk towards the fire. This is not a decision on my part. It seems that the way from the tree to the next segment of my life runs past the remains of the last segment of my life.

The fire is too hot to approach closely. The heart of the fire is flame, but round the edges I can see half-charred blocks, or bricks. One is on its side. Not blocks, not bricks. Books. All the books are the same: black hardbacks, like bibles. Then I see one lying on the edge of the fire that's been singed but not burned, and I run into the heat before I can think better of it and pull it out. The heat hits me like a wall and I spring back but I have the book.

I move away into the cold morning and look at the ash-coated volume. It is of course in this language that I don't understand. I can see what I take to be the title on the title page but the words look like nothing I've ever met. The author's name, as I suppose, is printed beneath the title. It is LEON VICINO. So it's not a bible. I turn the pages. The text is laid out in separate paragraphs of varying length, page after page. Whatever they say must matter to somebody a whole lot or they wouldn't be burning them.

Then it strikes me that these books are what Marker was smuggling into the country. The porno videos were just part of the cover. It gives me a strange wobbly feeling to know that the most criminal, the most dangerous, the most secret part of his cargo was not the fake Nike trainers or the pornographic videos, but plain old-style books. Words on pages. Just like this, that I'm writing now and you're reading.

Meanwhile quite close to where I'm standing, in fact just precisely in that section of the field at which I take special care not to look, there lies a dark mound. I'm reasoning with myself. Why go over and look more closely? It'll only make me more sick and more afraid. There's nothing I can now do. I owe it to myself to remain as fit, mentally and physically, as I can. Better to leave this place and not look back.

And yet I must see. What has happened must be known. If I don't look now, I'll never stop looking for the rest of my life.

I walk towards the dark mound. The body lies in a crouch, on its side, as if to protect as much of itself as possible from assault. I see the hunched back in the ski jacket. The worn jeans. The mud-stained leather boots. I walk round. His hands are clutched over his stomach, and are stained with blood. Something glints on the ground before me. I nudge aside the half-covering dirt with my boot, and I'm looking down at a pair of long-nosed pliers, the kind you use for pulling out staples. I look at the pliers stupidly, as if looking at them will make sense of their being here. I reach down and pick them up. I don't know why I do this. Some instinct against waste that says this perfectly good tool has been lost and should be returned to its owner, or failing that, used. I put the pliers in my coat pocket.

Then I look at his face.

Not everything needs to be described. In that one look I understand the horror of what has been done, and I understand the scream. But why did they do it? That I will never understand. They asked him no questions. They wanted nothing from him they hadn't got. Why inflict such suffering? Death is death. Isn't the victory enough?

One look is all I take, but it pierces every defensive barrier in my mind, and causes me to know for ever how passionately men can hate. This is lust for pain. This is hatred without limit.

But it wasn't done to me. I have survived.

There was no way I could have saved him. There were too many of them. They were armed professionals. What was I supposed to do, go out in a blaze of glory? 'For evil to triumph,' said someone I don't recall, 'it is only necessary for good men to do nothing.' But I never said I was a good man. I never said anything. I didn't ask to come to the show, so don't tell me I have to pay for my ticket. This someone should stand where I'm standing and see what I'm seeing. For evil to triumph it is only necessary for the bad guys to be the ones with the guns.

I walk away, moving briskly, not running. When I reach the road I walk along it, on the verge, paying no attention to the occasional passing car. I'm so frightened I want no one to notice me, but I'm also in urgent need of ordinariness. I want to be among shops and houses and people going about their everyday lives. I want to find a phone. I want to go home.

5

My head is throbbing. The town is quiet. There are people on the streets but they look down and don't meet my eyes. Something is wrong with the shops. I stand looking in the window of a pharmacy wondering if I should attempt to buy some paracetamol when I realise what it is that's wrong. There are no advertisements. The window display has no images of smiling models with white teeth, or happy babies in disposable nappies. I look up and down the street, and there's not a single billboard anywhere. Nor are there any other splashes of colour. The buildings are made of grey cement, or grey-hued stone. The roofs are dark-grey slate or dark-grey tarred felt. The roads and pavements are tarmac. The people wear heavy coats of grey or black or brown. The cars parked along the kerbs are all old models, all grey, or navy blue, or black. It's like I've stumbled into some black and white movie, only there's no music. In those old movies, there's always music.

I feel faint. I go into a bar. The minute I step through the door I get this feeling I've been here before. It's a bare room with the floor painted in grey and white squares and a tall fireplace and a beamed ceiling. There are three people at a table on the left: two men sitting down, and a woman in a red skirt standing with her back to me, holding up a glass of white wine. The barmaid is crossing the room towards them with a bowl of something in her hand. She wears a dirty brown apron and has red shoes. They all turn and stare at me as I enter, and then look away. The barmaid puts the bowl on the table before one of the men, and goes back behind the bar. It's a bowl of soup. The woman in the red skirt drinks up her wine and leaves, letting the door shut with a bang behind her. The man at the table starts to slurp the soup. He's eating too fast.

I cross the room, treading on something that crunches underfoot. I go to the bar and ask for coffee, which I'm hoping is one of those words that sounds the same in most languages. Also I point at the man's soup, and then at myself. The barmaid says nothing at all and still doesn't look at me but she starts to get out cups and bowls so I take it she understands. I go to the only other table in the bare room and sit down and wonder why I'm feeling I've seen all this before, and what it was I trod on. Tiny fragments of white clay.

The two men are staring at me. Or rather, they're staring at the book I've put down on the table top.

Until I put it down I'd forgotten that all this time I've been gripping it with one hand. The book bothers them. The soup drinker wipes his mouth with the back of his hand and gets up. So does his companion. I decide to put the book away. I push it into my coat pocket, where it doesn't quite fit. The two men leave.

My coffee comes, and my soup, and a bill. I give the barmaid a ten-euro note, which I have left over from my change in Germany. She stares at it like it's burning her fingers, but she takes it. She goes back behind the bar and out through an inner doorway screened by dangling blue and green plastic ribbons. From an inner room I hear a telephone dialling, the old kind that sounds like winding a clock. Then her voice, a low mumble.

The coffee tastes of mud. The soup is unidentifiable but filling. Even here, in the midst of fear and strangers, the meeting of basic needs delivers its reward. I start to feel better.

The street door opens and a young woman enters, moving fast. Her black hair is cut short, she wears no make-up, her slight body is wrapped in a well-worn leather overcoat. She looks at me without smiling. She is beautiful. A pale face. Wide dark eyes beneath strong eyebrows, full lips. Am I expecting her?

She looks quickly towards the empty bar, sits down before me at my table, and turns her eyes fully onto mine. I'm about to speak when she puts one finger to her lips. She takes out pen and paper and writes:

MEET – CAR PARK. Her eyes on mine again: have I understood? I nod.

She goes as quickly as she came. Only as the door closes behind her do I realise I don't know where the car park is.

The barmaid returns to her place behind the bar. She shows no sign of bringing me any change. No doubt she's been calling the police about me.

I pull on my coat and leave. Out in the street I catch sight of the young woman with the short hair walking rapidly down the pavement some way ahead. I follow. As I walk I tell myself I know nothing about her, I may be falling into a trap. Thieves use attractive women to lure their victims. So do secret police organisations. I don't have to follow her just because she looked into my eyes and wrote MEET – CAR PARK. Nevertheless I am following her. I'm alone and afraid and I've made a snap judgement that she's a good person based solely on the fact that she looked into my eyes. Not much of a basis for tagging along, but like they say, if you can't be with the one you love, then love the one you're with. So I'm actually speeding up, because I don't want to lose her. At least she understands English.

She turns down a side street and passes out of sight. I break into a run. When I get to the side street, I can see there's a car park at the far end. I look for a band of robbers, but there's only parked empty cars. Old cars, all of them, some of them seemingly abandoned. She's standing by a car waiting for me. It's an early model

Volkswagen Golf, with a long crack down the windscreen.

I go to her. She has one of the rear doors open.

'Get in.'

I get in. Why am I in the back? She's got into the driver's seat.

'Down!' she says. 'There is danger.'

So I get down, squeezing myself into the space between the front and back seats. She starts the car and off we go. Once again I'm on the floor of a moving vehicle and I don't know who I'm hiding from or where I'm going, but I do know she's right about one thing. There is danger.

After a few minutes on the floor I start to feel sick. I need to see where I'm going. I need to know who she is.

'I have to get up.'

'No!' Her voice is urgent. She sounds afraid. This is convincing. 'No one must see you. No one must know you've come.'

She speaks good English but with a strong accent. I try to place the accent. Russian? Meanwhile I decide to stay on the floor. I don't know what she's afraid of but nor do I want to meet men in bomber jackets wielding pliers.

Then she says, 'Everything's ready.'

'For what?'

'For you to do what you have come to do.'

She thinks I'm somebody else.

'No,' I say. 'That's not me. I'm not who you think I am.'

'Of course,' she says. 'I know nothing about you. I must know nothing.'

I try again. I speak slowly and clearly.

'I've no idea where I am, or what it is you expect me to do.'

'The less you know the better,' she says. 'Everything's going according to plan.'

Now I'm quite sure she's mistaken me for somebody else, but this is neither the time nor the place for an argument. Since there clearly is danger of some sort, I decide to do as she says until we reach wherever it is we're going. I wriggle my bruised and exhausted body into a marginally more comfortable position. I review my situation. Helpless and afraid, I fall back on the faithful standby of all lives that are spinning out of control, the numbered list.

First: I don't know where I am or what's going on.

Second: I've done nothing wrong.

Third: None of this has anything to do with me.

Fourth: I should get out as soon as I can.

I tell myself that so long as I hold hard to these four points, everything will end up alright. I can be accused of naivety, for entering an unknown country in the vehicle of a criminal stranger, but I myself have committed no crime. The worst they can do to me is send me home.

'We will have music.'

The young woman switches on the car radio and suddenly I'm listening to the sound of Simon and Garfunkel singing The Boxer. I first heard this song played in my father's workroom, long ago, before he left. It used to be one of his favourites. I'd gone into his workroom to ask him to help me with some school stuff and he let me stay to the end of the song. Usually he didn't like us to go into his workroom. I must have been about eight. I didn't understand a word of the song but my father liked it and so I liked it.

So I'm lying folded up on the floor of this car listening to The Boxer and feeling how all my body is throbbing and remembering my father with his funny crinkly smile, and I start to cry. I suppose I've just about come to the end of whatever it is that keeps people going because now as well as crying I'm slipping away into sleep.

I wake in stages. First I'm only aware that I'm waking. Then I feel the position of my body, which is sitting in a chair. Then I let my eyes open and see I'm in a dark room. Nothing's moving. No sounds.

Little by little my memories catch up. I was in a car, with a young woman. How did I get here? I have no way of answering that. So I wake up some more, and look round me. At least I can establish where I am.

I'm in a long room, which seems to be some kind of a reading room. There are bookshelves down both sides. The books have uniform backs, like reference books or collected editions. There's a door at the far end of the room, open to a passage. I'm sitting at the head of a long table that runs down the middle of the room. A faint light filters through the open door, not a direct light, but a light entering the passage beyond from some other room. So it's not easy to see.

However I can see the gun. It lies on the table right in front of me. It's a handgun, with a stubby barrel and a knurled grip. There's nothing else on the table. But now as my eyes adjust to the low light I see there's someone sitting at the table's far end. He's slumped over, so that his head lies on the table itself. I start to have a very bad feeling.

I get up and walk slowly towards him, one hand touching the edge of the table as I go. Now I can see that his head lies sideways, with one cheek pressed to the table's surface. Round his head the table seems to be darker. I come closer, now dreading what I know I will see.

There's a hole just above his nose. Nothing else registers: not the eyes, or the colour of his hair, or the clothes he's wearing. Only that dark hole, and the ribbon of darkness that runs from it to the puddle of darkness on the table.

A second door, a closed door behind me, now opens, and the young woman in the leather coat comes into the room. She moves briskly, purposefully, entirely unsurprised. She examines the dead man, and gives a quick nod of satisfaction.

'Good,' she says.

'I don't know—' I begin.

'No time. Get your gun.'

My gun?

But she's already on her way out. So I grab the gun and follow her. There's an unlit hallway, with a hard marble floor. A door out onto a long street. It's night. A car waits, its engine running, a young man at the wheel smoking a cigarette.

'Get in the back.' To the young man she says something in the language I don't know. The young man smacks the steering wheel with both palms, and turns to me as I get in.

'You do good!'

As he drives us at speed down the long dark street the woman leans over the front seat and fixes me with her eyes.

'The movement will show its gratitude.'

'I don't understand what's happened,' I say. I feel giddy.

'Do not understand. It is better so.'

It's like she doesn't hear me when I speak. I want to shout. But when I speak it sounds more like I'm crying.

'Please. Listen to me. I don't know who you are. I don't know where I am. I don't even know who the dead man is.'

'Of course,' she says. 'You are a professional. You kill without knowing who you kill.'

Everything's ready for you to do what you have come to do. Except I didn't come to do anything. I'm the original man without a purpose. Don't go pointing your finger at me. If I wasn't feeling dizzy I'd laugh.

'I didn't kill him.'

At this point the driver interrupts in his own language, and the two of them have an exchange that I don't understand. This gives me a few moments for private reflection. The outcome is an uncomfortable new thought.

What if I'm wrong?

Maybe I did kill the man in the book-lined room. I have no memory of entering the room. How can I be sure that during that time of which I remember nothing I didn't take the waiting gun and shoot him dead? It looks that way. This young woman believes it. Whether I actually did it or not begins to seem irrelevant. I had better start finding out the consequences.

She turns her attention back to me.

'We are taking you to a house where you will be safe for the rest of tonight. As soon as you are rested, you must move. You must leave the country.'

I ask the only question I can think of that will produce an answer I'll understand.

'What's your name?'

'My name is Petra.'

She gives me an unexpected and dazzling smile. She doesn't ask me my name.

6

I'm sitting at a table in a big kitchen warmed by a tiled
stove, eating some more soup I can't identify, while
the others smoke cigarettes and flick the ash into an
empty beer-can and argue in low voices in the
language I can't understand. There are four of them, all
quite young. The beautiful Petra has now shed her coat
to reveal a figure so desirable I can hardly eat. I keep
staring at her breasts without realising I'm doing it.
She sees this but acts like she doesn't. It's not that her
breasts are huge or anything, just very well defined by
the tight T-shirt she's wearing. Then there's Egon, who
is lanky and drooping and sunk in a permanent gloom.
This has something to do with Petra, who I sense is his
girlfriend, or perhaps was. Anyway he watches her
with accusation in his eyes, and she takes care never
quite to look back. Then there's Stefan, who drove the
car, who is the youngest and doesn't say much. And
last there's Ilse. Ilse is watching me. She's the only one

who seems aware of my presence. This is not so much a source of excitement for me, because Ilse is strikingly ugly. Not only does she have too much nose, but her skin is pocked all over like bubble-wrap. I don't like to be superficial in my judgements but it's not easy to rise above this first impression. Sometimes you get ugly people with so much vitality and charm that they don't seem ugly. But more commonly ugly people are so exhausted by their ugliness that they've just given up, and make no effort to join the human race. They accept their role as losers, punished for no fault of their own, and stare with wounded eyes from the corners of rooms. Ilse is one of these. She's looking at me with no indication that she sees me. I'm just the latest manifestation of a world she views with a kind of generalised resentment.

Petra is the energy source for the group. She does most of the talking. They're talking about me and what I've done, while I eat my soup. It seems they've all eaten earlier, no doubt while I was in the reading room shooting dead a man I've never met. I still have the gun, it's in one pocket of my coat, which is hanging on the back of the kitchen door. Apparently it's my gun. This is not the only gun. The room is full of guns, on the table, on the bench, against the fridge. They leave guns lying about like other people leave umbrellas. Also on the table between them is the book I pulled from the fire. I've already told them how I came by it, and about Marker, and how he died. Apparently the men in bomber jackets are a branch of the interior ministry police. The pliers are something of a trademark.

Petra now turns to me.

'This man with the truck. Did he say where he was taking the books?'

I shake my head. They go on talking among themselves. I finish eating. It's time I learned what's going on.

'Excuse me,' I say. 'There's things I need to know.'

They all look at me.

'So?' says Petra.

'Who is this man you say I killed?'

Petra starts to answer and then changes her mind. Stefan asks her what I said and she tells him. Egon looks at me and I meet his eyes and it's like going out of a doorway into winter rain, the chilly drizzle of his unhappiness. Unexpectedly, this makes me like him. Maybe I've been there too. Anyway, it's Egon who gives me an answer, or part of an answer. His English isn't as good as Petra's, but at least he's talking.

'He is chief of security,' he says.

It's a start. Little by little I piece together the situation. I'm in a country that is currently under a state of emergency. The authorities are crushing all opposition groups, using as cover the claim that they are fighting terrorism. The group protecting me is a cell of an underground organisation which they call the movement. This alone, they tell me, among all the groups that oppose the police state, has the will to inflict real

84

damage. My action in the reading room is proof of this.

'But of course,' says Petra, 'you are now in very great danger.'

Thanks for telling me. That makes me feel just great. I guess she sees how thrilled I am because she puts out one hand and rests it on my arm and says:

'The movement will protect you.'

Here I am in very great danger and all I can think about is Petra's breasts. Mankind is not as evolved as we suppose. On the other hand maybe this is my way of dealing with an unmanageable situation. These people seem to think they hired me to carry out an assassination, which I would class as a simple case of mistaken identity were it not for the corpse in the reading room and the gun in my coat pocket, and none of it makes any sense, so I might as well focus on tits.

Ilse is still gazing at me. Now she speaks.

'They will hunt you,' she says. Her voice is unexpectedly soft, coming from that corrugated face. 'They will hunt you and kill you. They have information. They are well trained. They will find you.'

She almost sounds like she's pleased about it.

'That's enough, Ilse.' Petra's voice carries authority, like a mother correcting a wayward child.

'Yes, Petra,' says Ilse, soft and submissive. 'That's enough.'

To me Petra says again, 'The movement will protect you.' Then, prodding the book on the table, 'These people will not protect you. He will not protect you.'

She means Leon Vicino, author of this book that it seems she does not respect, but for which Arnie Marker died.

'Who is he?'

'An old man. An irrelevance. A failed poet. An exile.'

That's a lot of dismissing for someone who doesn't matter. Egon starts to shift in his seat. He looks at me, and alongside the sadness there's a wrinkle between his brows that looks like a plea.

'I admire him,' he says. His tone is regretful. 'He was a great man once.'

'Once,' says Petra. 'Twenty years ago. Thirty years ago.'

'Why did they burn his book?'

'Anything which questions their authority makes them afraid. What Egon said is true. Vicino is well known. He has influence. This book of his, it makes people question the actions of the state. So they ban it.'

'Is Vicino part of your movement?'

'No.'

Her answer is swift and sharp, as if she's snapping shut a lid on a box I'm not to open. Stefan asks her what I said and she tells him. There follows a brief argument between her and Egon. I gather that Egon is urging her to tell me more than she believes is necessary. So, grudgingly, she tells me a little more.

'The movement understands that the police state can only be overthrown by the use of force. We do not shrink from what is necessary. Leon Vicino is an old man. He is sentimental. He tells us to fight torture with poems. His approach has failed. His methods are discredited. His day is over.'

Again I get the feeling she's burying Vicino under too many words. It's like she's afraid of him. I reach out for the book and turn again to the title page. It's frustrating, staring at printed words and getting back no meaning at all.

'It's called *The Society of Others*.' This is Ilse again. Now she wants to please me. 'I have a copy in English, if you like.'

'The book is unimportant.' Petra speaks sharply, and her eyes reprimand Ilse. 'Our friend must sleep. Before dawn we will move on.'

She stands and stubs out her cigarette and puts the butt carefully in the beer-can.

'I will show you where you can sleep.'

Egon stands too, and holds out his hand for me to shake. A curiously formal gesture. As I hold his hand I feel his brief grip and I sense that he is trying to communicate to me some wordless fellowship. This is like being befriended by the class loser in school, and I don't much like it. We have nothing in common. Except maybe being told what to do by Petra, and wanting to touch her, and never getting close.

So meek as a dog on a lead I follow Petra into the little outer hall and up the stairs. We are in a suburban house built cheaply maybe thirty years ago. The unseasoned timber has warped and none of the doors close properly. Upstairs, the rooms are unheated.

I am to sleep in what is clearly the main bedroom. The bed is wide, and there are curtains on the window. Petra turns on the single centre light and closes the door. We're alone together in a room with a double bed.

'I hope you will be comfortable.'

'I'm sure I will.'

Why has she closed the door? Or almost closed it, because it no longer fits its frame.

'Is there anything else I can get you?'

She's looking at me in this odd way.

'I guess I'm okay for now.'

'We are grateful,' she says.

Then she comes right up to me and puts one hand on my shoulder and looks into my eyes. What am I supposed to think? Beyond her I see the door quietly open a few more centimetres. Ilse is standing on the other side, watching.

Petra kisses me.

Nothing makes any sense to me. I don't know how I got into this mess or how I'm going to get out of it, but just for now this is feeling good. Petra's lips taste smoky from her cigarette. She's pressing her body against mine. Ilse is watching through the crack in the door, expressionless.

'You want me?' whispers Petra in my ear.

'Yes.' It's not like I can hide it.

'Desire is power.'

'I'm sorry?'

'I too feel desire. I use my desire to make myself strong. We must be strong, all the time. This is how we will win.'

Now she's kissing me again. I don't follow her reasoning but I am picking up the general idea that I'm not about to get lucky.

She whispers in my ear again, very softly.

'Only the free can love.'

With that, she turns and goes. She walks right past Ilse without a word or a glance. Ilse acts as if nothing out of the ordinary has happened. Maybe it hasn't. Maybe this is Petra's party trick and she does it twice nightly. That could explain Egon's long face.

Now Ilse is coming into the bedroom and pushing the door shut behind her. For a panicky moment I think she too plans to contribute to the power of my desire, but it turns out she has a book for me.

'I think you like it,' she says.

It's Leon Vicino's book, in English. *The Society of Others.*

'Thank you.'

She fixes me with her eyes and says in her little-girl voice,

'Use your power gently.'

Then she too goes.

I'm astonished. Her words are of course familiar to me, since they were my words first. I said them to the mother of the screaming children in the motorway service station somewhere in southern England, some time that seems a whole lifetime ago. Arnie Marker heard me, bent over his all-day breakfast, and wrote them in his notebook. And now here they are again. There's a connection here somewhere, a common thread linking me and Marker, this book that he was smuggling into the country, and Ilse who has just given me an English copy.

The book has a paper bookmark in it. I let it fall open, and read: *Use your power gently.*

So Ilse is quoting Vicino, not me. This removes one part of the puzzle. But how come Vicino is stealing my lines? I check the publication date of the book, and find it was first published thirty-two years ago, ten years before I was even born. So I've been stealing his lines.

I turn to the opening page. The first paragraph is a single line of print.

Life is hard and then you die.

I start to feel giddy. I have never read this book before. I'd never even heard of Leon Vicino until yesterday. Yet it's like I'm reading my own mind. I read the second paragraph.

Do not expect to be happy. Happiness is your horizon.
It will retreat before you if you pursue it.

At least I never said that. I might have said it, if I'd been a lot smarter. I certainly agree with it. I decide not to go to sleep yet, but to read on. After all, I've already done some sleeping earlier in the day, if you can call it sleeping when it's combined with assassinating security agency chiefs.

Observe other people closely. Contrary to your expectations, they see, feel and think differently to you. They inhabit undiscovered countries on the far side of lost oceans. Your life is a voyage of discovery. You are an explorer.

On I read, deep into the night. Somewhere around page ninety I feel myself falling asleep. I close the book and slip fully dressed beneath the bedcovers, suddenly aware how cold my body has become. For a few moments, as I wriggle in the bed to create warmth, Vicino's ideas and phrases dance in my head.

Imagine that you have a beloved ghost brother, who is always by your side. Every move you make to hurt others hurts your ghost brother too. Every blow you strike against an enemy causes your ghost brother to flinch in pain. And when at last you meet your enemy face to face and kill him, you slay your ghost brother also. From that day on you will carry his unseen corpse with you, until your life in turn also comes to an end.

As sleep creeps over me this ghost brother of Vicino's merges in my mind with the man who will hunt me and kill me. He is well trained. I am in very great danger. I must jump and run and hide. But first I will sleep.

7

Stefan wakes me. How long have I slept? It feels like no time at all, but my watch tells me five hours have gone by. The others are up. Coffee is brewing. We are to go shortly. I look out between the curtains. The last of the night.

Downstairs in the kitchen Petra and Egon are huddled together in a fog of cigarette smoke studying some sheets of paper covered with type. The guns have been gathered up into a large canvas hold-all. Ilse pours me a mug of hot black coffee and cuts me a slice of white cheese. As I sip the coffee I see an envelope lying open on the table. It looks familiar. I turn, and see that my coat is no longer hanging on the hook behind the door. It's spread out on a bench, and the contents of the pockets are laid out as if on display. I find this humiliating.

The envelope is the one Marker gave me. They've opened it. They're reading the contents.

I recall the terrible urgency in Marker's voice as he cried to me, *Got the envelope? Got the envelope? Eat it! Burn it!*

'What exactly do you think you're doing?'

Petra looks up in surprise.

'You have a problem?'

'Yes, I have a problem. What gives you the right to go through my pockets?'

'I don't understand.' It's there on her face, she truly doesn't understand. 'We work together.'

'That doesn't mean you can do what you want with my belongings.'

'Your belongings? You have no belongings. I have no belongings. All we have belongs to the movement.'

'It's not my movement.'

They all stare at me in silence. I've shocked them. Petra speaks in their language, I guess repeating my words for the sake of Stefan and Egon. Then Petra says to me:

'Please understand. Only the movement can save you. Alone, you will die.' A pause, and she adds, just in case I don't get the full picture, 'First you will suffer. Then you will die.'

'Oh, well, then. Fine. I'll join.'

I mean my words to have a bitter ironic ring, but Petra takes them literally.

'That is good.'

They return to their discussion. I see now that Marker's papers are a list of names and addresses.

I eat my piece of cheese. Then I get up and one by one put all my belongings, which I still consider to be my property, back into the pockets of my coat. As I do so I try to decide what to do. I feel angry and helpless. I feel guilty because I didn't destroy the envelope. In fact, I forgot all about it. Then I tell myself Marker had no right to expect me to carry out any kind of assignment for him. He never told me what he was doing. It's not as if we were linked in any other way than by chance. My guilt, I now see, is generated by the fact that he was killed. But dying in itself has no special merit, does not validate a cause. A man can be misguided, and still suffer a painful death. Look at the suicide bombers.

There's another aspect to this train of thought. This group, this cell of the movement, is currently protecting me. I am, it seems, on their side. But this too is chance. How do I know they have right on their side? This isn't my country. Why must I choose a side anyway?

Then I see again Marker's face after the goons have finished with it, and I know there's no argument after all. I can never be on the side of the torturers. Therefore I'm against them. I have joined the movement.

I go to the group round the table and indicate the list they're all studying.

'Do you know what it is?'

'Yes,' says Petra. 'These are local area leaders. The people to whom he was to deliver the books.'

95

I look blank.

'Vicino was the leader of a political party. That of course was banned. So the party became a society, a network of so-called reading groups. The reading groups are not banned. But the police watch them closely. They suspect them of political activity.'

'Reading groups?'

'Reading, yes. And discussing. Debate as a substitute for action.'

She lights another cigarette from the glowing butt of the last one, and speaks to the others in their own language. It seems from her tone of voice that she has reached a decision, and is inviting them to endorse it. One by one, they raise their hands. I suspect this is for my benefit: democratic decision-making in action. It looks more to me like a teacher instructing a class of small children.

Petra folds up the pages of names and addresses and returns them carefully to the envelope. I see now that the envelope has been opened without being torn.

'What will you do with the list?'

'Egon will give it to his contact in the interior ministry.'

Now I'm lost.

'The security police?'

'Egon feeds them harmless information. In return, he learns of their operations. This is how we have avoided capture. This is also how we knew the movements of the man you killed. But now, because of the assassination, Egon will come under suspicion. The handing over of the list will be a proof of his continuing loyalty and usefulness.'

My head is swimming. I try to follow this tangle of motives, but something here smells bad.

'What will they do with the list?'

'There may be names here they did not previously know were active in the society. That is of value to them.'

'Does it put the people named in danger?'

'Of course.' She had a look on her face I've not seen before: fixed, almost expressionless, but serene. 'They will be interrogated. They will disappear.'

'What does that mean?'

'The authorities never permit those who've been interrogated to make public their methods of interrogation.'

I stare back at her, profoundly shocked.

'Why?'

'What is your question?'

'Why are you handing these people over to torture and death?'

She blinks a little at my direct language, but is not otherwise disturbed by my question.

'It's necessary.'

'Why?'

'The followers of Vicino are very many. Add together the active members, and their families, and their friends, and you have almost the entire educated class of our country. Many thousands. At present this class does not understand the need for radical action. They refuse to open their eyes to the reality of state oppression. When their leaders begin to disappear, their eyes will be opened. They will understand that there is only one way to resist, and that is the movement's way. The movement will grow, until it achieves critical mass. Then we will sweep away the oppressors.'

She pauses, drawing on her cigarette, watching me to see if I have followed her so far. She softens her tone, aware that I'm new to this line of thinking, and need reminding of the final goal.

'It is a great sacrifice. But it will bring liberation.'

I say nothing. The truth is I'm confused. I feel like I'm in a class and I've just had a theory explained to me and I know something's wrong with it but I can't tell what. It reminds me of this argument I had with an American boy once, about capital punishment. He just couldn't see what was wrong with executing murderers. I said it didn't work as deterrence, because America has the death penalty, but still has a much higher murder rate than countries that don't. He said it was a matter of simple justice. I said you can never be sure you've got the right man. He said, suppose you were sure, suppose there were video shots of the murderer murdering, would it be okay to execute him then? I said no, it wouldn't, but I couldn't say why. It was only later that I worked it out. If the state kills a man, the state is saying killing is a legitimate tool for achieving a good end, and it just isn't.

On this point I have Vicino on my side.

The curious fact about violence is that each act of aggression is believed by the aggressor to be defensive. He strikes to make himself safe. But in striking, he makes his opponent afraid. That fear generates a violent retaliation. The aggressor, finding himself attacked in his turn, becomes more afraid, and more convinced that only greater violence will protect him. So it goes on: two ageing boxers trapped in a bout that has no end, condemned to punch each other until they can no longer see or stand or lift their fists. At last they fall, these battling heroes, and in falling achieve the peace for which they fought, simply because they no longer have the resources left to fight.

Naturally none of these lines spring readily to my lips. Petra's beautiful eyes disconcert me with their gaze. Smoke curls from her beautiful mouth. All I can think of is that no one will give up the habit of smoking cigarettes so long as the act of exhaling smoke is so sexually alluring.

'Please ask me any time any questions you need to ask,' she says. 'But now we must go.'

Lesson over. I'm not sorry. I need time to think about all this.

The group is taking everything, leaving the house

empty of all signs of human habitation. Stefan has a big black plastic bin-bag with all the rubbish. Ilse scours the room to make sure nothing has been over-looked. Egon shoulders the hold-all with its arsenal of guns.

In the little hallway, Egon offers me his hand once more, and his doleful gaze.

'For the children,' he says. 'We make the good world for the children. Not for us.'

'You have children, Egon?'

'How I wish.'

There's an idealist for you. Suffer for the next generation, then die childless. Walk the lonely road of destiny. What can I say? I feel for the guy, but he asked to be here and I didn't. Me, I'd sooner make the good world for myself and let the children do what they have to do when their turn comes. I'm with the movement all the way till the music swells, then I'm out of the door before they roll the first credit. That's my tip for survival. Be the first to leave. Go without making any fuss.

Outside in the silent suburban street we split up. Petra, Stefan and Ilse, me, the guns and the garbage all go in a waiting pick-up. It has a double cab. Stefan takes the driver's seat, with Ilse beside him in front. I sit in the row of seats behind, with Petra.

Egon and the envelope go in the VW with the cracked windscreen. He leaves first, heading into town. Then we too set off, turning in the other direction, down a road that leads to a bigger road and takes us out into open country.

As the day begins to break, I see mile upon mile of flat mud-coloured land broken by dark bands of trees. Squat red-roofed farm buildings huddle here and there beside the road. We pass farm workers trudging on foot towards their day's labour. For a while, a sluggish river runs on our left. But mostly there's nothing to see but the land and the trees and the heaped clouds that crowd the enormous sky.

My gaze lingers briefly on an overgrown ruin, beside a farmhouse on the right of our road. The structure is fronted by a great arch, like the entrance to a railway tunnel, but there's no railway to be seen. This arch, half hidden among dark-leafed trees, stays in my memory as it disappears into the distance behind us. For what purpose was it built? What long-lost glories does it recall? And why do I feel that there's some information here that is eluding me?

Petra asks me if I still have my gun. I do.

'There may be road blocks,' she says. 'If we're stopped, stay silent. Stefan will do the talking.'

I nod.

'If things go wrong, don't let them take you alive. Save a bullet for yourself.'

Oh sure. Like I'm a martyr with a dream of paradise. However, this is not the place to explain that if faced with a choice between a painful death and revealing all I know I lean towards singing like a choirboy.

'Don't hesitate. It's your duty. To the movement, and to yourself. If they take you alive, you will not like it.'

So here I am, being driven over badly repaired roads to somewhere I don't know, where I don't wish to go, and there's a reasonable chance that someone who doesn't know me will try to kill me.

Little by little the flat farmland gives way to a wilder terrain, and the road starts to climb up into mountains. There is snow here and there, lying where rocks or trees shade the ground. The cab is not well heated, and I start to feel cold. Petra senses this.

'Share warmth,' she says.

We huddle close together on the back seat. She puts an arm round me, and I put an arm round her. She smells of smoke and longing. I want her admiration. I want her body. I want her warmth.

Some vehicles pass us, travelling at speed: a closed truck, and a big grey old-model Mercedes. As the car goes by, I catch a glimpse of a tall dark-haired man sitting alone in the back. All I register is his silhouette against the snow. Petra sees him too. She curses softly to herself. Ilse starts pulling guns out of the hold-all and handing them out. They confer, in short decisive phrases. They wind down all the windows. Petra hands me an automatic pistol.

'You'll get in more shots with this.'

'What's happening?'

'We think they will stop us. If so, we come out shooting.'

I feel the weight of the automatic pistol. I've never used a weapon like this in my life, and don't intend to now. This doesn't seem the time to say so.

We round a bend and there ahead is the truck, pulled up on the side of the road, with the grey Mercedes behind it. The tall man is still sitting in the back of the car, his driver still at the wheel. Half a dozen men of the kind I have seen before stand by the truck, guns dangling, watching us approach. One of them waves his arm up and down, to tell us to pull up. Stefan slows to a crawl and stops a few metres short of the truck. He pulls some papers out of his breast pocket and hands them up for the men with the guns to see. The one who waved him to a stop now gestures for him to get out, and sets off towards him. Stefan opens the door on his side, puts down his papers, takes the gun Ilse has pushed across the seat towards him, and shoots the man dead.

Petra and Ilse start shooting out of the windows. Stefan rushes the truck, pumping bullets. Petra breaks out of the cab and stands rock steady on the road shooting from the hip. Ilse stays in the front seat, picking off her targets shot by shot. The men round the truck are hit and falling, but they're also shooting back. A bullet slams into the cab roof close to my head. A man runs towards me, his gun reached out before him. He stops, and staggers, and falls. I feel an unfamiliar vibration in my clenched hands. Men are bleeding on the road, trying to crawl on their elbows.

Petra takes careful aim, and they jerk, and lie still. The grey car pulls out and races away, abandoning the truck and the dead and dying men. Stefan fires at the car as it accelerates down the mountain road. When he stops firing, there is silence.

The shooting seems to me to have lasted for several hours, but this is not so. Barely a minute has gone by since Stefan opened the cab door and raised his gun. The second surprise is that I have the automatic pistol in my hand and it's warm. I have been shooting too.

The other three are moving forward now, checking the dead men. They roll them over with their boots, and strip the guns from them, and the belts of ammunition. They squat down and unzip their jackets and pull out wallets and papers. They don't seem bothered by the blood.

Stefan's standing over one of the bodies when it moves. He shouts out, and the others join him. Stefan rolls the man over, and Petra binds his wrists tight behind him with a belt. Then Stefan and Ilse haul him to the cab.

I am super-calm because I'm in shock. I realise I must look like the others: hard eyes, blank faces. Veteran urban warriors who kill and feel nothing. But this is only the anaesthetic of fear.

Now I've got a dying man beside me. It's hard to tell how badly wounded he is. He seems not to be able to use his legs, and he's clearly in great pain. But mostly he's frightened. He looks at me with this helpless terror. He's got pale-blue eyes. He's young, younger than me. He's whimpering.

The plunder goes in the back of the pick-up. Then they're returned to their seats, and we're on our way. Stefan drives as fast as the road allows. As we go, they light cigarettes and inhale deeply and speak together in low serious voices. Ilse says something that refers to me. Petra nods and says to me,

'You were good. You performed well.'

I performed well. This is how they refer to the fact that I killed a man, maybe two. The firing all happened at once, so no one can be sure. I do not feel good about this. I don't know what I feel. The men we killed would have killed us. Perhaps it was necessary. But one of them is not dead. He sits beside me, shivering.

'What will happen to this one?'

'He comes with us. He will help us. There are things we must know.'

In a little while the pick-up turns off the road onto a dirt track. The track winds between trees for several miles, and we see nothing. Then without warning the track emerges into the light, and there before us lies a wide view of the plains below. Here we stop, and I get out.

I stand staring stupidly at the view. Somehow, in my shock and confusion, it comforts me. There's a lake, and three white specks on the water, ducks or maybe swans. Some sheep, with a shepherd among them, in a russet-red coat, talking to a boy. Beyond him reach belts of trees, and winter-ploughed fields; and further off, in a distant strip of land lit dull gold by the morning sunlight, there is a windmill. I can make out the spire of a village church, and far away, another spire. Over all, the clouds roll grey, rimmed here and there with bright whiteness, where the light pushes through. Guns and terror seem to have no reality in the face of this majestic commonplace.

Behind me, where the track ends, the pick-up is now pulled up before an abandoned hunting lodge. It's a high-gabled house made of brick and slate, with the ornate detailing of the late nineteenth century: trefoils in the window mullions, finials on the roof ridge. One section of tiles has fallen, forming a grass and nettle covered mound beside the front door. The glass is gone from the windows. The lead has been stolen from the guttering. But the main structure stands.

This is where we are to hide out. There's no electricity, no running water, but several of the rooms are more or less weatherproof. In one, there's a stack of food supplies under a plastic sheet. Clearly they have used this house before.

Stefan carries the prisoner out of the cab as if he's a child, and ties him to a tree. Ilse scavenges for dead wood to build a fire. Petra starts shifting the contents of the pick-up into the house. They seem to have divided up the tasks without discussion.

I help Petra with the baggage.

'Shouldn't someone see to his wounds?'

106

I nod back at the prisoner, who sits hunched and shivering at the base of the tree to which he's tethered.

'After he's helped us,' says Petra, 'we'll let him go.'

I feel a surge of relief. I realise I've been expecting them to kill him. Somehow it's one thing to kill a man in the heat of battle, and quite another to see him trembling and hear him whimpering and then to end his life.

As we come back out of the house, Petra stops by the stairs and picks up a loose brass stair rod. Outside, Ilse has made her fire, and already has a blaze going in a sheltered clearing between the trees. I begin to have hopes of hot coffee, or even better, hot soup. Petra wraps a glove round one end of the stair rod and, kneeling before the fire, holds the other end in the flames. Ilse and Stefan light up their everlasting cigarettes and stand there waiting. In a little while Petra draws the brass rod out of the fire, and I can see that its end is glowing red. She speaks to the others and they flick away their cigarettes and go over to where the prisoner sits.

'What's that for?' I say stupidly.

'To help him help us,' says Petra.

I still can't believe they're going to do it. But the prisoner believes it. He's struggling and jerking and whimpering, trying pathetically to shuffle away. Stefan and Ilse between them yank him back against the tree. He's very weak, quite unable to resist. Stefan holds his head back by pulling on his hair. Petra comes to him and holds the red-hot rod where he can see it and says something to him. Then she does something I don't watch and he screams the scream I've heard before. Then the prisoner starts to talk in gulping choking broken sentences. I turn and walk away through the trees.

After a while I hear a gunshot. I make my way back. The prisoner has fallen forward, still tied to the tree, and blood pours from the side of his head. The others are smoking again, and silent.

'You said you'd let him go.'

'He's gone.'

All I can think is: I must get away. These people are not my people. They do not protect me.

Petra's watching me. Maybe she guesses what I'm feeling. If so, she doesn't care. Either I'm useful or I'm not. If I become a liability, then I can go. Like the boy with the blue eyes went.

Stefan boils a pan of water on the fire, and puts in rice and beans from the stored supplies. The three of them seem subdued. This at least shows they have some humanity left. Nobody speaks to me. They don't speak much to each other. I sit myself down with my back against a tree, in a position where I don't have to look at the dead man. Then I close my eyes, so I don't have to look at anything.

I'm sitting in the car with my father, in the old Buick he used to drive, with the bench seats. He loved the Buick because it was a relic of the early sixties, and showed he wasn't the sort who upgrades his car every two years. Also because it was very wide, and filled the road. Right now, in my memory, it's dark beyond the windscreen and the lights of other cars are coming at me and Cat is by my side with her hair in plaits. That makes her about nine years old, so I'm eleven. My mother has told us my father won't be staying with us so much any more, and this is him explaining, and it's not making sense.

'I'll see just as much of you as before,' he says. 'You won't even notice any difference. I love you just as much as before.'

So what's changed? Cat is crying beside me but not making any sound. My father drives and doesn't even know Cat is crying, she's too small for the lights of the oncoming cars to reveal her face. She's crying because she won't notice any difference other than that everything is changed for ever and there's no safety after all. Things turn out not to last. I don't remember Cat wearing her hair in plaits after that. It was like the plaits went with how we used to be, before the time when we wouldn't notice any difference. Afterwards she had her hair in a ponytail, and later she cut it very short, which made her eyes look bigger, so I called her Goggle-eyes.

I find myself wondering what my father said to my mother. Maybe the six words. 'I love you, let me go.'

I'm remembering that car ride to nowhere because I

have the same feeling now I had then. It feels like loss. Loss for ever.

When I open my eyes a few moments later, I'm alone. The others have vanished. I stand up and look round, bewildered. I hear the sound of an approaching car. I dive into the trees to hide.

It's the old VW with the cracked windscreen, driven by Egon. He pulls the car up beside the pick-up and goes to the house and calls out. He hasn't seen the dead man.

Petra steps out of the trees, her gun in her hand. She goes to the VW and reaches inside and finds Egon's gun. Egon turns and sees her. Then he sees the tortured body of the prisoner. Then he sees Ilse and Stefan also coming out of the trees, also holding guns. His eyes travel back to the VW. Petra holds up his gun, not to give it to him, but to show him she's got it. I watch each move, and see how they stare at him, and I start to understand. The quietness after the torture was not pity. It was caused by the information the dying man had revealed.

Egon has gone white. He looks from side to side, as if calculating his chances of getting away. He has no chance. He sinks to his knees in front of the derelict hunting lodge. He mumbles some words. Petra speaks, cool and clear, to the other two. Yes, they say in their language. Yes.

Now Petra is looking towards me, and holding out Egon's handgun.

'Executioner.'

I stare back. Is this supposed to be me?

'He asks for it to be quick. One shot.'

Egon looks at me. This is exactly the look he has given me each time before, only now, framed by its true context, it makes sense. He is asking me not to kill him. He wants to make the good world for the children who will never be his. How I wish.

'No.' My own voice surprises me. I speak clearly and loudly.

'He has betrayed us.'

'Not me.'

Petra slightly raises her eyebrows, but does not repeat her request. Instead, she walks over to Egon's side as if she has something to say to him, and puts her gun to his brow. He looks away from me, to spare me at the last. A single sharp report, and he buckles sideways to the ground.

I turn and run. I hear them coming after me, calling to me, crashing through dead wood and leaf litter. I run faster and faster, not knowing or caring which direction I take, plunging between tree trunks. Their voices echo about me as they give chase. I find a descending gully and bound down it, clearing the brambles with great leaps. Then the gully sheers away to nothing, and I'm falling, turning as I fall. My flailing legs strike the branches of young trees, and I tumble and crash down the mountain slope, over and over, down and down, now snagged by brambles, now

111

smacked by frozen snow, now clubbed by trees, until at last stunned and reeling, bundled in pain, I roll to stillness.

I am lying in a singing bed where kind hands caress me, and all my hurt is soothed away. At last I feel nothing and want nothing and am nothing.

Dimly, as if from far away, I am aware that I've fallen into a fast-flowing stream. The mountain water is cold as ice. I must not let myself go to sleep. Must not sleep. Must not. Sleep.

8

There was once a countryman who lived in a cottage by a beech wood. The cottage was very small: one room just of a size for the countryman and his wife to cook and eat and sit by the fire in the corner, and a second room for their high-sided bed. In front of the cottage there was a small garden where hollyhocks grew in the summer, and a cobbled path that led to a road. Behind the cottage a path ran through the beech wood to a potato field where the countryman grew potatoes for market. Morning and evening the country-man walked this path, in the white frost of winter and the dappled sunlight of summer. In May the leaves glowed green as dawn, and in October they flamed golden as sunset. The potato field was stony, and planting, tending and digging up the potatoes was hard work for little return, but there was always a pig fattening in the pen beneath the apple tree, and in the autumn there were apples.

Then one day while turning over the soil of the potato field, the countryman came upon a stone that showed a gleam of gold. He took the stone to town, and a gold expert told him that it was indeed gold, and if he dug further he might find more gold. The countryman dug further, and so it was. There was gold in the potato field, there was gold in the back yard, there was gold in the front garden. The countryman used the gold to hire labourers, and his team of men dug up the land, following the seams of gold. Soon the potato field was gone, and the front garden with its hollyhocks, and the back yard with its pig pen and its apple tree. It was plain there was gold beneath the floor of the cottage, so they dug there too. 'Where are we to live?' cried the countryman's wife, gazing on the diggings. 'Don't worry about that,' said the countryman. 'We're rich now. We'll build ourselves a mansion.'

They were rich, and they did build a mansion. Meanwhile the teams of diggers followed the seams of gold, and they dug up the cottage altogether, and they cut down the beech trees and dug up the beech wood and all the land round about. By the time they stopped digging, the countryman was the richest man for miles around, and he and his wife were living in a mansion with twenty-four rooms and five servants. The days of digging potatoes and chopping wood were over.

Sitting together one evening in the spacious drawing room of their centrally heated mansion, the wife said to her husband, 'I do miss a fire.' 'You're right,' said her husband, and he ordered a snug fireplace to be built in one corner, the way they'd had it in their cottage. Sitting before the fire, the wife said, 'This room is so big it makes me feel cold.' 'You're right,' said her husband, and he had the room made much smaller. After that, the rest of the mansion seemed too big. 'What do we want with so many rooms?' said his wife. 'I hate to see them standing empty.' So they reduced the mansion to six rooms: a hallway, a drawing room, a kitchen, and three bedrooms. The extra bedrooms were for guests.

'I miss our little apple tree,' said the wife one day. So they planted an apple tree behind the mansion, and then, for old times' sake, they built a pig pen beneath it and kept a pig there. They had guests to stay, but the experience made the wife anxious, and they decided not to repeat it. The cook who made their meals turned out to be robbing them, and had to be dismissed. 'Don't worry,' said the wife, 'I'll cook for us myself, the way I used to.' She didn't like being in the kitchen while her husband was in the snug little room next door with the fire, so they had the stove moved in to join him, and the sink and the dresser. Now that there were no guests there seemed no point in the extra bedrooms, so they had them taken down.

'You know what?' said the wife. 'This is so like our old cottage that I'd like to make a little front garden the way we used to have it.' So they made a little front garden with a cobbled path, and even built a road for it to go out and meet; and so that they could see it through the window the way they used to, they took down the hallway.

By now the mansion was just two rooms in size, and so very like the old cottage that you would hardly have known they had ever moved. The countryman and his wife were much happier. 'Really we had everything we wanted before,' they told each other, 'but we didn't know it. We can thank the gold for teaching us to be content.'

So everything was just as it had been before, except that the beech wood was gone. The countryman planted a new beech wood, but trees are slow to grow. Long before they were tall enough to form a shady path down which he could walk in the white frost of winter and the dappled sunlight of summer, the countryman was dead.

This story is told by Leon Vicino in his book. I find it very touching, because Vicino refuses to sneer at his country couple, either for their pursuit of gold or for their limited ambitions. Also I'm impressed because he allows the story's moral to remain complex. Yes, the countryman has lost his beech wood, but he's also been saved the drudgery of digging his potato field, and he's been granted the subtle blessing of knowing what brings him contentment. He has been saved by the gold from bitterness and envy. Win some, lose some.

That isn't the end of it, either. The more I read Vicino, the more I realise his subject, his area of enquiry, is what he calls 'the well-lived life'. Vicino wants to understand, and wants us to understand, the nature of contentment. What is it, he asks, we labour to achieve, earn money to buy, fight wars to defend? When the battle is over and the long day's work is done, what is our chosen reward? I read on eagerly, hoping for answers.

I have been ill. Over many long days, lying in bed too weak to move, I've read Vicino's words and thought his thoughts. The good people who are looking after me speak no English, so we communicate with mime. Hanna, the young mother, is so amused by my mimes that she reproduces them for her husband when he comes home at the end of the day. He gazes at her like one of his own oxen, willing but slow, entirely unable to grasp the meaning of her dumb-show. Hanna is as short and wide and sturdy as her husband, but she is far more mentally agile. When I became strong enough to want to read, I mimed fetching the book from the pocket of my coat, and mimed turning its pages. She herself I'm almost certain can't read at all, but she understood my meaning at once.

Hanna and Lutz are in some ways like Vicino's countryman and wife. They live a life of hard labour and extreme simplicity, without the help of electricity or piped water. Their house is a big deep-roofed barn, divided down the middle by a timber paling. On one side, Lutz's herd of thirty cows passes the winter, filling the house with their heat and stink. On the other side there is a tiled stove round which the bunks cluster, and a fireplace rising to a brick chimney, where hams hang slowly smoking. The roof thatch is exposed on its underside, and the eaves fall low, to within four feet of the ground. The windows are small, and now in the cold weather permanently shuttered. Hanna cooks and washes and minds the baby in an eternal twilight. For my reading I have a fat candle, which stands in a clay saucer of melted wax.

The night after Lutz brought me here, carrying me in his arms like a calf, the winter storms began. Snow has been falling for five days. When the outer door opens I can see how deep the snow lies. Lutz keeps the path clear, shovelling the snow morning and evening into heaps on either side. This is the way to the privy, the small wooden shed where there is a box seat with a deep hole beneath. When at last I grew strong enough to walk, Lutz led me out here, through still-falling snow. Sitting on the smooth wooden seat, straining for a result, shivering in the cold, I racked my brains to discover how I had emptied my bowels during my days in the bunk by the stove. I concluded I hadn't. I carried within me the waste matter of six days; though it's true to say that for most of that time I've eaten nothing.

My illness is not really an illness so much as a

collapse. The fall down the mountainside hurt me, but did no lasting damage. I was badly chilled by lying in the stream. Had Lutz not found me I would now be dead. But I believe the root cause of my fever is moral shock. In the days since I entered this miserable country I have seen too much suffering and hatred, too much cruelty and death. I've not been prepared for this. I have no picture of the world into which it all fits. I feel as if I've lost all bearings, or as if my life up to this point has been a dream, and now with merciless brutality I am thrust into the waking world. Why this should be so I can't conceive. Is this punishment? If so, what are my crimes? Silently, within myself, I cry the aggrieved cry of the eternal child: It's not fair, why are they picking on me, I didn't do anything.

It's true. It's not fair. They are picking on me. But it begins to strike me that it's the same for everyone. They pick on everyone. I am not alone.

You see why I read Vicino with such eagerness. His voice is wry and undeceived, but he has hope. He loves the company of other people.

Lutz's father, the old man, is singing. He sits on a bench with his back to the stove and a wool hat pulled down low over his withered face and croons to himself. He sings sweet songs with simple repetitive tunes that go round and round for ever. The old lady, his wife, shuffles about the house moving implements and dishes back to what she considers to be their proper place. There are no shelves in this long-roofed barn:

everything hangs from hooks attached to the rafters, or slides into pockets made of netted string. The old lady is permanently annoyed that Hanna doesn't know the right hook for the stew pan, or the right pocket for the heavy white plates. She never tells Hanna she's made a mistake. She just shuffles about, breathing heavily, and puts things back where they should be. Hanna too never remarks on this, or even seems to notice. But I am watching from my bunk, and I see how whenever the old lady is at her rearranging, Hanna becomes especially preoccupied with the needs of her baby.

This baby is a boy named Manfred, who they call Man. They all adore Man, and compete in worshipping him. He is a delightful good-natured baby, about six months old, and always smiling. When Hanna is raking out the hot embers from the stove she puts Man in the bunk with me, and we sit and smile at each other. He finds me enormously interesting. After gazing at me for a while he reaches out one hand, and I lean my face close and he feels my face with his fingers. He pokes his fingers into my mouth and nostrils and eyes, and bats at my nose and chin. This is exactly how he treats the huge shaggy dogs that come loping back with Lutz every evening. The dogs react as I react, with patient submission. The prod of Man's little hands feels like an honour.

These people have taken me into their home without questions. Of course I have no means of answering them, even if they were to question me, but their every action has shown that they have no doubts about what they are doing. I'm a fellow creature in need, and they have the means to help me. They're not especially virtuous people. Hanna's steady good humour conceals a stubborn insistence on getting her own way, and Lutz almost certainly has a secret supply of alcohol somewhere outside the house. His mother, the old lady, devotes her life to silent but determined demonstrations of her daughter-in-law's fecklessness; while the old man has clearly decided that his working days are over, and now in his final years has opted to do nothing whatsoever. I doubt if he's much over sixty. So contented peasants they are not, with the possible exception of Man. However I believe they enjoy frequent moments in which they have, for a little while, all that they require. Vicino calls this 'the Great Enough'.

In the midst of aches in the joints, anxiety over the payment of bills, concern for the safety of those you love, envy of the rich, fear of robbers, dog-weariness at the end of a long day, and the unacceptable slipping away of youth, there does occasionally appear, like a ray of light piercing the clouds, a moment of joy. Perhaps you have entered the house and sat down before removing your boots. A friend has pressed a drink into your hands, and is telling you the latest news. You see from his face that he's glad you've come in; and you are glad too. Glad to be sitting down, glad of the warming glow of the drink, glad of your friend's furrowed brow and eager speech. For this moment, nothing more is required. It is in its way unimprovable. This is what I mean by the Great Enough.

Lutz comes back accompanied by a boy of twelve or so. The boy has a tale to tell, to which the others listen in silence, occasionally glancing at me. Then the boy comes over to where I lie and solemnly offers me his hand.

'Hello sir,' he says. 'I am name Bruno.'

He speaks carefully. He has planned this sentence in advance. Still, at last I can talk.

'I'm happy to meet you.'

I echo his courteous formality.

'I am son of brother of Lutz,' he tells me.

Then in awkward stumbling English, he explains why he has come. It seems two policemen called on his father's farm, some way down the valley, to warn the family that there were dangerous men in the area. These men carry bombs, with which they blow up innocent people.

'Why?' I ask.

'They are terrorist,' says Bruno.

'Why should terrorists want to blow up innocent people?'

'Because they are terrorist,' he replies. It's as if I've asked why foxes take chickens. That's what foxes do.

Then I remember Petra fixing me with her beautiful eyes and telling me, 'It will be a great sacrifice, but it will bring liberation.' Bruno is right. The movement sacrifices innocent people because that is their mode of operation.

'I think the police come here too.'

He looks at me steadily as he says this and I understand that he believes I am a terrorist. Despite this, he has come to warn me. I think this is because the code of hospitality is stronger than the fear of terrorism that the authorities are seeking to cultivate. I have slept under his family's roof, I have broken bread with them. I have asked for and been given refuge. For all these reasons, these puzzled people are in some way obligated to me. Perhaps there's nothing here to do with country custom after all, perhaps it's simply that I have become real to them. No real person is a terrorist.

And yet Egon was real to Petra, and she killed him. As Vicino writes: *Other people's lives are more mysterious than the moon and the stars.*

'I'm not a terrorist, Bruno.'

Those grave eyes. Children grow up young here.

'That is good.'

Nevertheless I have no wish to be discovered by the visiting policemen. This is entirely understood by the family. Hanna brushes dry soil from a section of the floor, and lifts a hatch. A ladder leads down into a lightless cellar, where the winter's supply of tubers is stored.

'They come,' explains Bruno, 'you go here.'

Now it seems he plans to go, even though darkness has fallen. He holds out his hand for me to shake once more.

'Please,' I say. 'Tell your uncle he has saved my life. I owe him my life.'

Bruno passes this on. Lutz shrugs and looks down and mumbles a few words.

'He says anyone would do this.'

'Tell him, I don't wish to place his family in danger. As soon as I'm strong, I'll go on my way.'

On my way. What way is that? From an unknown resting place to an unknown testing place.

As a gauge of my returning strength, I go out with Lutz for the day. We leave the house at first light, with the dogs at our heels. I have not been further than the privy for a week, and the effect of the sunrise is startling. It's a bitter cold, still, clear day, the Morning Star still hovering over the horizon. Snow covers the valley and the tree-clad hills that rise steeply on either side. The sun is about to appear above the eastern range of mountains, and already it is reaching out from behind gold-rimmed clouds three fan-shaped beams of amber light. These beams shine upon the underside of a second, higher layer of cloud, turning the pale grey to a warm silver. Then as the burning orb of the sun itself climbs into view, the dazzling light spills down the valley, and all the snow turns gold before our tramping feet. Lutz has lent me a long warm coat and a fur hat with ear flaps that I suspect belong to his father. I am glad of them: I'm shivering with the cold. The sunrise brings no addition of warmth, but the celestial glory of it takes my breath away. Lutz says nothing as usual, but I glance at him and see that he too is appreciating it. Then, as quickly as it began, it's over. The sun has risen into the cloud belt, and the valley is mortal again.

We are going to fetch wood for the ever-hungry stove. The wood-pile by the house is well stacked, all down one outside wall beneath the eaves, but as it is used it must be replaced. We carry axes, to cut the timber into lengths that will fit into the iron mouth of the stove. I follow Lutz and his dogs down a path he has tramped before. His boot marks are before us, frozen in the snow. No one else has been this way. The path leads over the stream, up the hillside, to a small clearing in the trees. The clearing is Lutz's own creation: each stump the remains of a tree felled by his axe. Across the clearing lies a tall birch felled by Lutz on some previous occasion. Our task is to cut it up.

He takes the base end, where the trunk is widest, and suggests to me, by pointing and making chopping gestures, that I cut off the feathery branches higher up. He then stands alongside the tree trunk and swings his axe with light circular strokes as if he's skipping rope, and a section of timber half a metre wide falls away. When I tackle a slender branch, aiming to shear it off where it joins the trunk, my blow misses entirely and I bury my axe-blade in the ground. For the first time in my life I find myself wondering how you aim an axe. You can't look down it. You can't track the line from the blade to the target, because when you start to strike the blade is high above your head. I watch Lutz. He doesn't seem to look at anything, and yet blow after blow lands in exactly the same place, until the wood splits.

I can't stand still, it's too cold. So I decide to copy Lutz, and swing my axe as if it knows itself where to go, and to act as if wherever it lands is fine with me. So I chop away, and make criss-cross marks in the hard ground, and chip the sides of the trunk, and slice off the odd twig, and at least I get warm. I also get blisters. Lutz works steadily on, slicing rings of tree trunk and stacking them behind him, paying no attention to my ridiculous miming of chopping wood.

Now my hands hurt quite a lot, and I decide I might as well stop. Lutz does not stop. He's getting close to my part of the trunk, where the side branches begin. He moves towards me, and with small sideways snips of his axe he lops off some branches. Then he goes back to his stack of trunk-rings, and lays one by itself on the ground, and crack! crack! chops it into four triangular segments. This I now recognise as the final product, as stacked in the house wood-pile. He rolls another ring into place, and signs to me to try chopping it. I think of showing him my blisters and then decide not to.

My second blow splits the ring in two. I'm astonished, and proud. Lutz hasn't noticed. After that I swing away with a will. It takes me seven more blows to achieve the pure clean power that caused the timber to part, but now I have tasted success. On I work, becoming ever more capable, my arms and wrists and hands gradually learning the precise path they must travel through the air to deliver the irresistible blow. I catch sight of Lutz glancing in my direction. He says nothing, but no words are necessary. The split logs are my witnesses.

When at last we stop, my hands are actually bleeding, and I haven't been aware of it. Lutz sees, and frowns, and washes my burst blisters with snow. He produces a metal flask which contains schnapps, and we both drink from it. Then he pulls out two tangled bundles of string which turn out to be nets, and we gather up the split logs.

I carry my load the way he shows me, leaning forward on the balls of the feet, with the weight resting on the small of my back. The two main cords run over my shoulders and I hold them at waist level in both hands. We plod home down the track, over the stream and across the snow-covered fields. I am surprised to see from the length of my shadow before me that the sun is sinking in the sky. We have been chopping wood for nearly all the short winter day.

It strikes me that this is what Lutz does every day. There is no ploughing or planting possible in such weather. This must mean that the household burns as much wood in twenty-four hours as we can chop each day. He's like the fish that swim about all day finding food to give them the energy to swim about all day. This no longer seems ridiculous to me. I have joined the fish.

Back at the house, Hanna has hot food waiting in the stew pot. I have never been so hungry in my life. The smell of the stew alone makes me feel faint with anticipated joy. The actual eating of it, even with the distraction of the pain in my hands, is mouthful upon mouthful of bliss. When at last I stop, unable to eat any more, the overwhelming sensation of bodily satisfaction fills me from top to toe, and I sit and beam in glowing silence.

Lutz tells Hanna about my blisters. She comes and looks at my hands, and clicks her tongue, and fetches a jar of ointment. The ointment is cool and soothing. I watch her grave plain features as she applies the ointment, and suddenly I'm flooded with gratitude. What excellent people they are! How good she is, to fill my belly and ease my pain. How well Lutz swings his axe. How pleasantly the old man sings, and the baby gurgles. How obliging of the stove to keep me warm and the roof to keep me dry. How welcoming my bunk, how irresistible the nest prepared for me beneath the rugs. How sweet the warm motherly arms of sleep.

*   *   *

The police come. Their arrival is heralded by the roar of a four-wheel drive from far down the valley. Lutz is out, but Hanna remains calm. She lifts the hatch in the floor and I go down into the dark to crouch among the potatoes. Seeing nothing, I hear the boots of the policemen, and their voices and their laughter. I work out that Hanna is giving them a glass of schnapps and they are playing with the baby. I've no doubt little Manfred smiles on them as bonnily as he smiles on me.

Then they go, and I hear the roar of their vehicle departing. The hatch opens, and I climb out. Hanna makes no attempt to tell me what has happened, nor do I need to be told. The policemen have come looking for strangers. Hanna has told them nothing, and they have gone on their way. An everyday story of courage and kindness with no possible hope of reward.

When Lutz returns, he has Bruno with him. They know of the police visit. I say at once, through Bruno, that I will leave in the morning. They nod and accept this. Bruno will stay the night. In the morning he will guide me to the road that leads to their nearest town. They take it for granted that as a non-countryman I will want to go to the town.

That evening Hanna tells the story of the policemen, and there's huge amusement. Bruno, smiling, explains.

'The police say, these strangers, they cut the throat, they kill the baby, they steal the cow.'

I too laugh. But as I laugh I think how it might have been, if the police warnings had come before Lutz found me. Would these fears have sounded so preposterous then, if I had appeared as the predicted stranger? I can as easily imagine Lutz taking his axe and dashing out my brains, to stop me cutting his wife's throat and killing his baby, as doing what he in fact did, which was to lift me gently out of the stream and carry me to a bed by the stove.

I can give these people nothing in return for all they have given me. I offer them my foreign money, aware that if they try to spend it they will attract suspicion. They know this better than I. They shake their heads, and I put my notes away. Perhaps after all payment is not required. They have given me the purest gift known to mankind, which is to care for a stranger in need. My part is to receive the gift, and when my turn comes, to pass it on.

9

The narrow road down which I am walking is striped white and brown where passing cars have left their tracks in the snow, and flecked with broken reddish stones. On either side of the road grow tall thin-trunked branchless trees, that put out leaves only at the top, in uncertain bundles like the heads of mops. These trees, both straight and not straight, retreat before my eyes into the distance, a parade of homely standards that make of the road a ceremonial approach. Beyond them, the view is divided by their bent trunks into a line of vertical windows. I can make out the snowy roofs and soft red walls of a small town. There's a church with a square tower, capped with a cupola that's too smooth-sided to hold the snow and glints silver-grey in the morning light. The land on either side of the road is laid out in orchards, all now under snow. A man is walking towards me, with a shotgun over one shoulder and a dog at his heels.

I come to a stop. This is the town to which Bruno has directed me. I stand looking down the avenue of trees towards the church with its odd-shaped tower. The man with the gun approaches. I nod a greeting. He passes by with barely a glance, his dog behind him. Bruno told me there has been a bomb explosion in some other town, not far away, and people are afraid. The hunter shows no curiosity in me. This may be because I am wearing the long outer coat and the fur hat with ear flaps given me by Lutz. I look like all the rest of them, bundled up against the cold.

I have stopped because I have seen all this before: the avenue of trees, the church, the man with the dog. I tell myself this is the experience called déjà vu, which is no more than a kind of crossing of wires in the brain. The thing you think you've seen before is the same thing you're looking at now, only your brain has diverted the message via its ancient memories store, and it reaches your conscious mind labelled 'past experience'. This keeps happening to me: one of the symptoms of disorientation. A creepy feeling.

I set off once more towards the town. There are others out on the road ahead of me. No sounds: no bells or voices or passing cars or laughter. Everyone is afraid. Before Bruno left me, at the point where the farm track met the road, I asked him what it is the people fear, the terrorists or the police? Everyone, he answered. Everyone is afraid of everyone. It's not only the cold and the snow that keep people in their houses. Out on the streets anything may happen. Safety lies in not getting involved. Even witnessing one of the anythings is dangerous. The active parties don't like witnesses.

Bruno can read. That is, he can form the words represented by letters, moving his finger carefully across the page. He saw my book and read the name VICINO and recognised it. His teacher has a book with the same name on its cover. He admires his teacher greatly, he is brave and clever and wears glasses. His name is Eckhard. It is this teacher who taught him his English.

In the course of our early-morning trudge across the snowy fields I became quite impressed by Bruno. His solemn eyes turned towards me again and again, and I felt within him a quiet steady yearning for knowledge. Not knowledge of anything in particular, or for any purpose, just a reaching out of his young mind. He made me feel he was like a prisoner in a cell with one very small window, out of which he gazes all day in hope of building a picture of the great world.

He knew I was not from his own country. So where was I from? I said England. England! I might as well have said Eldorado. His eyes grew wide with wonder.

'What is it like in England?' he asked. 'I hear it's a very beautiful country where all the people are happy and free.'

What can I say? Two out of three? So I tell him it's

good in England, but it has its downside like every-where. He doesn't believe me. If he could go to England he would be happy for the rest of his life.

'What would you do in England, Bruno?'

'I would walk in the park and drink tea and watch television.'

Not a bad plan for a life. I've known worse.

The avenue leads me into a narrow street, and the street leads me into a small square. Here is the church before me now, unexpectedly large. There's also an inn, which seems to be closed, and a long tile-roofed arcade that I take to be the market place, and a square stone building at its far end that I take to be the school. All this following Bruno's careful instructions. The school has stone steps covered by a wooden porch, leading to an arched doorway.

Under other circumstances the scene would be charming. Due to the poverty of the region, the little town has not been developed since its last period of prosperity, which I guess to be some time in the seventeenth century. The effect, especially under snow, is picturesque. There are travellers who pride themselves on discovering unspoiled destinations, rather like men who like sex with virgins, so they can be the first to spoil them. They'd like this place. They'll be here soon. Then the inn will be turned into a small but luxurious hotel, and there'll be living statues performing under the arcade.

No signs of bomb-wielding terrorists or men in black

nylon jackets. I feel invisible in my long coat and fur hat. My sole objective now is to escape the men who pursue me, who have information, who are well trained, and to leave this country and find my way home to England, where I can walk in the park and drink tea and watch television. To this end I now cross the brushed snow of the square and climb the stone steps beneath the wooden porch of the school.

The door is ajar. No lights are on inside, and I can find no light switch. Blinds are drawn at the windows. Winter daylight creeps through cracks, and as my eyes adjust I find I can see well enough.

A small lobby, its walls lined with coat-hooks. Two doors, leading into classrooms. A staircase, with worn shiny metal edges on its treads. I push on a door and go into one of the classrooms, where a light is on. Long tables with benches, lined up facing a blackboard. On the blackboard, columns of words neatly written in pairs. The words are in English.

give	gave
meet	met
take	took
go	went
come	came
say	said

Without stopping to think why I do it, I read the words out loud. Maybe it's because I'm homesick.

'Give, gave. Meet, met. Take, took.'

A voice behind me chimes in:

'Go, went. Come, came. Say, said.'

I turn to find a bony man of maybe thirty with a face like a skull and round black-rimmed spectacles. He is sitting at a table in one corner, at work on some papers. This has to be Eckhard.

'You are English, I suppose?'

He speaks like someone who has read a great deal but has never heard the language spoken. The emphases fall in the wrong places.

'Yes. I am.'

'I love your language. Please speak some more.'

I stare at him like I'm stupid.

'I'm not really much of a speaker,' I say.

'Ah.' He sighs with pleasure. '*I'm*. That is the elision of *I am*, which is from the verb *to be*. *Be, am*. No structural connection at all. *I am, you are, he is*. All quite different word forms, yet all the present tense of the verb *to be*. Your language refuses to conform to any laws. This is why it has much moral beauty.'

This is quite an opening. His goggle-glassed eyes shine with enthusiasm.

'Right,' I say.

'Right! You say, *Right*. This word I think signifies: *maybe, okay*. But this is also the word that signifies, one, correct meaning, and two, that which by common custom is due to a person. The rights of man, yes? So this word has no secure meaning, or rather, no single

136

meaning. Would you say that the task of the auditor is to identify the one intended meaning from the context, or that all meanings are present each time of use, enclosed one within another, but as it were in changing orders of priority?'

I have no answer to this. I feel unable to say 'right' again.

'For example,' he pursues earnestly, 'your first meaning is: *yes, okay.* Your second meaning is perhaps that the reasoning in my statement is correct. But do you also mean to tell me that I have a *right* to my opinion? Not consciously, I think. But the language carries this possibility. Can you avoid it?'

This has gone on long enough.

'Would you be Mr Eckhard?'

'Would I be? This tense that you use, it is the conditional. Would I, if I could? You allow me the option of choosing to be someone other. So courteous, even permissive. And yet I must answer you in simple solid words, being a foreigner to your language, yes, my name is Eckhard.'

Progress.

'I need help, Mr Eckhard.'

His face clouds with caution.

'Help of what nature?'

I explain my dilemma, leaving out any details that might make him nervous, such as my alleged assassination of the chief of the security police. I have wandered into this country by mistake. I seem to have attracted suspicion. I wish to leave as quietly as possible.

Eckhard finds none of this surprising.

'These are bad times,' he says. 'People keep to their homes.'

'I need a guide to the border.'

'Yes. I understand.'

He understands but he does not volunteer to help. I don't blame him. Stick your head over the parapet round here and you're liable to have parts of your face removed.

'I have money. English money. I can pay.'

He shakes his head. Either he's not the acquisitive type or it's not clever to be caught dealing in hard currency. I try another approach.

'When you walk with a stranger you travel further than when you walk with a friend.'

He goggles at me as if I've just developed supernatural powers.

'You have read Leon Vicino?'

I produce the book.

'Ah!' He takes the book and fingers it lovingly. 'You have the English edition. It is well translated?'

'I think so.'

'By Vicino himself, of course. He speaks six languages. This book is much beloved. It is beloved by you too?'

I'm about to correct his use of the word when I realise I have nothing better to put in its place.

'It's getting to be quite beloved by me, yes.'

He beams and embraces me. His breath smells. I guess not being a fully developed consumer society they haven't reached toothpaste yet.

'A friend of Vicino's is a friend of mine. I will help you.'

So that's settled.

He gazes at me, and taps his teeth with one fingernail. He is running through the options open to him. You can always tell when people are processing like this, it's almost as if a little symbol appears on their face, an hour-glass or a spinning disc, like on a computer screen.

'They know you are here?'

'Yes.'

'You fear them?'

'Yes.'

'Why? You are English.'

I see I'm going to have to tell him a little more. So I explain about Marker and the burning of the books. Eckhard keeps nodding as I talk. It seems he knows part of this already.

'They found a list,' he tells me. 'It is very terrible. Many good people now hide.'

However this seems to have done the trick, because all at once he comes to a decision.

'There is a border crossing,' he says, 'where the guards may be bribed. It's far from here, at least four days' journey, because you must go by the back roads.

You will need a guide.' He thinks some more. 'I will guide you part of the way myself. Then others will complete the journey.'

'You're very kind.'

'Today, you had better stay at my friend's house. You will be safe there, and we can talk. I will take you.'

When he says he'll take me he turns out to be speaking metaphorically. His spirit will take me, maybe. Meanwhile his body will take damn good care not to be seen within half a mile of me. He draws me a little map. The main street of the town, a right turn, a longish walk, a house with a brick archway and red shutters that will be closed.

'You must knock on the door. You ask for Sabine, yes? You go through the front room to the room at the back. Yes?'

Not hard to follow. I tell him I'm with him every step of the way.

'The front room, it is not important. You will go to the room at the back. I will be there.'

He leaves first. I am to wait until he's well gone, then I'm to follow. I feel like I've been told to shut my eyes and count to forty. When I'm done maybe I'll shout out, Coming! Ready or not!

I'm beginning to feel hungry. Bruno and I left the farm at first light, but it was a long walk to the road, and a longer one down the road to the town. Already the time is past noon. I resolve to try to buy some bread or sausage as I pass through the town. Then I remember yet again that I have no local currency. So I walk faster, to arrive sooner at the house of Eckhard's friends. They will feed me.

All the houses in the street turn out to have brick archways over their doors; or, to be precise, red brick alternating with blocks of whitish stone. Many of the houses also have red shutters. Only one seems to have its shutters closed at this hour of the day. Its outer door stands open.

I look in, uncertain. The door opens onto a passage, which leads to a courtyard. I go through the passage, past a closed door. The courtyard is very clean, paved in cream-coloured brick. A broom lies on the ground, its bristles bound together with white cord, beside a wooden bucket. No one in sight. I go back out into the street, and look again at the closed red shutters.

I know this red. It's a soft dusty red, somewhere between earth and sunset. My mother took forever picking it out from a stack of colour cards in the Historical Colour Range. It's called Etruscan Red, and it's the colour of our front door. What is happening to me?

I go back into the passage and knock on the inner door. After a moment it's opened by a middle-aged woman wearing an apron and holding a coffee-jug in one hand. She lets me in without question. The room I now enter is quite dark. The woman with the jug precedes me, and then stops and turns to me with an indulgent smile, and points with her free hand. She's showing me the only other person in the room, a much younger woman, who wears a red sleeveless jacket over a rumpled white blouse. She sits on a chair, her head on her hand, her elbow on her knee, asleep.

The jug woman says something to me in her language, and laughs. Behind the sleeper is a bar. I look towards the bar and know I will see a cat. The cat has crept up onto the bar, and is stealing food left unguarded on a plate: a cold chicken, only its neck is too long to be a chicken. The wooden-boarded floor is painted in faded black lozenges, like a chessboard. I have known all this before. The woman sees the cat, and swipes at it, and puts down her jug with a bang. The sleeper wakes and yawns, and looks up at me without surprise or enthusiasm.

'Okay,' she says sleepily. 'Okay, okay.'

I say, 'Sabine.'

The jug woman raises her eyebrows and glances at the door behind her, then looks quickly away, as if she has heard nothing. The younger woman shrugs and settles back into her sleeping posture. I go through the door.

The back room is small and crowded. Two middle-aged ladies sit whispering and drinking, on either side of an old man who has fallen asleep sitting very upright on a high-backed chair, his hat still on his head. Further into the room, at a table covered with a red-and-black rug, sits a grave round-faced man,

142

reading aloud from a book he holds open in one hand, while a round-faced woman listens, a stringed instrument on her lap. It's a mandolin, or a lute. Eckhard himself stands behind the reader, his eyes tracking the words as they are spoken. The mandolin woman plucks the strings softly, ping-ping-ping. Not a mandolin, a theorbo. I wonder briefly how I know this arcane name. On the floor, left over from some earlier game of cards, lies an ace of spades.

Eckhard hears me come in and looks up, and gives a smile of pleasure. He comes over to me and pumps my hand.

'You are here! So good!'

He introduces me to the others with a small speech in which I recognise the word 'England'. They all clap, and the old man wakes up and takes his hat off. One of the middle-aged ladies pours me a glass of whatever it is they have been drinking. I seem to be a hit.

'These people,' Eckhard explains, 'their names are on the list. The police wish to interrogate them.'

'Why?'

He shrugs. 'The activities of the society concern them.'

The others in the room look so inoffensive, so utterly respectable, that I find this hard to believe.

'Are you all part of the resistance movement?'

'No,' he replied. 'The movement, no. But we are educated. We know that matters are arranged

143

differently in other countries. We think for ourselves. We are members of the Society of Others.'

'That's enough?'

He stares at me.

'Don't you know? It is enough to question the need for the state of emergency. It is enough to be the friend of one who has questioned the need for the state of emergency. It is enough to have your name in the address book of a relative who has a friend who has questioned the need for the state of emergency. They will interrogate you for that.'

He adopts the fierce demeanour of an interrogator, punching questions at me.

'Do you understand how great is the danger from terrorists? Do you agree that any measures, however extreme, are justified in the fight against terror? If not, you are yourself a terrorist! You are part of the thought-climate which makes terrorism possible! You are part of the rot that must be cut away!'

He speaks so vehemently that his pale cheeks become blotched with pink. What am I supposed to say to all that? Defensively, I drink my drink. Apple juice.

'Forgive me, please. These things make me angry. You have eaten?'

No, I have not eaten. They bring me food, slices of ham pie and cold boiled potatoes and pickled cabbage. It turns out the others all speak a few words of English which they're eager to try out on me, so as I eat I do my best to respond intelligently to a series of surreal statements.

'Please tell me where is the railway station.'

'I wish this bus to go to Piccadilly.'

'If the day is rain, I will have umbrella.'

'Will you to dance with me kindly?'

No actual answer is required, only my acknowledgement that the sentences are more or less correctly formed and have meaning. At the same time, I hear the unseen outer door open and close. I hear voices from the front room, followed by footsteps going up a staircase. Whoever it is has gone into the room directly above us. Shortly there comes the unmistakable sound of bedsprings creaking to a mounting rhythm.

Eckhard meets my eyes with another of his wry shrugs.

'This is why the police don't look here,' he explains. 'They have other interests.' A glance up at the ceiling.

I am in the back room of a small brothel favoured by the security police. There are three girls who work here regularly, all former students of Eckhard. One of them is the woman with the theorbo. Only now do I discover I have a pre-existing notion of the women who wait in brothels to give pleasure to men. I've never been in a brothel before, but I have this very clear image of a naked woman lying on a couch, before a red velvet drape. She's on her side, with her back towards me, so there's nothing on view that the censor would consider unacceptable. Even so, the curve of her naked back, the swell of her naked bottom, and in particular the dimple at the top of her left buttock, is seriously arousing. I would pay money to cuddle up to that. However the picture I have retained so fondly in my memory is not a whore at all but a goddess and a famous work of art; to be exact, the Rokeby Venus by Velásquez. She's looking in this mirror, her face is kind of smudgy, but it's definitely looking out at me. This is supposed to be Venus reflecting on her beauty. You go with that if you want to. I say she's looking at me with that smudgy face and saying, You want to fuck me, right? I should know. I've jerked off to her in my time.

Onto this image of languid invitation I must now superimpose the memory of a small front room where a tired girl sits asleep on a chair. It's not something I've given much thought to, but in the nature of things whores work mostly at night, and do a lot of waiting around. Not so easy to get up that bright-eyed enthusiasm the gentleman caller expects. I revisit her waking look and understand it all too well. Her expression says, Alright, let's get it over with.

'Okay,' she mumbles. 'Okay, okay.'

The chill dank day fades into a freezing night. Imprisoned with my companions in our back room, I let myself be drawn into a long evening that unfolds in the most unexpected way. Here I am in a brothel, where the working girls join us when business is slow, but the night's delight is not sex. It's poetry.

The matter of what to do with me has been discussed and settled. Eckhard will go with me part of the way, as far as the village where he has urgent business. There the Society will provide a second guide, who will take me to the border. We will travel on foot. We are to leave in the morning.

Now Eckhard produces a small dark-blue volume that turns out to be the *Oxford Book of English Verse*, an old and well-thumbed India-paper edition from 1930. He shows me the dedication.

To

THE PRESIDENT

FELLOWS AND SCHOLARS

of

TRINITY COLLEGE OXFORD

A HOUSE OF LEARNING

ANCIENT LIBERAL HUMANE

AND MY MOST KINDLY NURSE

He asks me to read this dedication aloud. As I do so, tears form in his eyes.

'A house of learning,' he repeats softly. 'Ancient. Liberal. Humane. For you, this is ordinary. For us, it is the city on the hill, the earthly paradise. We too wish such a kindly nurse.' He intones aloud, savouring each syllable with a reverent longing, 'Trinity – College – Oxford.'

The old man points towards the book and speaks to Eckhard. Eckhard nods and turns the pages. Here and there I see pencilled comments in English, scribbled in the margins by some long-dead former owner. He hands me the book open at a poem called Exequy on his Wife, by Henry King. I can't pronounce the title, let alone understand it, but it seems the old man's wife is dead, and so is the poet's.

> Sleep on, my Love, in thy cold bed,
> Never to be disquieted.
> My last good-night! Thou wilt not wake
> Till I thy fate shall overtake:
> Till age, or grief, or sickness must
> Marry my body to that dust
> It so much loves; and fill the room
> My heart keeps empty in thy tomb.
> Stay for me there: I will not fail
> To meet thee in that hollow vale.
> And think not much of my delay:
> I am already on the way,
> And follow thee with all the speed
> Desire can make, or sorrows breed.
> Each minute is a short degree
> And every hour a step towards thee . . .
> 'Tis true – with shame and grief I yield –
> Thou, like the van, first took'st the field;
> And gotten hast the victory
> In thus adventuring to die
> Before me, whose more years might crave
> A just precedence in the grave.

But hark! my pulse, like a soft drum,
Beats my approach, tells thee I come;
And slow howe'er my marches be
I shall at last sit down by thee.

The old man's eyes are streaming with tears by the time I'm done, and though it's no barrel of laughs even I get a small buzz from it. They all clap, in a genteel poetry-loving sort of way, and after this there's no stopping them. They're shy of trying their English on me directly and speak through Eckhard, but they seem to understand the poems as I read them.

I've never been much of a one for poems. I can't really see the point. Actually it's more than that. My instincts tell me the emotion in poems is fake. I mean, suppose you love a girl and she dumps you. Do you write a poem about it? Like, for who? The answer is, for a book. Poems are for showing how clever you are, and for putting in books, and for making people write about in exams. They're just another way to make people like me feel stupid.

This long-ago guy who owned this particular anthology is wonderfully bossy. I catch his comments as I peel the pages. Beside a poem by someone called John Cutts he puts, *As vulgar as Tennyson at his worst.* At the end of a poem by Thomas Campbell that goes, 'Now joy, old England, raise!', he scrawls, *Oh dear! oh dear!* And poor old Edgar Allan Poe gets this: *The vulgarity of Poe is positively shattering.*

So partly it's this feeling that I don't have to admire the poems just because they're collected here, and partly it's the feeling I get from looking at the faces of my companions as they listen, but this time it's different. This time the poems are making sense to me. I mean, I can see how you might want to read them, even if you weren't studying them in some class.

There's this poem by Leigh Hunt called Jenny Kissed Me.

> Jenny kissed me when we met,
> Jumping from the chair she sat in;
> Time, you thief, who love to get
> Sweets into your list, put that in!
> Say I'm weary, say I'm sad,
> Say that health and wealth have missed me,
> Say I'm growing old, but add,
> Jenny kissed me.

That's not so terrible. At least I can understand it. I have this idea, maybe I'm wrong, that Jenny's this kid, around seven or eight years old. It's nice when kids do that.

I'm amazed how well these people know this anthology. It seems English poetry books aren't encouraged under the state of emergency. They're not exactly banned, but if you go round reading them in public they think maybe you're part of the thought-climate that needs to be eradicated. This makes the poems dangerous and exciting.

Eckhard says they want me to choose a favourite poem of my own to read to them. I'm about to tell them I don't know any poems when my page-turning fingers come to a stop at some lines I know very well indeed. They're printed here as this anonymous poem, but I know it as a song. I read it to them, hearing as I do so my mother's sweet voice singing as she drives me and my sister to school.

> O waly, waly, up the bank,
> And waly, waly, doun the brae,
> And waly, waly, yon burn side,
> Where I and my love wont to gae . . .
> But had I wist, before I kissed,
> That love had been so ill to win,
> I had locked my heart in a case of gold
> And pinned it with a silver pin.

I want so much to be home, and to see her again. I want to thank her for singing to us in the car, and for showing us the pictures she loves. Slowly, from a long sleep, I am awakening.

Now they call for Wordsworth.

'The great Ode! Please, the mighty Ode!'

This turns out to mean the Intimations of Immortality, which I read at school. Now, reading slowly and carefully for my listeners' sake, I discover it for the first time.

Our birth is but a sleep and a forgetting:
The soul that rises with us, our life's star,
Hath had elsewhere its setting
And cometh from afar:
Not in entire forgetfulness
And not in utter nakedness
But trailing clouds of glory do we come
From God, who is our home:
Heaven lies about us in our infancy!
Shades of the prison-house begin to close
Upon the growing boy,
But he beholds the light, and whence it flows,
He sees it in his joy;
The youth, who daily farther from the east
Must travel, still is Nature's priest,
And by the vision splendid
Is on his way attended;
At length the man perceives it die away
And fade into the light of common day.

They're all weeping. Actually so am I. Here are these people living in real and constant danger and what they're hearing is how everything comes to an end but along the way there's stuff worth having been born for. Even the woman with the theorbo for God's sake is sitting listening to me like this is going to save her life. Petra said about Vicino, like it was self-evident garbage, 'He tells us to fight torture with poems.' But she's the one holding the red-hot stair rod. Give me Wordsworth any day.

'You must be so proud,' says Eckhard. 'Your country has so many great poets.'

So now I'm proud.

10

Eckhard and I set off in the morning, though not together. He directs me which road to take out of town, and tells me to keep my eyes down as I walk. If I look too interested in the scenery it marks me out as a stranger. A mile or so out of town I'll come to a filling station. I'm to wait for him there.

So I find this filling station and it has only one pump. While I'm waiting I stare at the pump and ask myself what kind of filling station has only one pump. It's an old pump, an industrial antique, the kind you expect an attendant in overalls and a cap to operate for you. A tall thin pump that looks like a person with a big head and no arms. An out-of-date pump for out-of-date vehicles. Only now does it strike me that the cars in this country are all old. This is where all our rich-country cars go to die. Not that there are any to be seen on the road right now. This is not a country with a traffic problem.

I get the feeling that the little hut by the pump is

154

empty. I peer in its window. There are signs that it's in use: a mug hanging on a hook, a small television. But no attendant. This is a ghost filling station.

Eckhard shows up at last, with an army-style kitbag on his back and a wool hat and scarf to protect his face from the cold. He's seen me looking in the hut window.

'They've taken him away,' he tells me.

Now they're rounding up filling-station attendants?

'He reads books.'

I'm getting the picture. Books are the source of ideas. Ideas make you think. Thinking makes you ask yourself if maybe the authorities are running the country in their own interests rather than yours.

'Television is okay with them?'

'Of course. Everything on television they put there. Television is the babysitter for the people. You who watch television, you are the baby.'

He doesn't mean me personally, though I have been known to watch TV, and do not feel in any way infantilised by it. Actually I find his anger at TV hard to fathom. Okay, so it's not high culture, but you can't be burning rocket fuel all week. Sometimes you need to coast.

'It is better,' says Eckhard, 'to look at the wall. You look at the wall, you have your own thoughts. You look at the TV, you have the thoughts of the state.'

'Not where I come from,' I say. 'We don't have state-controlled television.'

'You have the thoughts of corporations who want your money. That is no-thoughts.'

I'm not arguing. I'm the one who watches TV with the sound off. It's my living mural. I read once about this hip hotel in Los Angeles where they have TV-screen-shaped holes in the walls, and as you go by you see soft flickering light. If you put your head in the hole there's a TV down there alright, only you don't see it as you go by, you just see the colours bouncing off the white paintwork. So all those eager people telling you all those urgent messages end up as a jiggle of cyan, a jiggle of magenta. I really liked that. I don't tell Eckhard. Somehow it seems like it's going to take too much explaining.

We have left the road and are hiking across country. We're following a well-worn trail. Eckhard says this is the way the drovers bring the flocks of sheep in the spring and autumn.

He starts to tell me about this novel he's writing.

I should have guessed. People who hate TV always turn out to be writing a novel. They don't like the competition. They don't like the way everyone watches TV and no one reads novels. So why don't they go and write for television? Because they're not smart enough. You can work on a novel for years and all that time you can tell yourself every day you're a genius, but go work in television or movies and pretty soon someone wants to see what you're doing and then of course you're fucked because it's actually crap. People who write novels never show them to anybody. They're like ageing women who've stopped looking in mirrors. That way you're always young, always beautiful.

Eckhard's novel is about a writer who's in the middle of writing the greatest novel in history when he falls in love with this girl and she gets pregnant and he has a dilemma. The dilemma is: does he ditch the greatest novel in history and get a job so he can look after the girl and their baby, or does he ditch the girl? Eckhard tells me about this with ferocious passion and multiple hand gestures. The choice, it seems, is impossible. The hero is as it were pregnant with his great work and can't abort now. However he loves the girl with all his heart and soul, and she too is past the thirteen-week mark.

So what does he do? I'm on the edge of my seat. Fast forward to the denouement. I run through the plot options in my head. He abandons the novel, blames the girl, grows bitter, and leaves her. He kills himself. He kills the girl. A Mayerling-style love pact in which they die together.

None of the above. He puts the novel aside, marries the girl, and gets a job as a teacher.

This is when I realise the novel is autobiographical. Eckhard's urgent business which makes it impossible for him to take me all the way to the border is his own wedding, scheduled for tomorrow. Since it seems I will be on site at the time of the wedding, would I honour him and his bride by reading an English poem at the ceremony?

'Her name is Ilona, which is the name you call Helen. There is a poem to Helen. By Edgar Allan Poe.'

The vulgarity of Poe is positively shattering. Yes, I'll read his poem. The honour will be all mine.

'So you've stopped writing your novel?'

'Yes,' he says. 'The same day my Ilona told me the baby was to come, I went back to my job as teacher. Now the baby is my great work.'

'You don't mind?'

'No. I love my Ilona very much. I love our baby very much. These days we are afraid, you know. But I am so happy.'

I can see it on his face. When he speaks about his fiancée and his baby, his face glows. I think of poor doomed Egon, who said, 'We make the good world for the children.'

'Everything is changed for me.' Eckhard waves his arms up at the sky as we walk. 'I see clouds and I think, I will show my child such clouds. I will tell my child how there is a country in the clouds, and how when the sunbeams reach down from the clouds to the earth, the cloud people ride down them on sleds to visit us. That is what my father told me. I believed it was true, for many years. Maybe I still believe it is true.'

He gives me a quick smile, afraid that I will laugh at him for this.

'I wish my father had told me that,' I say.

'And when my child is older,' says Eckhard, happy now in my approval, 'I will read him the poems I love. Then he will love them too.'

'Your child will be a boy?'

'A boy, or a girl. It is equal. I will so love a daughter also. She will look like Ilona, I hope, not like me.'

'Is Ilona beautiful?'

I ask him this to make him happy.

'You will not think so,' he replies. His voice goes quiet with reverence. 'But to me she is beautiful. She has dark hair, and a light face. A quiet face. You will see. Her beauty will remain. Sometimes when I watch her, I can see how beautiful she will be when she is old.'

This is quite a testimonial. I can see how the novel can't compete. Why write it when you can live it? *Aut tace aut loquere meliora silentio*, right? Either be silent, or let your speech be better than silence.

It hits me then that something like this must have happened to my father. Not quite the same sequence, because he'd already written *The Mercy Kiss* when my mother got pregnant with me. In his play Judas rejects martyrdom, saying, 'I will not die for what I believe in because what I believe in is life.' Martyrdom comes in many forms, and suffering for the sake of art could be said to be one of them. Is this the choice my father also made, and made with deliberation, even pride? I'd always supposed he went into movie-writing to pay the mortgage, and that was the end of his great dream. But maybe it was the start of another dream. Maybe he'd looked at the clouds too and thought how he'd tell his child stories about the sky. Not that he did, since I'm the child in question, and I would know. But the general point holds. Maybe he loved me more than he loved being a famous writer. Maybe he still does. Only now he's got Joey too.

All this gives me peculiar feelings in my intestines and I start to look around for somewhere that offers privacy and to wish I'd thought to carry toilet paper. However before I can act on this I hear the sound of distant engines.

Eckhard has stopped. His face has gone white.

'Police,' he says.

I don't see how he can know, but here they come: two motorbikes approaching, bouncing over the sheep trail.

'I will speak with them,' he says quietly. 'You do not speak.'

'They may not stop.'

'They will stop.'

I pull my coat close around me and as I do so I feel the heavy weight of the gun which has been in my coat pocket all this time. I slide one hand into the pocket and clasp the gun's handle. In the other pocket, with the other hand, I feel the pliers. I register Eckhard's extreme fear, and realise that it is caused by my presence at his side. I endanger him. They won't hurt

160

me, because I'm a foreigner. They'll hurt him. That makes me feel angry.

The motorbikes reach us. Uniformed police. They roar past us and swing round, showing off like they're cowboys on wild horses. They cut their engines and swing their leather legs off the leather saddles and walk towards us with that crotch-bucking swagger that says, Here come the hard men. Make my day. You feeling lucky? It makes me sick to my stomach to watch and not because I'm afraid of them, but because it's all so recycled, an act based on an act dreamed up by some sad fantasist in Santa Monica compensating for his undersized dick. So what I'm saying is before I do what I do I'm feeling this violent need for authenticity.

They're only young, not much older than me, maybe even younger. They walk the walk because they've got the big boots and the padded leather jackets and the guns in their holsters smacking against their thighs. Also because their total job experience up to today is unarmed citizens of their country standing in line and shitting themselves when the motorcycle cops roar by.

Eckhard is behaving as per regulations, hands by his sides, eyes on the ground. They reach him first. They say something to him. I don't know the words but I know the tone, halfway between a command and a jeer. Before Eckhard can answer, one of them reaches out his gloved hand and whacks him across the face, knocking his spectacles to the ground. I can't believe what I'm seeing. My friend hasn't spoken

161

a word, and this baboon is smacking him about.

Eckhard makes no protest at all. He picks up his spectacles and fumbles in one pocket for his papers, but his hands are shaking too much. That's because of me. The baboon whacks him again, making him stagger. I don't like this. I am seriously not amused. I mean, fuck them, right?

I take out my gun and shoot one shot into the ground. This gains their attention. I yell out in English.

'One FUCKING MOVE and you die!'

'Don't!' says Eckhard.

'You want to DIE?'

They've seen enough movies. I'm screaming like a madman and just in case they don't get it I'm pointing my gun at their heads and moving towards them and on my face is a look that says, Just give me one chance, please do something stupid, because I really, really want to blow your face off.

I am the executioner.

Don't ask me where this is coming from. It's like a wild fury has exploded deep inside me and I'm singing a song that goes, Fuck you! Fuck me! Fuck us all!

Time to take charge.

'If they touch their guns, I SHOOT! Tell them!'

Eckhard tells them. They don't touch their guns. They're staring at me like I'm a serial killer with an anger-management problem. But it's going to get worse, boys. They're suddenly so young, I see it now, eighteen at the most. They've never had anyone fight back before. They're not just afraid of my gun. The rules of the game have changed. They're bewildered. The peasants aren't supposed to shout.

'They do EXACTLY what I say! EXACTLY! Tell them.'

Eckhard tells them. They're listening.

'Or I put a bullet in their spines. Tell them.'

Eckhard tells them.

'The bullet doesn't kill them. It paralyses them.'

Eckhard stares at me.

'Tell them.'

He tells them. Now their eyes are jumping out of their heads. The next part doesn't need words, in my language or theirs. I take out the pliers and I hold them up so they can see. It's there on their faces. They know what bad guys do with pliers to people who can't run away. After this I have willing co-operation.

I order them to remove their outer clothing, their gloves and biking leathers and boots. I tell them to lie face down on the ground. Just to help them along I fire two more shots, quite close to them. I strap their ankles to their wrists with their own belts. Eckhard watches me as if I've morphed into the Terminator.

'Can you ride a motorbike?'

'What?' he says. 'What?'

'Ever ridden one of those?'

I gesture at the cops' bikes.

'No. No. No.'

'Me neither.'

However the fire is in my belly and the man who has just reduced two evil goons to jelly is not intimidated by a heap of machinery on wheels. I tell Eckhard to put on the leathers, as I now proceed to do myself.

'You're crazy,' says Eckhard, his teeth chattering. 'They'll kill us.'

'How are they going to do that? Huh?' I get angry, to wake him up. 'HUH? Did they see your papers? No! Will they recognise your face? No! You're all scarfed up. Will they know where we've gone? No! So how are they going to kill us, HUH?'

'You,' says Eckhard miserably. 'You. They'll know you.'

'So they kill me. You're okay. I'm dead, you're not. Okay? OKAY?'

'Okay,' he says, looking down.

Now I've turned into a goon. Time enough to deal with that later. Right now Eckhard has to be woken up so we can get out of here.

I examine the motorbikes. How hard can it be to drive one of these things? I knew a boy once who was so stupid he had to stop walking if you asked him a question. I mean, literally suspend the brain operations required for motion and engage the brain operations for speech. This boy owned and rode a motorbike. In my present full-on mode, in which I'm already rolling so fast that I'm committed to take-off and all out of runway, I believe myself capable of anything. In order not to alarm the natives I tell a very small lie.

'Get on behind me. I can ride this fucker.'

It's not so much a lie as an advance on the truth. Very soon now I will know how to ride this fucker. Eckhard to give him his due never questions my giant self-assurance, not even when we jump forward and stop dead and the engine cuts and we fall over.

'Cheap garbage Eastern European shit!' I shout, kicking the toppled bike. I've become bad. This is new.

Now we're back in the saddle and we're on the move, though just in one gear. I have no idea how to change gears but what the hell, I've found the throttle and I've found the brake. As a show of confidence for Eckhard's sake I circle the two half-stripped cops lying trussed on the ground and let off a last couple of shots to keep them docile. Then I swing back onto the sheep track and Eckhard holds on like he loves me and I open up the throttle and we rock and roll.

This is without doubt the way to go. If you want to eat countryside and possess a carefree attitude to personal injury, motorbike travel is for you. Also it helps if your skeletal structure is bendy in several places because it is likely to get bent. So I race down the trails with the wind in my face and speed-tears in my eyes and I really get the feel of the machine. Fortunately I'm not called upon to stop because the only way I've found how to brake is completely which would not be good at this speed. I can hear Eckhard whimpering behind me, due I imagine to an exaggerated attachment to life, which I do not share. I'm discovering that there's a big buzz to be got from risk. Mortal danger is the true zingaroo. Why did nobody tell me this before? From now on I spend my life in war zones.

We hammer over winter-hard earth and down into a lost valley and I see a stream ahead. Somewhere buried in my brain are images of pursuit and tyre-marks and tracker dogs so without further analysis I ride us into the water and charge down the stream bed kicking up a wake like a power boat. I think maybe Eckhard is screaming now but what's the problem? We're not drowning. The stream is shallow. So long as we keep moving at this speed which I guess to be roughly a thousand miles an hour why should we fall off?

There's a road ahead which will be a friend to the coccyx so up, up, up, spitting gravel on the stream bank and smack onto the crumbling tarmac. The racing rubber chews the road and off we go, faster still. The sudden absence of crashing and splashing makes speech possible so long as we yell.

'ARE WE ON THE RIGHT ROAD?'

No answer.

'ECKHARD! TALK TO ME! DIRECT ME!'

'YES! RIGHT ROAD!'

All is well. The god of adventurers has guided us on our rampage. Now the god of connubial arrangements sees us to our destination. We thieves, we wild men, we gun-toting terrorists, have a wedding to attend.

The road rolls us into a village. The people who are out on the single street stare at us in fear and hatred, which seems to me to be out of order until I see myself reflected in a dark window. I am of course a cop.

I slow down and swerve into a side lane and execute an imperfect stop. Eckhard falls off. I swing my leather leg from the leather seat and feel like a cop. Enough.

'Is this it?' I say. 'Is this the right place?'

He's climbing to his feet. Not in a good way.

'You don't understand,' he says. 'You don't understand.'

'They're not going to find us, Eckhard! We could be anywhere! We got away!'

'You don't understand.'

This is not the gratitude I deserve. For the first time in my life I have imposed my will on others, set the agenda, broken out of passivity and given the orders. I am the leader. I am the man with the gun. So what exactly is it I don't understand?

'They will find us.'

I see it in his eyes: he's lived all his life in a police state, he's endowed the authorities with god-like powers. He simply can't imagine that defiance such as ours will go unpunished. Nothing I can say will reassure him because I don't live here and I don't understand.

'How close are we?'

'What?'

'How close are we to where we're going?'

'We're here. It's here.'

This is Ilona's family's village. Ilona's family's house is just a few minutes' walk away. I suggest we strip off our cop suits and lose the motorbike. This he understands. We have pulled up beside an open-fronted barn, in which several carts and wagons are standing. Every one of them is broken in some way, a missing wheel, a snapped shaft, a buckled bed. The barn is a wagon cemetery. Together we roll the bike into the barn and lay it down right at the back, and cover it and the stolen leathers with a tarpaulin borrowed from a wood-pile.

'Later we move it,' says Eckhard. 'If they find it here, they will take the farmer.'

'They won't find it. They don't know where to look. We got away.'

'No. You don't—'

'Yes, okay. I got that bit. Let's go.'

I've become so dominant. I wish my father could see me.

As we reach the village street, which is also the main road, a car is approaching. It cruises on by without stopping, a big old grey Mercedes. He's sitting in the back, his head leaning on the head-rest, as if he's been sleeping. As he passes, he glances towards me, and I know he sees me. All I see of him is an impression of a dark furrowed brow and piercing black eyes, but I sense that he's young, not much older than me. This is scary, because he's the one in the back of the car, the one in control, the one who is following me. I'm wearing a farm coat, a farm hat, nothing marks me out as a stranger. Why should he notice me or remember me? But I know he does. He has information. He is well trained. He is the hunter. He will follow me for ever, and I will not escape him.

I come to a standstill and shake my head, to throw off the sudden jolt of fear. The grey car is already out of sight. I force myself to think more rationally. If my pursuer is so all-knowing, how come he doesn't stop the car and come after me? What's happening here is classic guilt projection. I feel deep down that I should be punished for my badness, and so I project superhuman powers onto the first available authority figure. I'm worse than Eckhard. Analyse the situation objectively: a man in a passing car has looked at me; possibly, but by no means certainly, a man I have seen once before. I have no idea what he actually looks like, so the chances are he has no idea what I look like. This does not add up to a pursuit by avenging furies. And now he's gone.

'That car,' I say to Eckhard. 'Is that a common sort of car in your country?'

'A grey car?'

'A grey car like that one.'

'You mean some grey cars are different from others?'

Right. The man's a novelist. You don't find him

studying the new models in *Auto World Monthly*. However, my capacity for world domination is dwindling. If it was the same man in the grey car, then it may be that he will return, looking for me. In which case, in fairness to Eckhard, I should fuck off out of his life. We're walking down the village street towards his fiancée's house. The man is about to acquire a wife and child, currently packaged as a single item. He does not need an associate who is an alleged assassin.

'I think I should leave you here.'

We're in front of a doorway. An ordinary home with a faded timber door.

'Why?'

'I don't want to get you into any more trouble.'

Now that I'm sounding less sure of myself Eckhard regains some of his former courage. This is how it goes. In any given group of people there's only so much will power to go round. One very wilful individual can corner the entire supply, and then everyone else goes floppy and does what he tells them. As we stand before the doorway, the certainty is bleeding out of me because of that glimpse of the man in the grey car, and Eckhard is soaking it up.

'I'm in trouble anyway,' he tells me. 'My name is on the list. One day they will come for me. But not today.'

He raps on the door.

'I'm a danger to you,' I say. 'And to these people.'

'It's okay,' he says. 'It's okay.'

The door opens and we go in.

11

They're all teachers. Eckhard is a teacher. Ilona is a teacher. Her father is a teacher. In this country, it seems, it's a considerable deal to be a teacher. I think of my own schooldays and how my teachers drove sad old Fiestas and pretended that not buying their own cigarettes meant they weren't smokers and how they stank of staleness and failure. Who'd be a teacher if you could hack it in the world of grown-ups? We all sensed it. They'd come to our school because we were the short people, and that made them tall. But we grew, every day we grew. Now of course when I meet one of my old teachers in our town I'm taller than them and they're all smiles and deference and I just feel pity.

But here it's different. For a start the authorities don't trust teachers. That alone gives teachers status. Then there's the interesting fact that the authorities are right. These teachers have a mission. They see themselves as the lamp-holders, the one source of light in a shadowy world where their people are close to drowning in darkness. They have no ambition to overthrow the state. They want only to keep the light of knowledge burning, and to spark an answering flame in as many hearts and minds as possible, while the dark clouds roll on by overhead.

Not so long ago I would have laughed like a duck laying an egg at a phrase like 'the light of knowledge', but it doesn't seem so funny any more. I have fallen into a shadowed land. I am hungry for the light. I think of the dawn of a new day, of the light of the rising sun spilling into the kitchen at home, and the memory moves me almost to tears. Not that I have any actual memory of ever being out of bed early enough to see the dawn, but I must have done it once because the image is lodged within me.

Also I'm beginning to understand the connection between the many little things teachers do, day after day, in all the ungrateful classrooms across the ungrateful world, and the one big thing we all seek, which is the contented life. You can't enjoy a poem until your belly's full and the barbarians have stopped raping your sister, but you can still dream of the day. How else are we to go on? In smug sea-hugged England I have been unaware that I am the recipient of a bequest. Teachers are millionaire donors, they pass on the wealth accumulated by past generations. Teachers are warriors, they fight the forces of darkness. And everywhere, always, in the end, they win.

This is not my own insight. As before, I echo Leon Vicino. In his writings I too am finding the articulation of a new faith.

However powerful our enemies grow, they can never defeat us. We pursue a goal to which they too must come in the end. When at last their anger and their fear are exhausted, they will ask, how now am I to live? From that day on they will join with us, of their own free will. They will say, as we say: life is short, let us live it well.

Live life well. Not much of a rallying cry when the time comes to man the barricades and start the revolution, but then they have no revolution in mind.

Beware of victory. Beware of all stories that end in the sound of applause. For us, there are no endings. The clapping fades, the company disperses, and life goes on. So I say: beware of glory.

Ilona is, as promised, no beauty. Her hair is a dull brown, cut like a helmet, and her face a little longer than is strictly the fashion. But she loves pop-eyed bespectacled Eckhard, no two ways about that. I watch them sitting side by side at table and I can tell by the way they're each eating with one hand that the other hands are clasped out of sight. Afterwards, Eckhard strokes Ilona's bump where the baby is, though if

173

you'd asked me I'd have said there wasn't a bump. He whispers to the baby, which should be embarrassing, but isn't at all because his face is so serious. He looks like the characters you see in movies visiting their loved ones in prison: leaning close to the bars and speaking low and wanting terribly to be able to touch.

While he's doing this Ilona is stroking his hair and looking far away. I can feel how she too is communicating with her baby, from what you might say is the other side. Not saying anything that requires words, just sending her love. This baby is getting it from all directions. It had better be grateful.

Then for a moment I feel it too. It's only a flash, but it's unmistakable. I feel what it's like to be that baby, and to be so loved. In fact this isn't a transference, it's a memory. I was there once. My mother and my father adored me beyond reason. I was the baby god, I drank their worship as my due. I lay on my back, defenceless, trusting, omnipotent.

Where did it go? That blithe self-love, fed by innocence and my parents' generosity? How soon did it go? The world betrayed me as it betrays us all. Shades of the prison-house begin to close upon the growing boy. But there was a time, by me forgotten until this moment in a lost village in a lost country, when I too was all in all, and wanted for nothing, and was beautiful.

* * *

Eckhard has told Ilona's family nothing about our recent adventure. He tells them I am English, and that I need to leave the country without attracting attention, and that I will stay long enough to read a poem at the wedding. So now I am an honoured guest in this house, where everyone is preparing for the celebration.

Ilona herself, assisted by her mother, her sister and her aunt, prepares the food in industrial quantities. Mostly this consists of pies. I am in the land of pies. Meat pies, egg pies, leek pies, onion pies. Also soup, in huge aluminium pans big enough to bath a child. And small sweet sticky cakes, shaped like the hulls of boats. So much food presumes a big party, and I wonder very much where they will all go, in the little rooms of this house.

In the evening after supper the extended family sits on at table and talks. I don't understand the words, but it's clear from their faces that this is real talk, in which people listen to ideas and challenge them and arrive at new insights. At first I find the earnest faces comical, like a parody of a college discussion group; but after a while I'm impressed. They pass round bottles of wine, from which I too drink, and they keep the fire burning with an occasional log. The talk rises and falls in volume, fingers wag, palms slice the air: such animation, as if what they say could make a difference. From time to time a wave of laughter ripples outwards, most often from Ilona's father, who seems to act as the umpire in the debate. At one point his eyes fall on me, and he speaks to Eckhard, and Eckhard, turning with a friendly smile, speaks to me.

'We talk about the duties of marriage,' he says. 'What to do if your spouse does not please you. Can the person who is not pleasing become pleasing by taking thought?'

Having supplied this précis in his grave voice, Eckhard returns to the discussion. I'm left thinking what a peculiar puzzle they've set themselves. As I turn it over in my mind I realise it's a question that is no longer asked in my society. If one partner doesn't please the other partner it's presumed they're not suited, and should look for happiness elsewhere. The notion that one can become more pleasing to another by taking thought seems archaic, almost sinister. What is involved here? Calculated pleasantry? Forced attentions? But then as I muse on, obliged to supply both sides of the debate for myself, I remember my father telling us the tale of the Great Petrol Row. Back when Cat and I were little children, my parents had just the one car. Mostly it was my mother who drove it, because my father stayed home and wrote his books. But every time my father drove it, or so he claimed, he found the petrol tank was empty. The amber warning light was flashing. So he would fill it up, and all the time he was standing by the pump he would be thinking, How could she do that? How could she not see the warning light? This happened about a hundred times, according to my father, and every time he filled the tank with petrol he filled himself with anger. He didn't show how angry he was because actually my mother was doing all the driving, which she didn't much like, so that he could get on with his great works, which were turning out to be not so great. But the anger went on gushing into him until there was no room left, and then the time came when it all came gushing back out.

He went out to the car one winter day and found the amber warning light came on, so instead of driving wherever it was he needed to go he came back into the house and yelled and stamped up and down the kitchen and said it wasn't fair and it was dangerous and my mother was indolent and never thought ahead and if he ever had to fill up the car again he'd explode only he wasn't ever going to fill it up again and she could damn well run out of petrol on the motorway and damn well walk all the way home. My mother was completely taken by surprise. She said she knew she was on the optimistic side when it came to fuel gauges but she had no idea it was upsetting him so much, and now that she knew, of course she'd fill the tank sooner. And she did. From that day on, she changed her behaviour. The entire problem evaporated. This was the punchline of my father's story as it used to be, with him as the dope. He should have told her years ago. It just never occurred to him that the solution could be so simple.

But he still left.

I never asked him why. After that ride in the Buick, the moment never presented itself again. My father was right in a way. We didn't notice much difference. The leaving never quite started and never quite ended. He was often away, in Los Angeles, or on film locations. There were no screaming fits, no scenes of high drama: just a little more being away, a little less being at home. A dwindling away of dreams. The place he lives in now began as an office, a quiet flat where he went to do his work, only a short walk from home. But a short walk is much like a long walk if you stop walking it. Don't ask me what went wrong because I don't know. It's only now, sitting by the fire with a glass of warm wine in my hands, watching the earnest faces talking round me, that I feel ashamed not to know. We never talk like this at home. I've been too afraid to ask, not wanting to see the shape of my mother's unhappiness, not wanting to know that somehow it's all my fault. Vanity, of course. Vanity takes so many forms. With me it's not the mirror-hunting self-admiration, it's the vanity of guilt, the vanity of fear, the vanity that forces my own self into the centre of other people's unhappiness. I see now how ridiculous this is. Why should my father have left home because of me? Why should that shroud of sadness that hangs about him have been woven out of disappointment in me? Surely the only true and potent disappointment is with one's self. My poor smiley father must have been in very great need of whatever it is that a new, young and beautiful partner can give: something so much more complex than sex. Or so much more simple. Self-belief, I suppose.

We should all talk more. Television isn't talk, nor is the internet, nor, contrary to appearance, is the phone. What Eckhard and Ilona and her family and friends are doing round me is conversation. Conversation uses words, voice tones, faces, smiles, silences, hand gestures, leg movements, comings and goings, all the knit and tangle of humanity. Why don't we value conversation any more? Why do we go chasing after louder sounds, brighter colours, hotter liquor, higher highs? Why do we behave as though talking with friends is for the old, the poor, the sad? This is one of the very few roads out of the land-locked country of vanity. One of the few gates into the society of others.

The last paragraph of Vicino's book goes like this:

If you ask me, What then is the nature of the well-lived life?, I must paint you a picture. In a warm room a group of old friends sit round a table. They have eaten an excellent meal, and now as they finish their wine they push back their chairs and stretch out their legs and the conversation flows. Their subject is, perhaps, What is the nature of the well-lived life?

The wedding takes place at noon the next day. I am immersed in a world that is so domestic, so familial, that the danger from which I'm fleeing seems unreal. Later I will be guided on my road to the border. This morning, today, we celebrate.

Eckhard and Ilona have put on their wedding clothes. Eckhard wears a navy-blue suit and looks like a low-paid clerical worker, but for the flower in his buttonhole. Ilona wears an ankle-length dress with a short veil. The effect is peculiar. To my eyes she looks as if she has put on garments that are several sizes too small for her, but everyone else admires her so I suppose this is the fashion round these parts.

The family is assembled. There seem to be no guests. Who will eat all those pies?

The strains of a fiddle sound outside the front door. The wedding party all smile and nod at this, and the door is thrown open wide. Outside stand a fiddler and an accordion player, playing a jaunty tune. Eckhard and Ilona step out of the front door onto the village street, and the musicians set off to the right. We follow, all moving at the same jigging step without fully realising it, in time to the beat of the music. The door of the neighbouring house opens and an entire family troops out, dressed in their Sunday best, to fall into place behind us. So with the next house, and the next. The fiddler and the accordion player lead an ever-growing procession that winds up one side of the village street and then down the other, their music sucking wedding guests from every door and alley they pass. By the time we reach the gates to the church, the entire village is lined up behind us, tapping their toes to the chirpy little tune.

The church doors open and the bells start to ring. The musicians retire. Into the church go the bride and groom, down the aisle to the waiting priest. In flow the people after them, spilling down the pews to right and left. Vows are exchanged, lickety-spit, and the couple clasp hands and turn to the congregation, and everyone cheers. It's all disconcertingly rapid, businesslike, and joyful. And so out we go, Eckhard and Ilona in the lead once more, and the people unloop from the pews like a garden hose being dragged behind us.

The fiddler and the accordion player are already in position in the village hall, along with a third band member, a bass player. They serenade the wedding party as we arrive. Here too are all the pies, lining the walls like a guard of honour on brightly draped tables. Behind the pies stand bottles of wine, all uncorked, and thick-rimmed wine glasses, and tall jugs of water. *Diddle-dee diddle-dee diddle-diddle-diddle-dee* goes the band, and Eckhard and Ilona take to the floor. They dance with a funny little bouncing gait, like cock pheasants squaring up for a fight, though this dance ends with arms linked and a swirling spin. Now other guests are dancing, step up, step back, in and out, over and under. I tap my feet and drink my wine and begin to get the measure of it, so that when Ilona's sister comes up to me, hand outreached, I'm willing to try my chance.

I muddle my way through with my partner's assistance, and catch smiles and nods of appreciation on every side. It turns out to be hot work, this dancing, and I pause to unbutton my coat and throw it under a table. My partner is a plain girl but she dances well, and so by some strange slithering of mental categories her spirited dancing makes her pretty. This is also true of Ilona, who looks radiant, as is only proper in a bride.

After the dancing there's eating and drinking, and after the eating and drinking come the toasts. I drink throughout and am definitely drunk when it dawns on me that they're all looking at me and Eckhard is holding out his old blue-bound copy of the *Oxford Book of English Verse*. My moment has arrived.

This poem I'm to read, To Helen by Edgar Allan Poe, isn't about a real woman at all. It's about a mythic woman, Helen of Troy, the one whose face launched a thousand ships, according to some other poet. They've all written about her. She's anybody's, a kind of poetic slag. What relevance has any of this to Eckhard and Ilona, who will struggle to make a half-decent life in an impoverished Eastern European country under a state of emergency?

You tell me.

Being drunk, I read rather well.

> Helen, thy beauty is to me
> Like those Nicean barks of yore

That gently o'er a perfumed sea
The weary way-worn wanderer bore
To his own native shore.

On desperate seas long wont to roam,
Thy hyacinth hair, thy classic face,
Thy Naiad airs have brought me home
To the glory that was Greece
And the grandeur that was Rome.

Lo, in yon brilliant window-niche
How statue-like I see thee stand,
The agate lamp within thy hand!
Ah! Psyche, from the regions which
Are holy land!

When I finish there is silence. How many of these villagers understood a single word? Impossible to say. But then there rises up a nodding murmur of satisfaction, and it appears that there is a general approval, even a kind of pride. It comes to me then that this not-very-remarkable poem is a link with the tales, the dreams, the passions that have animated the peoples of Europe for centuries. The light of Helen's lamp shines even into this village hall, and for a moment this land is holy too. The glory of Greece is here, and the grandeur of Rome. Not tribal attributes, sealed in history, but part of a shared inheritance, kept shining and new by every poet who returns to the treasure chest to add his portion of wonder. So the Helen of Troy becomes the Ilona of this village, and both lives are enriched, and grow in beauty.

The band begins to play again, and we return to the dance. Nobody is leaving. Outside the day is fading into early winter night. The smaller children are making themselves nests out of coats under the tables, and curling up to sleep. The old folk are sitting down and talking among themselves. But everyone else is dancing, including me. We dance and dance, dizzy with the spins and the swirls, faces red with wine, and I begin to feel there's no reason why the dancing shouldn't go on all night, and all the next day, and for the rest of my life.

Then it seems to me the music has stopped. I look round. The dancers have fallen still. Faces are turned to the door. Through the dull boom of my blood and the smoky haze of the air I gather that something is going wrong. There are bright lights outside the windows. Men in the doorway. The buzz of fearful voices.

Now hands are seizing me by either arm, and I'm being dragged back into the crowd, a crowd which melts away to let me pass, to a small back door. These are Eckhard's friends who hold me. They are taking me away from danger. Out through the narrow door into the night, and the cold night air smacks me awake.

'No!' I say.

The men with the bright lights have come for me. If

they don't find me, these good people with whom I've been drinking and dancing will be made to suffer. I can't allow this. No courage involved, at no point does this feel like heroism or self-sacrifice: it's simply the thing that has to be done. Not to do it, to jump and run and hide, to hear the screams in the distance, would be unendurable. No great moral debate, then, just the shock of the icy night and the imperative of pure instinct.

'They've come for me. It's me they want.'

I break free and push back through the door. Across the floor to the men who stand framed in light in the open front doorway of the village hall. Some of them wear the uniform of the regular police, others the black bomber jackets of the interior ministry. I hardly see them. My eyes reach past them, out into the street beyond, where an old grey Mercedes waits, its engine running, its headlights blazing, and a man sits motionless in the back.

I raise both arms in the international sign of surrender. From behind me I hear Eckhard's voice shouting out.

'No! You don't understand!'

Oh, I understand. Actions have consequences. Either I take responsibility for what I've done or I live my life as a child.

A policeman shines the beam of a torch onto my face. I shut my eyes against the blinding brightness. Voices shout orders. Once more, hands grab my arms.

I am propelled forward, slammed against the side of a car, searched. They find nothing. My coat is under a table in the hall, forming a pillow for a sleeping three-year-old.

They push me into the police car. I give a wave in the direction of the wedding party. There's not all that much you can say with a wave other than goodbye. I try to say thanks for the party, and for loving each other, and good luck with the baby. But one of the policemen smashes me hard in the solar plexus and for a while I have to concentrate on learning how to breathe again. Shortly before I die I get the trick back and realise the car is in motion and we're speeding down the road. The grey Mercedes is ahead of us. I can see the back of its passenger's head.

Now I remember with chilling clarity Petra's words to me. 'Only the movement can save you. Alone you will die. First you will suffer, then you will die.'

12

This windowless room in which they have locked me is not like a prison cell. It's square, with orange-painted walls and blue-grey carpet tiles on the floor. On one wall hang two paintings which I've been looking at longer then they deserve: blodges of mauve and brown, sub-Rothko style, knock-off modernism from the early 1960s. There are also four armchairs with bent-wood frames, upholstered in stained turquoise fabric, and a coffee table made of laminated wood. Above the door there is a red light. These visual clues seem to be telling me something about the nature and purpose of the room, but I don't know what.

I have nothing to do but wait. So this is a waiting room.

I'm afraid. But I'm also strangely detached. Whatever will happen will happen. Only, nothing happens. After a while I curl up as best I can in two of the armchairs, and settle down to an uneasy sleep.

*　*　*

She's sitting watching me. She speaks in her own
language to nobody. Then she nods, like she's getting
an answer. She's maybe thirty-five years old, tanned
and handsome, very well-groomed, wearing quietly
expensive carefully casual clothes.

'So,' she says, this time in English and to me. 'You are
awake.'

I sit up, feeling like shit.

'Some coffee and some toast will come.'

I try to straighten my sleep-crumpled clothes. I need
to piss, clean my teeth, take a shower, get fresh
things to wear, shave. A man can dream.

'You need the rest room?'

I nod. She calls out, and the door opens. There are
two goons standing outside.

'It's down the passage to the left.'

The goons escort me down the passage to the left.
On the passage walls are black and white photographs
of smirking men and women, some holding guitars.

In the rest room, I piss for England. God it feels
good. Then I wash as best I can in a basin that has
push-down taps and no plug. Why do they do that?
Are there people who come in and steal the water?
Actually I know the answer. We're all taught to wash
our hands after going to the toilet but none of us ever
quite do this, certainly not after a piss. But if you push
the tap down and sort of wet your hands it's a token
that you've tried, and you can pull out a paper towel

and leave. The brief gush of water the tap grants you is your absolution from the demands of hygiene.

There's a paper-towel dispenser but no paper towels. A soap dispenser but no soap. There's a condom dispenser on the wall but I bet it has no condoms. This whole toilet is trying to look like it belongs in a modern Western European country where things work, but actually it's a knock-off like the not-Rothko paintings in the waiting room. Even so it's not what you expect in a police station or prison or wherever I am.

The goons escort me back. The men with guitars smirk at me some more from the walls. At the end of the corridor past the waiting-room door I see a heavy door with a sign above it that lights up, but is currently dark. In the waiting room, the handsome woman is standing, a paper folder in her hands, talking to the air again. There's a tray come for me. Coffee and toast as billed. Without stopping talking, she nods to me to drink, to eat.

We finish at the same time.

'So,' she says. 'They are ready for us. We will go.'

She opens the door for me and there are the faithful goons. This time we turn right. The sign over the heavy door is lit up. She heaves the door open and beyond there's a second door, and then the clues begin to fall into place. I'm entering a small provincial television studio. The sad gloss of a long-lost modernity, the once-bright colours, the pleading faces of performers with unfashionable haircuts, the airport-hotel décor from around 1975: if they hold their nerve for another decade or so it could become the look again, but they won't. Someone will slip them a contraband batch of *The World of Interiors* and they'll lose their innocence. These thoughts sustain my pretence that I'm a detached observer of my surroundings. The truth is I'm deeply scared and finding all this somewhat unreal.

Lights shine on a little stage. Two armchairs wait on either side of a coffee table. On the table, a jug of water and two glasses. Behind, a piece of scenery designed to look like one wall of a suburban living room. The goons have remained outside in the passage. My smart companion and I appear to be alone in the studio. She beckons me to one of the chairs in the circle of light.

'Don't worry if you make mistakes,' she tells me. 'We always tape more than we need. We can edit out the mistakes later.'

I have been adopting a policy of saying nothing in case I incriminate myself. But all this is so far outside my understanding that I decide to change my policy and start asking questions.

'Why am I here? Where am I?'

She sits down and opens her folder on her lap and smoothes her quite short skirt towards her knees. Her legs are tanned, and she does not wear tights or stockings. She has excellent legs, they're her best feature.

'My name is Magdalena,' she says. 'I'll be talking to you on the show today.'

She flicks heavy shiny hair from across her eyes.

'What show?'

'Aha!' She wags a finger at me. 'I ask the questions!' She smiles as if this is a joke between us. 'Soon now we start the show, and then the tape is recording and we miss nothing, you know?'

I don't know. But now I sense movement around me. There are three television cameras, big old EMI cameras, standing in an arc before us, and their lenses are in motion. Some remote operation is causing the barrels of the lenses to turn, and as they turn they reach towards us and withdraw again. At their feet are television monitors on which I can see myself growing bigger and bigger, and then, on a sudden cut, reduced to the smallness of full figure, the two of us seated in our fake suburban living room.

Magdalena is listening to a voice in her ear. I study the space around me. High up in one far wall I find the sound-proof window through which I can see the technicians who are controlling the cameras. Three men, each illuminated by a tiny light on the desk before him. And behind, in shadow, a tall gaunt figure that I know at once to be the man who has haunted me, and is now my captor.

This is some kind of interrogation.

'We are ready now,' says Magdalena.

She turns her face towards one of the cameras and

puts on a dazzling professional smile. A red light springs on. She starts to speak to camera, in her own language, in a bright voice punctuated by a series of gestures that she believes to be charming. She flicks back her hair, opens her palms to camera, bobs her head in eager little nods. I think she looks wacko.

Then she turns to me.

'So,' she says, leaning forward and touching my knee. 'Welcome to the show. This is your first visit to our country. We're all so interested to know how you find it.'

This has to be some kind of joke.

'I'm sorry?'

'Your first impressions. Is it so different from England?'

'This is a trick, right?'

She shakes her head at me, still smiling.

'We'll edit that out,' she says. 'You are a little abrupt, forgive me for saying. I know you don't want to sound discourteous. You are in a way an ambassador for your country.'

'Listen.' I'm beginning to feel pissed off by this game, as well as scared. 'I was picked up by armed police and brought here as a prisoner. Don't give me this ambassador shit.'

'A prisoner?' She looks horrified. 'Oh, no, no, no! You are here as our guest.'

'So I can go?'

'Of course. But first, if you please, the interview.'

'I don't want an interview.'

'But all is ready. It would be of such interest to our viewers. It would create a good impression, you know?' She's giving me a pleading look. 'I understand your papers are not entirely in order.'

Her eyes are begging me: play the game. Don't go. I look back at her, trying to figure out what's going on.

'Just lay it out for me, okay? If this is a deal, tell me.'

'Our show is very popular. It is seen by everyone in the country. We have only one channel, you know? And no commercials.' Her smile is getting positively desperate. 'The show will make you famous. You will be a star.'

'I don't want to be famous.'

Now her eyes register shock.

'Of course you want to be famous. Everyone wants to be famous.'

It now occurs to me that maybe she's as much of a dupe of the interrogation process as I am. Also that she's nervous.

'Are you famous?' I ask.

'Maybe a little.' She calms down. Pulls her skirt towards her knee and strokes one shapely calf. 'I think it begins for me, yes.'

'So you're new at this job?'

'A little new,' she concedes.

This gives me confidence.

'Well, you see the man standing at the back of the control room up there? He's an officer of the state

193

security police. He's not here to learn my impressions of your country.'

'But we are all so interested! Someone from the West!'

It must be question one on her list. She's not bright enough to move past it until it's been answered. I meet people like this all the time. They're expecting a certain kind of answer from you and if you say something else they simply don't hear you. Your words have no place ready to receive them in their brain, so it's like you haven't spoken.

What the hell. I have nothing to lose. Also I doubt that I'm being given the choice of walking out. I decide to play their game and see where it leads.

'Okay. What do you want to know?'

'Ah! Now you make me happy! Now we have a wonderful time, and we make a wonderful show!'

'Don't count on it.'

She smiles and once more wags a mock-angry finger as me.

'Oh, you! We've done our research. We know all about you.'

So she composes herself on her chair and we start again. The spiel to camera. The turn to smile on me. There's my face on the floor monitors. I seem to be talking.

'My first impression of your country,' I'm saying, 'is that everybody is afraid.'

The smile modulates into a look of concern and understanding.

'Ah, yes. You refer to the state of emergency.'

'I don't know what it is. Just, everyone's afraid.'

'These are very difficult times for us. We have a very serious problem, the terrorism. But you know this.'

'I know there's some kind of war going on.'

'A war, of course. For five years now the terrorists have fought a war against us. They bomb our shopping centres and our public buildings. They assassinate our senators and our judges. We are all so afraid. Even I am afraid. Those who have children are most afraid. I have no children myself at this time, though of course I love children, and I hope that when I am less busy, and when the right man—' She stops, blushing and feeling her earpiece. She nods and looks down at her notes. 'The terrorism, yes. Over two thousand people have been killed since the state of emergency was declared.'

She pauses again to listen to the voice in her earpiece.

'We will edit in some news clips here, of the atrocities. You would like to see?'

On the floor monitors I now see a succession of mute news items, showing mostly the aftermath of bomb explosions. Smashed buildings, running people, police waving onlookers away. Then close shots of dead bodies, all mutilated by the blasts: arms ripped off, torsos disembowelled, faces smashed

195

beyond recognition. The camera lingers in a way we never see on our television screens at home. It's too much. I look away.

'Yes, these things are more than one can bear. They are the work of the terrorists. This is why people are, as you say, afraid.'

'That, and the police.'

She blinks at me, confused.

'The police protect us. We have nothing to fear from the police. Only terrorists, and those who support terrorists, need fear the police.'

I shrug. Not my country.

'But you English understand these things. In your country you have terrorists also. Your police do their best to track down these evil men, who murder innocent people.'

I nod.

'And England is a free country.'

I nod. Then I catch sight of the monitor on the floor just behind Magdalena. It has been showing a shot of me, but now it's showing something different. At first I think it's another close-up of a corpse. The screen is black and white, the image-definition poor. Then the focus shifts and I see it's a living face, badly wounded. The eyes move. Whoever it is must be close to death. The nose, the cheeks, are raw, torn, bloody.

Magdalena talks on.

'We too are a free country. My country is famous for

its writers and poets, for its cheeses, and for its beautiful women.'

I'm staring at the wrecked face. I know that face.

'I'm told I'm quite typical of my people.'

'What is that?'

She looks back at me, waiting for the compliment.

'What are they showing on that screen?'

As I ask the question, the grisly image goes, to be replaced by my own agitated face. Magdalena looks round, following my gaze, and finds nothing out of the ordinary.

'That is the output of Camera Two, which is your camera. Mine is Camera One. Camera Three has the two-shot. We will have to edit, yes?' This to the silent listeners in the control room. She attends to her ear-piece, nods, checks her notes. Then the puppyish smile is back, eager to please. 'We continue?'

I shrug. Why not? I want them to show me that injured face again. It was for my benefit, not Magdalena's, that much is clear. She knows as little as me about this process.

'So I am very interested to ask you this question,' she says, reading from her notes. 'What would you do in England, which is a free country, if a foreign visitor entered the country illegally and gave assistance to terrorists?'

I go very still. She's looking up again, eyes bright, wanting to hear my answer. She has no idea of the implications of what she has just asked. Why tell her anything? But she's not the only one listening. Maybe it's time to put forward some kind of defence.

'Well,' I say, playing for time, 'did he know what he was doing, or was he an unwitting tool?'

Magdalena gazes at me with glossy unseeing eyes, the look she wears when listening to the voice in her ear. Then:

'Suppose he's an unwitting tool, but he's murdered a member of the security forces.'

'He could still be innocent.'

'How?' She's puzzled: that question's her own. Then comes a piped question. 'If he's innocent, naturally he would go to the police at the first opportunity. But what if he doesn't? Suppose he runs, and hides, and is protected by dissidents. Suppose he attacks and robs more members of the security forces. What – in your country – would happen to him?'

'Justice,' I say. 'A fair trial.'

I'm trying as hard as I can to go on looking like none of this is a big deal, but the truth is this interview is starting to spook me. I know she's just a dummy mouthing someone else's words, but the ventriloquist is listening too.

'So you wouldn't send him home?'

I shake my head.

'How long would the process take?'

'Quite a long time.'

So this is the threat. Not all the threat, however. The monitor behind Magdalena is showing me a man tied to a steel chair, with his forehead strapped against the chair back. His tongue hangs out of his mouth. Two crocodile clips are clamped to his tongue. Wires run from the clips to somewhere out of frame. There's no sound. The man's eyes are swivelling from left to right in desperation and fear. Then his body goes into spasm, all the muscles of his face turn rigid. He strains against his bonds, his tongue flaps up and down, sweat streams from every pore. This is a man helplessly in the grip of unbearable pain. I look away the minute, the second it begins, but it's too late. I've seen it. Magdalena of course has not. She is checking her list of questions.

'Now we move on to your impressions of the people. As you may know, we are called "the happy hosts", because we are a hospitable people. You have already made friends in our country, you know?'

As she speaks, the image of the tortured man on the monitor is replaced by the image of a woman dancing. The shots have evidently been taken with a secret camera. The woman is dancing in a nightclub with a much older man. She wears a tight-fitting top and a micro-skirt. She turns and sways closer to camera, and I see that it is Petra.

'No,' I hear myself saying. 'I've made no friends so far.'

'But I think,' Magdalena teases me, checking her research, 'maybe a pretty little girlfriend?'

'No,' I say. 'Nobody.'

On the monitor I'm seeing a dark bedroom, an indistinct impression of activity on the bed. After a few moments, the movements stop and someone gets off the bed and heads for a door. As the door opens, light enters the room and reveals Petra lying naked on the bed, on her side, her back to the hidden camera, her bottom rising in a voluptuous curve.

By now Magdalena has taken in that I'm more attentive to the monitor than to her. With a little pout of irritation, she turns to see what I'm looking at. As she does so, the image changes again and I'm seeing a tennis game. A sixteen-year-old girl is playing, extremely well. Petra again, from some years back. A service and a blistering return, and there's my face back on the monitor.

'So,' says Magdalena. 'This is from the archives. This young lady, she was one of our tennis stars, I think the best.' The shots have confused her. She listens to her earpiece, nodding. Then she checks her notes. 'You wish to know more about her?'

'Yes,' I say.

'I have the details here. Yes. I may tell you. Her father was a very successful businessman. Her mother a famous actress. She went to the best private schools. She was a tennis star. Later she was a model. Such a person has much to thank her country for. You agree?'

I nod.

'Well. She is a terrorist.' I can see from Magdalena's face as she reads this that she is astonished. 'She has chosen to destroy her homeland. This gifted young woman had everything she could desire. And she chose destruction.' She looks up at me. 'Can you understand that?'

I shrug. Don't ask me, ask a shrink. Though as a matter of fact in a very small way I can understand it. I come from a privileged background and have been given just about everything I want. For some perverse reason if people go on giving you things there comes a time when you want to smash the gifts out of their hands. It's as if the act of giving is also an act of oppression. All this is very ungrateful of course but being grateful can get to be wearing. Even so I've never quite made the move into terrorism.

'This young woman,' Magdalena is reading to me, 'has convinced herself that she is permitted to use violence as the means to further what she believes to be a noble cause. However, she deceives herself. The acts of violence themselves are her end, and the noble cause is her means to that end.' She blinks. 'This is a report from the psychologists. You see, we do our best to understand the motives of the terrorists.'

'Why have you been asked to tell me this?'

Magdalena's fingers scurry through her notes. 'I think you know this young lady.'

Time to cut to the chase.

'Am I under arrest?'

This calls for higher instruction. Her fingers fondle her earpiece.

'That has not yet been decided.'

'What am I charged with?'

Pause.

'That too has not yet been decided. It's possible you have been an ignorant dupe, whose subsequent actions have been driven by fear.'

Yes! I shout within myself. Yes! That's how it all happened! Don't blame me. Don't hurt me.

'It's also possible you suffer from a dangerous psychotic condition, like our young friend here.'

A nod back at the monitor, on which I now see only my own strained face.

'I'm not psychotic,' I say, trying to stop my voice from cracking as I speak.

'Of course not. You're a visitor to our country. Due to a series of unfortunate mistakes you have been drawn into events you don't understand.'

Suddenly there's the bloody face on the monitor again. Of course I know that face. It's Ilse. Poor ugly Ilse, who gave me the English translation of Vicino's book. She's ugly no more. The ugliness has been torn off her, and all that is left is the suffering.

'Now, however,' says Magdalena, 'it is time for you to understand.'

From her folder she takes out several sheets of paper closely covered in type. I feel a sick sensation in my stomach. It's Marker's list.

'You have seen this before?'

For a fraction of a second I consider denying it. But

202

by now I'm getting a picture of just how much they know about me and my activities since entering the country, and it adds up to roughly everything.

'Yes. I've seen it.'

'Do you know how it came to be in the possession of the police?'

'Yes. I know.'

'How?'

She says it like she doesn't know, and would like to know.

'Petra arranged for it to be handed over.'

'Petra?' Magdalena wrinkles her brow and returns to her notes. 'There is no Petra. Ah, yes. I understand. She gives herself this new name, Petra. Her real name is Edith.'

The camera catches the effect of this information on me. I show nothing. What do I care? Though of course little by little the image of Petra I have retained in my mind is crumbling. The actress mother. The rich father. The tennis prodigy. The time spent as a model. The betrayal of Marker's list. The contempt for Vicino. The burning stair rod. All this, and her real name is Edith.

'Why did she arrange for the list to be handed over?'

What can I say other than the truth? I'm not Petra's protector.

'To radicalise the followers of Leon Vicino.'

'To do what? What is that?'

Not the brightest candle on the tree, our Magdalena.

'The police would arrest the people on the list. That would make their friends realise they must take action.'

'I see.' She ponders. 'If I understand you correctly, the intention behind this action was that all these people would disappear, leading to a violent reaction by thousands more, who would then themselves, in committing acts of violence, force the authorities to be violent in their turn. This would generate a rising cycle of violence, until our society falls apart, destroyed by hatred and suffering.'

She ends with her weird bright smile. Not such a dumb speech. Maybe I'm wrong about Magdalena. Maybe I'm wrong about everything.

'I guess so.'

'How did she get the list?'

'She got it from me.'

'Did you know what was on the list?'

'No.'

'Did you know it had some importance, and must not fall into the wrong hands?'

'I guess I did.'

'Do you feel in any way responsible for the list falling into the hands of the terrorists?'

'Yes.'

'Would you like to put the situation right again?'

'How?'

'This list gives the names and addresses of all the key people in what was once a political party. The members of this organisation see themselves as occupying the middle ground between two extremes. We believe that view is dangerously mistaken. There is no middle ground between terrorism and order. Our job is to persuade them to understand where their interests lie, and to join us in the task of identifying and eliminating the terrorists.'

This all comes out with practised fluency. It's evidently a speech she's given many times before. But I'm not entirely stupid. There's a missing link in her story. The guys in black bomber jackets don't behave like your friendly neighbourhood watch officer.

'Like with pliers?'

She takes it in her stride.

'Unfortunate incidents sometimes happen. Violence breeds violence. We too have elements that get out of control.'

'What are you talking about, out of control?' I gesture at the floor monitor. 'I saw that guy being tortured. That wasn't out of control.'

She looks puzzled.

'What guy being tortured?'

'The guy in the video clip. With the electrodes on his tongue.'

'You believe you've seen a video clip of a man being tortured?'

'I don't believe I saw it. I saw it.'

'You must realise that's impossible. Why would you be shown any such clip, even supposing it existed?'

'To scare the shit out of me.'

'Why should we want to scare you? We want you to help us.'

Even as she speaks, there it is on the monitor again: the rictus grin on the tortured face, the twitching wires.

'There! There!'

But of course it's gone by the time she looks. If she doesn't know what's going on, she's putting on a good act. I don't know what to think any more. To be honest, I'm terrified.

'There's nothing there, you know?'

'Okay. Forget it.'

So here it comes, the deal: some of it in words, some of it in pictures only I get to see. I play the game or I get the tongue-clips. Or at the very least, an unspecified number of years in jail waiting for a rigged trial.

'All we ask is that you tell the truth. You, as a foreigner, as an Englishman, will be believed.'

'Which truth am I to tell?'

I mean this in a spirit of cynicism.

'The truth about the list. How the terrorists gave it to the police. How the terrorists want more violence, not less.'

Now I find myself in quite a dilemma. I have no respect for Petra's betrayal. I reject her movement's methods and goals. And anyway, judging from Ilse's condition, Petra is most likely already dead. On the other hand, I have no wish to be an agent of the equally violent authorities. On the other hand again, I want to get out of this fucked-up country as fast as I reasonably can.

This reminds me of my nemesis. I look up at the control-room window. He's still there, watching me.

'If you do this for us,' says Magdalena, 'you will demonstrate your concern for our country. Then we will know that you have been misguided, rather than criminal.'

'And you'll let me go home?'

'Naturally.'

It's all very well to say I just have to tell the truth. I'd still be doing it to save my own skin. Actually I'm super-eager to save my own skin, but that just makes it harder still.

'I wouldn't begin to know how to tell them. I mean, where are they? They're all over the place.'

'Every year, the members of the society gather in a secret meeting. This meeting is due to take place on Sunday, this very week. Not so far away.'

'And you know all about this meeting? Even though it's so secret?'

'Of course.'

I start to consider ways of working this. If I agree to the plan, I get to leave the studio without getting the tongue-clip treatment. After I've left, I'll still have time to think. The show's not over till the thin guy sings. And anyway, it's perfectly true about the list. And

207

what good do I do to anybody by staying here and screaming? It's not like they'll hear. So I look up at the softly lit sound-proof window of the control room and see him standing there in the shadows and I say,

'Okay. I'll do it.'

I see the watching man give a little nod. So he's happy, which is something. Maybe now he'll stop staring at me from the backs of cars.

'Oh, that is so wonderful! I am so happy!'

Magdalena is mostly plain relieved. She needed to get this agreement and now she's got it. I find myself wondering again if she's one of the manipulators or one of the victims. In her relief she has her hands on my knees and she's stroking me.

'It was a good interview? My questions, they were good?'

'Yes. Sure.'

'My show, you think it will be a success?'

'Why not?'

'You have a fiancée?'

Where did that come from? I look up towards the control-room and see that the lights have gone out. The floor monitors too have gone dark. The remote-operated cameras are no longer moving. We seem to be done.

'What?'

'You have a girlfriend, who you will marry?'

'Marry? No.'

'Then you are free.'

Only the free can love. Here in the country of the

happy hosts. She raises her hand and strokes my face.

'Such an English face! When my show is a success I will be famous.'

All at once, the studio lights go out. I'm trapped in a darkened studio with a wannabe television star. This is not a situation for which I'm equipped.

Her voice comes out of the dark.

'May I tell you my secret dream?'

I think I can guess. I get up out of my chair, and hear her rising also. I'm wondering which way is out, and whether the goons are still on duty.

'It is to make love in front of television cameras.'

Somehow she's found my body and is pressing her body against it.

'You're crazy! Back off!'

'I will take off my panties?'

'No! You're nuts!'

I step backwards in the dark, and fall off the edge of the little stage. Magdalena follows. So now we're on the floor, locked in what a casual observer might call a passionate embrace.

'Please, English! Please!' Magdalena whispers urgently in my ear, and then starts to lick it. A certain amount of wriggling takes place, caused by my attempts to get up off the floor and Magdalena's attempts to undo my belt. In the end I win.

She lies there on the floor illuminated by the faint light from the EXIT sign: an international word, and my guide out of here. Her skirt has ridden up to reveal the pale glow of her unstockinged thighs, and the white triangle of her crotch. Undignified but erotic.

'Please, English!' she whispers, making no effort to stand.

I pass on the offer. As I negotiate the camera cables on the way to the exit I hear her plaintive voice calling after me.

'I will be famous!'

The passage is empty. I go down it to the far end, walking fast. The door opens into an entrance lobby, where a receptionist sits at a desk, talking on the phone in a way that sounds like gossip with a girlfriend. She looks up as I cross the lobby and waves at me, without breaking off her phone conversation. I stop, unsure what she wants. She holds out an envelope. I go to her and she gives it to me. She chatters on.

I leave the building with the envelope in my hand, and make my way out into a snowy city street. Have I escaped, or merely been released to carry out my side of the bargain? Am I being followed? I look round, but see no signs of surveillance. So I stand at a tram stop and open the envelope.

Inside there is a printed invitation: a date and a time, and lines that look like an address. I take it this gives me access to the secret meeting that takes place on Sunday. But I have no idea how far away it is, or how long it will take me to get there. Nor do I have the faintest idea what day it is today.

13

The more I think about it all the angrier I get. The mock television interview, the waiting envelope. Either arrest me or let me go. Why the big mystery? If they want me to go somewhere, lay on a car and driver. If this is some kind of test, I'm not taking it. So fail me. I don't do tests. I'm on a journey without a destination. This is the pigeon's lesson. This is why I'm here. If they want me to do this thing for them they're going to have to make it happen, because me, I'm just rolling along.

Roll like a pebble, fall like a leaf, sail like a cloud.

This thought, once brought to the forefront of my mind, has a radical effect on my mood. I stop hurrying. Why walk fast? I'm going nowhere. Enjoy this sharp white winter day. Be kind to old ladies. Smile at policemen. I'm living under the protection of their purpose for me. They can do the heavy lifting.

So I saunter down the broad tree-lined boulevard.

The buildings on either side are faded-grand, which is the best kind of grand, with long unbroken facades. I seem to be in a capital city. The street is striped by passing cars. The snow on the pavements is well trodden. I'm passing the front of an ocean liner of a hotel called the Bristol. This name I can read. There are luxury hotels called the Bristol all over the place, which is a joke, because Bristol is this city built on the slave trade that got bombed flat in World War Two and isn't in any way luxurious. It occurs to me that inside there will be hotel bathrooms. I would really like a hotel bath.

When my father first got rich, and before he left home, he took us on holidays where we stayed in luxury hotels. I don't think he enjoyed them much, but me, I really appreciated the bathrooms. I love all that chrome, all that mirror, all that white ceramic. It makes me feel like everything that doesn't work in my life can be washed away and I can start again. I'm not too interested in all the little bottles of free stuff beside the basins. It's the big towels, the big tub, and the general feeling that I'm going in used and coming out new. Whenever I hear that religious imagery about washing away sin I'm right there, only my version isn't so much to open my heart to Jesus as to go and have a bath.

Everything about me is currently soiled. My money is gone with my coat. The receptionist at the Hotel Bristol is not about to offer me the presidential suite. So I walk on by.

There's a policeman ahead acting like he'd direct the traffic if only there was any to direct. There are some cars hissing by but they don't go fast and they stop at the lights the way they should. The pedestrians are a law-abiding crowd too, bunching up by the crossings and only stepping out onto the street when the little green man appears. Then I see another policeman, and another. None of the policemen give me a second glance.

Now I'm passing a men's clothing shop. To my surprise there's some decent stuff in the window. If I ever had the urge to look like a millionaire playboy which I don't this is the kind of stuff I'd go for. Very casual but very expensive. How is it that in these very poor countries they have these very rich shops? I guess it's tough work running a police state. The elite need their little perks of office.

There's a suede blouson jacket that would look acceptable on me. It's a honey-gold, you can tell even through the window that it's supersoft silky suede. You wouldn't want to wear it anywhere it might get damaged, like out of doors or in the rain. But in a club or a bar, maybe. And not with jeans. My father wears jeans for Christ's sake. I'd go with khaki work pants, high-ankle boots, Timberland or Caterpillar. Not that I do all that label crap in everyday life, but here I am far from home and I can play around just for a laugh. Except I have no money.

They should have thought of this. How am I

supposed to live while getting myself to the address on the envelope? What do they care?

This is when it strikes me that not only do they care, but they must be watching me right now. I look up and down the avenue. Quite a few people coming and going. No one who looks like an agent of the interior ministry. But they have to be there. That studio stunt took some setting up. They need me alright. So they're out there, minding the baby.

I decide to test the system. It comes to me in a flash of brilliance. The upside of being in a police state is there's always a policeman handy when you want one.

I go into the luxury men's clothes shop, take the gold suede jacket out of the window, nod to the sad old fruit at the back, and walk out again. I don't do it fast, I take my time. I make no attempt to hide the jacket once I've got it. I start to stroll away down the avenue.

There's some yelling behind me. A policeman comes running. I turn, very relaxed. He cracks me on the side of my head with his stick, which is not part of my plan. My ear bleeds onto the stolen suede jacket as I fall to the pavement. The policeman is waving to a black van that's charging down the street towards us. I'm an undesirable element about to be purged.

Then my angels show up. They're a little late. My ear hurts like fury. Two guys in civilian clothes and dark glasses. I can hardly believe the dark glasses. I mean, it's winter in Eastern Europe or Central Asia or wherever the fuck we are. Maybe they're planning on going skiing. Meantime why not just wear a flashing lapel badge that says SECRET POLICE? However they do the necessary. The street cops back off ultra fast and the sad old fruit from the clothes shop, who's out in the cold to see me get my ribs kicked in, is displaying the body language of a property owner with no intention whatsoever of pressing charges.

By the time I'm on my feet they've all gone. So this is just great. I've got a bust ear and an ache in my head and every passer-by is looking through me like I don't exist and I still don't have any money. So fuck you all.

I go back into the luxury clothes shop. The sad old fruit starts out with a smile because he imagines the suede jacket is coming home to daddy. Think again, pal. I move round his emporium bleeding on the cashmere and picking myself out some gear. I've been a peasant long enough. I pick out a deep-grey linen shirt and a loose cotton-knit navy pullover and a pair of khaki pants and some socks and some underpants and a pair of boots. I try them all on except the socks and the underpants and he just watches with a kind of mournful gaze. Then I take my pile to him and mime putting them in a bag, and he does all this neat folding and puts them all in crisp carrier bags and never once suggests I go and fuck myself.

All this is quite exhilarating. For the first time in my life I am the beneficiary of a totally unfair system. You don't read much about the young Hitler or the young Stalin dreaming of going into a clothes shop and

picking out all the gear they want and not even looking at the prices, but it is definitely a motivator for the
wannabe dictator. Actually those guys went several
steps further and invented their own uniforms and
had them made for them by top tailors. Seize power,
look cool. Fun with nation states.

I take my carrier bags and I say thank you to the sad
old fruit and he just shrugs and looks tired. Then I
walk out of the shop and head directly towards the
Hotel Bristol. I am forming a plan. Please remember I
still look like a seriously not-wealthy hobo with a
bloody ear. It's true I'm carrying three bulging carrier
bags that display the name of a luxury store, but on the
whole the enormous doorman of the Hotel Bristol is
not excited by my entrance. He doesn't know about my
angels.

'You speak English?' I say to the lady at the desk.
She's one of those sleek young women they breed in
Milan to do this job: hair strained back, high cheek-
bones, dark-grey tailored suit, crisp make-up, smiling
but never intimate.

'Of course,' she says, the smile slowly leaking out of
her face for lack of input.

'I'd like a room,' I say. 'A good room. A very good
room.'

She doesn't look down at her screen to check room
availability. She just holds her default expression
that's designed to offend no one and to put no creases
in her make-up.

'How will you be paying, sir?'

'Oh, I won't.'

I'm enjoying this.

'I just want to use the room,' I amplify. 'I don't want to pay.'

'I see.'

I've not broken her cool. She transmits a micro-glance towards the doorman. He's been waiting for this. He comes over and takes hold of me by one arm and propels me with irresistible power towards the door.

'Police!' I yell. 'POLICE!'

This is not the way the doorman has been expecting events to unfold. He's got the door open and I'm about to be hurled onto the snowy pavement only I'm yelling 'Police!' like I'm the injured party. The police, ever ready to help a stranger in distress, are right here. Also my friendly ski instructors.

Once again low words are exchanged, and I am a free man. I take up my carrier bags and re-enter the hotel. The lady at the desk is disconcerted. Not much. Just a tremor of one pencilled eyebrow, but it's a start.

'As I was saying.' I savour the moment. 'I'd like a room.'

She looks past me. I don't even bother turning round. I know there'll be a man in dark glasses there making hand signals that say, Do it. She does it.

The key she gives me has a lump of metal attached

to it the size of Hong Kong. I love that. It's supposed to stop you leaving town with the key in your pocket but to me it's the material signifier of the hotel's status. If you can hardly lift the key you're in the right economic bracket. So I follow a young bellboy to the lift and I live for the moment.

It's not the presidential suite exactly but it's not bad. The bellboy moves around switching on lights and opening doors in that dance they go on doing till you tip them, but I have no money so he's wasting his sweetness upon the desert air. He shows me the mini-bar and the bulky closet which succeeds in hiding the TV but very obviously has no other function, and the balcony with the view of the cathedral.

'Sorry,' I say. 'No money. But next time you're in trouble with the police, call me.'

He gives me a long interested look, featuring my mashed ear.

'You want girl?'

'No. I want bath.'

'Okay.'

He cracks a grin that says, Good for you if you can swing it, and he goes. I check out the bathroom. Totally not renovated since I guess 1939, when hotels understood about bathrooms and majored on space. It's the size of a small concert hall, with loud shiny pipes six inches in diameter. I run myself a bath. The water comes out of the giant taps at a thousand gallons a minute, kettle-hot, and in seconds all the chrome and all the mirror-glass has a soft sheen of condensation. This is heaven.

I take off all my clothes and throw them on the bed. Then I walk naked into my steamy dreamland and just stroll about for a bit, from the bath to the double basins, from the double basins to the lavatory, from the lavatory to the bath, and so back again. I check the water temperature as the bath fills, and wallow in the knowledge that shortly I'll be pink and clean as a peeled tomato. Then the enormous bath is full. I turn off the taps. Silence falls, broken only by a distant whooshing. Slowly I enter the embrace of the steaming water.

This running of baths is one of the few matters on which I claim some expertise. The temperature of bath water is critical. Run it too hot and you can't get in without suffering. Run it not hot enough and you lose the entire point of taking a bath in the first place, which is to melt your unforgiving body. A lukewarm bath is worse than no bath at all. A lukewarm bath says your hopes and dreams will never come true. It's entropy in action, the dribbling away of energy in the inexorable downward slide to the death of the universe. So the water has to be hot, hot, hot: so hot that it takes half an hour to get in. Except for me. Here's the trick of it. Keep checking the mix as you run it. That means what it says: keep checking. Stay on the case. Don't wander off and re-stack your socks. Lose control for more than a minute and you'll start over-compensating, running all cold, then all hot, then all cold, and take it from me, it's over. Go run yourself a shower. The key to a fine bath is to keep it hot to your hand but bearable, remembering that it will feel much hotter to your body, and leave room for a major top-up of undiluted hot water once you're immersed. Maybe all this sounds obvious but don't tell me it's what you do because I don't believe you.

So then I just lie there for a week or two. My hurt ear buzzes and tingles. My entire body slowly turns to marshmallow. Then, one critical micro-second before the pleasure turns to disgust and self-hatred, I spring to my feet and soap myself all over and sluice myself down and lose myself in towels.

Never get dressed too quickly after a hot bath. Mooch about in a towel until you start to cool, then a bathrobe. I check out the mini-bar. There are rows of little tiny bottles of various alcohols and rows of little tiny bags of nuts and crisps and chocolates. I eat every-thing that can be eaten. Then I drink all but five of the little tiny bottles without getting overly concerned about what's in them. After that I'm king of the world.

I get dressed in all my new purchases, which is how I like to think of them because I paid for them with bravado. I discover myself in a full-length mirror behind the door and I look the way I feel. The honey suede over the navy cotton knit is so damn sharp I don't recognise myself, and when I do there's this ping in my brain of a new image being slotted into place.

I'm actually not a bad-looking guy. Even the black blood clotted in my ear looks cool in a mean sort of way. Up until this moment I've always thought my ears stuck out too much and my chin not enough, both of which are true. But here I am looking like someone you could mistake for a minor movie star after a night out with his mob buddies. So I drink the remaining five little bottles and I'm ready to assume power and run the country.

My bodily needs have been met. According to the psychologist Abraham Maslow I must now move on to the higher levels of need, which if I remember correctly are emotional, intellectual and spiritual. These needs can all be met by the one act of getting out of this country alive. Nothing stands in my way but the apparatus of the secret police. In my newly heightened state I see this as no insuperable problem. I will go out into the great maze that is a modern city and I will lose them. After that, I will seek help from teachers or librarians or whoever else I can find with a positive attitude to Leon Vicino, and ask for their guidance. But I'm not about to lead the boys with the pliers to do their business on friendly folk who are armed only with the *Oxford Book of English Verse*.

My filthy old clothes are scattered over the big bed. I ponder what to do with them. My roving eyes fall on the closed windows to the balcony. In one smooth movement that expresses my current twin sensations of omnipotence and contempt, I gather up my soiled garments, throw open the windows, and hurl them at the distant view of the cathedral.

Next stop those mean streets. This time as I leave the lobby the doorman holds the door for me, and I realise he doesn't recognise me. This is because I'm clean and wearing new clothes. It's also because the most striking part of my appearance is the golden-brown suede jacket, which I was not wearing on my way in. Once I'm out in the avenue and mingling with the populace this becomes even more apparent. Some people go for dark blue coats and some for dark grey. A breakaway minority make their statement in dark brown. But I alone look like egg yolk on legs. I am a beacon for all eyes. My minders will not be challenged in their appointed task. In this city you could pick me out at a distance of half a mile with your head in a paper bag.

This of course gives me my brilliant idea, or at least my brilliant idea Part One. I look round for my minders as I go and I can't see them. They're rather good at this. I infer their nearness from recent experience. But if you can't see people following you, how do you know when you've succeeded in losing them? For this, I have a plan.

I turn off the broad avenue and very quickly I'm in the real city, by which I mean narrow streets lived in by poor people. Some street doors stand open, revealing even narrower passages leading to tenement courtyards. On every corner there's a bar or a pawn shop. Small children sit on doorsteps practising being victims. Not so many people out on the pavements here. Once when I turn I catch a glimpse of two men in dark glasses, looking ridiculously overdressed for the milieu. But then so do I. If I'm not careful I'll get mugged for my jacket. So I'm being not careful.

I turn a corner walking fast and then I turn another corner and I run into a fight brewing outside a bar. These two guys with thick moustaches and dark work coats are yelling at a third guy with a thick moustache and a dark work coat and in between yells they're pushing at his shoulders. I back away, retracing my steps, and take a different turn, and there are the sun-seekers hovering at the far end of the street, so I head round the block thinking fast. I need a couple of minutes out of their sight and on present form I've got maybe thirty seconds. If I can lose them for two minutes I could be anywhere and that translates as everywhere and even well-trained secret police operating on home territory can't look everywhere.

This is where I have my brilliant idea Part Two. Lesser men would have dodged into a doorway or even tried to outrun the men in shades but I propose to go for the gold by disappearing altogether. So I turn the next corner and I've come all the way round the block and there at the far end is the bar brawl again, which has now ripened into a punch-up. I peel off my gold suede jacket and toss it through an open doorway. Then I break into a run, pound down the street to the yelling drunks outside the bar, and hit the one being hit by the other two. Not sporting but I have my reasons. He yells and hits me back. I go in with both fists. Being five miles high on a vodka-gin-Glenfiddich cocktail I feel no pain. As the angry octopus of the brawl takes me in its flailing arms and I become dimly aware that my ear is bleeding again the men in suits come loping by and never even give me a glance. They're not interested in a bunch of drunks beating the shit out of each other. I would guess that ninety per cent of the male population of the city gets blasted ninety per cent of the time. It's what you do when you have no money, no power, and a state-controlled television system. Nor am I surprised that they've let me join their mutual-injury society without any kind of introduction. The losers of this world have big hearts and open arms. Anybody can share in their leisure activities.

After the thumping has been going on for a while the lone brawler decides to call it a day, and backs off down the street, issuing a torrent of incomprehensible curses. His two assailants curse back with undimmed vigour until he passes out of sight. Then they shake hands with each other and shake hands with me and we all go back into the bar. They clap me affectionately on the back and we all compare wounds and I receive my share of dabbing with a wet dishcloth. A glass is pressed into my hands filled to the brim with some brand of firewater which my companions drink without pausing to take breath, so I do likewise, and the result seems to be a general anaesthetic because all the stinging and throbbing of my outer body ceases. My new friends ply me with questions but I've decided to be a deaf-mute and only answer them with nods and smiles. So I don't have a honey-coloured jacket and I'm not English and with luck I've disappeared.

By the time the party breaks up it's dark outside and my mood has changed again. I'm thinking of looking out a quiet cemetery somewhere and lying down to die. We all shake hands again and shake heads and give each other rueful smiles that I translate as, Life is hard and then you die. Then off we roll in our various directions. No goons loom out of the lamplight. The plan has worked. Whether I survive it is another matter.

The evening streets are quiet. Oddly quiet. Maybe there's a curfew or something and people out after dark get shot dead. I want very much to sit down and hold my head. I want very much to do this sitting down somewhere indoors, out of the vicious wind that has sprung up. My knitted cotton pullover and linen shirt are not proof against the night cold.

Ahead I can see a church with a small door standing half open and a dim light trickling out onto the pavement. I can also hear music. I head for this sanctuary. The music is a string quartet. For a moment I think I'm home again and coming down the path to the back door and the music is Radio 3 which my mother always has blasting away in the kitchen. But the door ahead is not our front door, it's a small arched entrance in the high side wall of a church. I stand in the doorway to get out of the wind and I close my eyes and I listen to the music and it occurs to me after a while that I'm crying, and that this is probably the most beautiful music I've ever heard in my life.

14

A deep thrill of sound streams through the shadowed church. I walk down ancient aisles, over honoured dead. Light in an end chapel, darkness elsewhere: the charged and mighty darkness of high stone vaults. *Da-da-da! Da-da-da!* Stabbed by sudden strings, the grave flow breaks, and resumes: and now I travel with it, tugged by longing for other worlds, for the journey that never ends, and I'm crying because I'm so smashed and fucked and pissed that I have no resistance left in me. The sweet-strange music carries me beyond hurting, beyond memory, into pure space. I sail like a soap bubble, weightless, transparent, rainbow-eyed. The music sings me and pierces me, bursts me and makes me nothing, as the enchantment of the violin steals through the church and lifts me on its thermal of hope and floats me up, away – *Da-da-da! Da-da-da!* Buffeted to earth, I come to a stop in the aisle, alone, and the music swirls about me, searching, turning, until the journey begins again, and now I know we're feeling for the way out, we seek rest, the music and I, we're caught in the twisted loop of eternity, we seek silence. The violins and I, we loop and twist, round and round, we dip low and rise, and – gone! – all sound gone! – we touch the cool cheek of the longed-for silence – and the questing murmur returns – and again! we slip out of time – and return – and sail on, only now we go nowhere, no goal, no strife, no journey, a surrender of the will, as the great cloud-massed chords return, so stately, so far above all human cares and joys, magisterial as mountains in the mist. So, slowly, the mist closes in, and the prospect fades, and without any moment that can be called an ending, the music has ended.

The musicians sit in a little circle before the lady chapel, candles glowing by their music stands, the last tremors of departing sound hovering about them. For a moment they are still, the music-making finished, the life not yet begun. I am standing in the aisle stupid with loss. How can such beauty have been made by such clowns? They look like refugees from a seaside bingo hall. Dress them in white and you'd have a crown bowls team. What I'm saying is they are all seriously old.

Two old men and two old women: two violins, a viola and a cello. The old women come in big and small, and so do the old men. The big man looks like General de Gaulle, the little man looks like a garden gnome. In a moment they will discover me. I brush my stained cheeks and marvel that these shrivelled oldies can make music that makes me cry. Some composition never knowingly heard by me before, without obvious shape or melody, has awed me into attention. I feel as if I have never truly listened to music until now. This much is clear to me. I have eaten music like comfort food, demanding foreknowledge of the experience in the shape of tunes, the way small children will only eat what they have eaten many times before. Never have I set out on music as on an adventure, trusting to an unknown guide. But never before have I been in the state I'm now in. So let me recommend disorientation, physical discomfort, and dread of the morrow, for your listening pleasure.

I am being awakened. Parts of me I had not known to exist are stretching and stirring and unfurling within me. Even as I long for home and warmth and sleep, I am waking.

The garden gnome is putting away his cello and speaking to me. It sounds like a greeting.

'Good evening,' I say.

My English of course surprises them. Their puzzled faces turn towards me in grave inspection. Candlelight is supposed to be flattering, but it is not kind to aged skin. It deepens wrinkles.

'You are English?'

Cello speaks my language.

'Yes.'

He raises the palm of his right hand as if in benediction.

'Oh to be in England, now that April's here.'

Another poetry lover. What is it about this country? Anyone would think they have a law that obliges them to learn English poetry by heart.

'Right,' I say.

'You are a visitor to our country?'

I don't deny it. I see his kind eyes probing the bruise on my face, and dried blood in my ear. He asks me where I'm staying and I tell a small lie so as not to distress them.

'The Hotel Bristol.' Then, to move the dialogue on past questions about my presence here that I do not altogether know how to answer, I add, 'What were you playing?'

'Shostakovich,' says Cello. 'The eighth string quartet. Dedicated to the victims of war.'

'You play beautifully.'

'Thank you. We are only amateurs, of course. We rehearse for the music festival.'

'The music festival. Right.'

I find myself wondering where the music festival is to be held. Is it for example anywhere near a border crossing?

'You must come.'

Cello nods at me, his eyes lingering on me in a curious gaze. He wears a black polo-neck jumper, which makes his bald head look as if it's floating in

230

space without a body.

'I'm afraid I don't have the time.'

'The festival begins tomorrow. But perhaps you are leaving tomorrow?'

'Yes.' I realise I don't sound at all sure of my own plans. 'I hope to leave tomorrow.'

They're all looking at me now, and I get the feeling they know there's something suspicious about me. Then they turn to packing up their instruments and music stands and ask me no more questions. The door of their curiosity opened for a few moments, and has now closed. I have maybe three more minutes before they blow out the candles and leave. The difficulty I face is that I can't ask them to help me without revealing my illegal status. How do I know they won't hand me over to the authorities? Why should they take even the smallest risk for my sake? And yet there is something about the little cello player that gives me reason to trust him. He has friendly eyes.

'If I run into difficulties over my travel arrangements,' I say, choosing my words with care, 'then maybe I won't be leaving for a few more days.'

General de Gaulle pulls a face, and speaks in a croaky voice edged with bitterness.

'For you, no difficulties. You show passport, you go where you like. London, Paris, New York.'

'First I must cross the border.'

This is as close as I dare come to the truth of my situation. They do not pick up the hint.

'I have seventy years,' grumbles General de Gaulle, 'and I never cross border. Never one time. When I am young man, I dream of Paris. But this is not God's will.'

He gives me a severe look. He thinks I'm ungrateful.

'Enjoy the rest of your journey,' says the little cello player.

Click-click. They close their instrument cases, and with parting bobs of the head they file off into the shadows. I make no more attempt to detain them. I hear the outer door clunk as they close it behind them. They have left the four candles burning, presumably for my benefit. What exactly do they expect me to do, alone in a foreign church at night? Pray?

I look round me, uncertain what happens next. Carved stone arches rise up on either side, joining high above to form a greater arch, beneath which stands the altar of the lady chapel. Behind the altar, framed in gilded wood, there is a painting of the Virgin and Child. The Virgin is sitting on a red seat with a high back and a red canopy over the top, and the Child is standing on her lap, looking sulky. The Virgin herself is rather ordinary, though she has a nice face, a little like Ilona's. I think of Eckhard saying, 'Sometimes when I watch her I can see how beautiful she will be when she is old.' This makes me feel lonely.

I take up one of the candles, and shielding its flame with the other hand, I explore the church. It's bigger than I realised. The door through which I entered and the music-makers exited is at the back of the building. Now, venturing up a side aisle and past the high altar, I see the nave stretching before me, column after column, far beyond the reach of my candle's light. So much darkness is scary. I retreat to the lady chapel.

The four chairs still stand in their circle, mocking me with my loss of company. The candles burn. I try to guess how long before they burn out. An hour more, or maybe two. I can't return to the Hotel Bristol, where my shadows will be waiting for me. Nor would it be useful to wander the streets at night. So it seems I am going to spend the hours of darkness in a church.

I move all four candles onto the altar so that they throw their light on the painting. I'm feeling lonely, and the Virgin and her Child are the only friends in sight. Actually there turn out to be two other figures, one on each side of the throne, one male and one female, saints or martyrs judging from their glum upward-rolling eyes. But I don't bother with them. I'm getting to know the girl.

She has her head a little on one side, and she's looking down and away, like she's occupied with some thoughts of her own. She's got on this simple pinky-orange dress and a blue hood and cloak and red sandals on her feet. She looks so young, fifteen maybe, and here she is with this great beefy Child standing on her lap. She's holding him upright, or almost holding him, letting him think he's standing all by himself, which is what mothers do and their sons never know it. So much giving for so little return.

The thing is she's not showing him off, this Child who's supposed to be God and is going to pull off the major trick of all time, which is coming back from the dead. There's none of that crown-and-glory stuff. She's got a halo but it's so minimalist I don't even see it for a while: just this thin trace of gold. It's true she's on this red canopied seat but you get the feeling someone said, Sit there, and so she sat there, but it's not hers. She's just an ordinary girl. Too young to have a baby really. Still a child herself, but now a mother. It happens.

I think of Hanna and her baby boy Manfred. Then I think of my own mother. In this thought I'm the sulky child on her lap, and it's my mother who's leaning her head on one side and looking far away. Is it me that makes her so grave? She holds me but she lets me think I stand alone. She loves me and she lets me go.

Oh my mother.

I never thanked you for holding me in your arms. I never knew that you were always there. I only knew that when I needed you, you never failed me. Did your life stop for me, or did it go on but in some changed way? Love me always but don't love me too much. I can't bear it. I can't repay. Please understand I'm not cruel and without heart, but I will leave you.

I am cruel and without heart.

They will crucify me and I will die but I won't rise again, that's only a story, and your heart will be broken. That's no way to go. Let's change the plot, you and me, tonight in the candlelight in the church. You've done enough loving. You get up off your red seat and put me down on the ground and walk away. I'll manage just fine. And in a little while when I don't need you any more I'll start loving you, and that way when you die I'm the one with the broken heart. Let that be my repayment.

Such strange thoughts. My mother holding my hand as we wait for the lights to stop the stream of taxis so we can cross the street, on the pigeon-pocked pavements of Trafalgar Square. The firm tug that says cross now. She seems so powerful, so in control. Red sandals on her feet. No, that's the Madonna above the altar.

When I come home I will kiss your feet and ask your forgiveness.

And the Child! He has his right hand raised like he's giving someone an order but his left hand is keeping hold of just the one finger of his young mother's hovering protective hand. He thinks he's God. I wonder if he hates me. Looking at his face, I don't think so. He too is looking far away, a little saddened to think of what's to come, but I'm no part of his thoughts. I'm the one doing the thinking.

The candles are burning down faster than I expected. Or maybe more time's gone by than I realise. I'm going to have to sleep here. The various alcohols I've ingested are coming to the end of their journey through my metabolism and I don't feel at all great any more. I shuffle about with a candle and find there are little tight-stuffed cushions in the pews, so I round up a herd of them and corral them between the base of the altar steps and the altar rail. I'm making my bed in the holy bit where visitors aren't supposed to go. I don't care. Gods are mortal, humans immortal, living their death, dying their life.

I stand the candles at the four corners exactly as if I'm in my coffin and lie down and don't care one way or the other if I wake up dead.

Some time in the middle of the night I have a mystical experience. My eyes open but the candles have gone out and there's no light at all. I don't know where I am but I don't feel afraid. In fact I feel immense. I feel as if I extend in all directions without limit and contain all things. A giant calmness possesses me, and I hear a voice which I know to be my own voice saying:

All is well! All is well!

It seems so obvious to me that whatever happens is for the best, and could not be otherwise. Like water that flows downhill, it's in its nature, it requires no effort, wherever it goes is right: so with the universe, so with history, so with my life, which are all the same thing. Whatever comes to pass is the right and only eventuality, and could not be otherwise.

When I wake again, I feel cold and hungry. I recall my night thoughts clearly but can't recreate the simple sublime conviction that sustained them. All is very far from well. I am in fact in deep shit. I stand up. My bones ache.

Grey light is creeping about the church. Little by little, as I see more, I take in the full scale of the building. This must be the cathedral, formerly starring in the view from my hotel window. The nave is about a mile long, and blue-grey as if carved in ice. The high gothic windows have lost any stained glass they may once have had and are glazed with opaque milky glass held in place with iron bars. Through this screen the daylight pours a soft white wash across the flagged floor.

I greet my friend the Virgin. She's still averting her eyes from mine but I understand. Then I hear a distant door open and someone comes in. He passes between the arches, from white light to shadow to white light, a man in a black soutane, a short man, a priest carrying a basket. He's evidently coming to me.

He raises one hand in friendly greeting and I realise that the priest is the cello player from the string quartet. Now that he wears a dog collar and a black robe he no longer resembles a garden gnome. He looks like a priest. Somehow it's normal for a priest to be short and squat and ugly. That's why priests can't be heroes in movies. Put a movie star in a priest costume and you know right off something's wrong. They just look too good.

He has brought the basket for me. It's my breakfast.

'How did you know I'd still be here?'

'Ah. Who can say?' He sits down in a pew to get his breath back. He's not fit, this one. 'A feeling?'

'I didn't know you were a priest.'

'Why should you? When I play music, I am not a priest. I am a musician.'

The basket contains a flask of hot coffee, a bread roll, soft cheese. And beneath these, washed and pressed and folded, my own clothes. My jeans and check shirt, my fleece, my socks. This is spooky.

'Where do these come from?'

'They were found in the street. They are yours?'

'Yes, but—'

I don't know how to begin to express the spookiness of what is happening to me. Cello seems to think it's all in the normal course of things.

'These are not clothes that can be bought here.' He fingers the labels. 'These are a foreigner's clothes. So when I heard they had been found, I thought of you.'

'Am I the only foreigner in the city?'

'I believe so. Yes.'

How can this be possible? Even at the height of the Cold War cities like Moscow and Leningrad had foreigners on visits. Or maybe they didn't. What do I know?

As I drink my coffee and eat my bread I ponder my situation and conclude that I have little left to risk. I like this priest. I'm grateful to him. He knows I'm in some sort of trouble. So I decide to trust him.

I begin with the question I swore I wouldn't ask.

'Where am I?'

'Where are you? You're in the cathedral church.'

'No. I mean, what city? What country?'

He stares at me.

'You don't know?'

'No.'

'How is that possible?'

So I tell him how I set out on a journey without a destination, and hitched a lift without knowing where I was going, and entered the country without going through the proper procedures. As I talk, he starts to chuckle, and then to laugh. I smile too, because I know his laughter is in delight and admiration at what I've done.

'Ah! That's precious!' he cries. 'That's rich!'

'But now,' I say, coming to the point, 'I'm in a mess, and I think I should know.'

'You think you should know?' He eyes me with his screwed-up little eyes, and the laughter subsides. 'Well, I'm not so sure about that.'

'What do you mean?'

'It's a fine thing you're doing. A fine thing. A species of meditation. Why not let it be?'

'But how can I? I'm lost.'

'You're no more lost than anyone else in this mortal world. Less lost than most, in fact. I could give you the name of a city. The name of a country. But would you then be found? Is it even necessary to be found?'

'It would be a beginning.'

'You think so? Might it not be an ending? Every name a nail. Bang! Bang! In goes the nail, and another living thing is pinned to a wall to die. Do I know your name? No, I don't. Do you know my name? Not at all. So you and I may be anyone and everyone. We may be whoever we wish. We may be all the different people we are, one by one. Now isn't that more profit to both of us than a mere name?'

This is all very well but I have things to do. He seems to follow my thoughts.

'You have some difficulties with your travel arrangements, perhaps?'

'The truth is, I need to find a way to get out of the country.'

'Without too many awkward questions being asked.'

'Yes.'

He contemplates me with his head on one side.

'I did rather guess as much.'

'I don't want to get anyone into any trouble,' I say.

'No, of course not. But I suppose if I were to give you a lift in my car to the music festival, in which you have already expressed an interest, well, I don't see why anyone should find anything out of the ordinary with that.'

'And the music festival is—?'

'A few hours' drive west of here. A charming old town. And not far from the border.' His eyes twinkle at me. 'So what do you say to an evening of Mozart? The great Mass in C Minor.'

'I'd be very grateful.'

'There, you see! All accomplished, and no names. The mystery endures.'

Speaking purely for myself I'd say I've had enough mystery in the past few days to last me for the rest of my life. Right now I'm in the market for the occasional answer. However this gnomish priest has his own game to play, which does not include enlightening me, except after the Socratic method. What is it about me that impels philosophy bums to pick me for their project? All I want to do is get to the border. But I know by the way he twinkles at me that he plans to spend the drive nudging me towards self-knowledge. It must just be one of those things that happens to people when they get old and wise. They can't stop themselves spraying their wisdom about the place. All you can do is keep nodding and not get too close.

15

Cello drives with a blithe disregard for all other users of the road. Fortunately there are few. Also fortunately his car, an ancient Renault 4, has very little power, and only achieves anything you could call speed on long downhill slopes. As well as Cello and myself we are carrying his instrument, his suitcase, and what seems to be an entire mobile library.

I have reverted to my old clothes, so unexpectedly returned to me. The smart new clothes needed washing, and anyway made me feel like a fraud. Now I am myself again.

I have decided to reveal nothing about my recent experiences to the little priest. The less he knows, the less trouble I will bring down upon him should things go wrong. However he clearly wants to talk about something, so in the interests of keeping the conversation focused on him rather than on me we talk about being a musician and being a priest and before I

242

can apply the brakes we're onto the existence of God.

I say I can't see it. I mean, it would be comforting and so forth, but check out the facts.

'Which facts do you have in mind?' he asks me.

Now this isn't a topic on which I've actually prepared an essay, but the surprising thing is I find I'm all full of arguments in support of what I'm saying. What's more, I turn out to be quite heated on the subject.

'Okay, so what's this God supposed to have done? Created everything, right? So why? For him to play with? Does he get off on watching us little creatures squirm or what?'

'That is something of a puzzle.'

'I mean, either do us a favour or leave us alone. I never asked to be created. You have to admit there's something a bit bent in this idea that God creates us bad and then tells us to get good before we're let into heaven.'

'A bit bent.' He chuckles at that.

'And I haven't even started on the Christian stuff. Jesus dying for my sins? Puh-lease! It's a set-up. God rigs the game and then sends Jesus onto the pitch to win it. I'm sorry, I just don't buy it.'

'It's an odd business. I admit that.'

He swerves to avoid an oncoming truck. As we have been driving, the early-morning cloud has dispersed, and there is actual winter sunlight gleaming on the snow. We are well out of the nameless city now, and crossing a broad flat plain. The clear light, and my

243

own forceful thinking, combine to make me feel powerful. Cello's gentle concession does not satisfy me. I want opposition or surrender.

'So you're agreeing with me?'

'Not agreeing, no. I'm listening.'

'I thought this was supposed to be an argument.'

'Not at all. Arguments are for winning and losing. What use is that?'

I'm a little taken aback by this question. I had rather supposed that winning was the point of more or less everything.

'If you win an argument, that proves you're right.'

'Not at all. It only proves you're better at arguing.'

'So that's good.'

'How is it good? It seems to me that it gets you no further than you were before. We might as well stand in the rain and piss at each other.'

'Oh.' I'm quite surprised by his language. 'So if we're not arguing what are we doing?'

'Embarking on a voyage of discovery.'

This is the sort of thing Vicino writes.

'To undiscovered countries,' I quote, 'on the far side of lost oceans.'

He nearly crashes the car.

'You read Vicino!'

'Yes. Some.'

'Then you understand! You and I, we are explorers. When I listen to you, I enter a new country where things are done in new ways. That is exciting. Why

244

would I wish to take you prisoner and drag you back to my country and force you to live as I do?'

'Right.' Put like that I see his point. 'Even so, we can't both be right, can we? About God, I mean.'

'Of course we can! Look ahead. What do you see?'

'A road. Snow. Sky.'

'And me, I see the ditch that runs beside the road, and the ice in the ditch, and the sunlight on the ice.'

'I see all that too. I could have said that.'

'But you chose to see one thing, and I another. We're both right. We invent nothing. We select. We each make our own world, out of the common store that is reality.'

I feel trapped. I'm sure he's wrong but he keeps wriggling out of my grasp. I'm puzzling over some better way to corner him when he sets off on a new tack.

'Tell me about your parents. Do they believe in God?'

'No. I don't think so.'

'You don't know?' This surprises him. He takes his eyes off the road to check my expression, in case I'm teasing him. 'How can you not know?'

'Well. The subject's never really come up.'

'Amazing! You amaze me! Well, well.'

'It just isn't a big deal back home.'

'Do you tell me so! What then is a big deal?'

He wags his head as he drives, clearly finding it hard to take in what I tell him. I for my part find it hard to answer his question. What is a big deal? Getting to be rich and famous? It sounds too crass. I play for time.

'Do you mean for people in general, or for me?'

'Oh, for you. There are no people in general.'

'If we're talking about me, the answer has to be that nothing's a big deal.'

'Nothing?'

I think back to my room, with the blind down and the mute television flickering away and the door locked.

'Nothing.'

'You are telling me that nothing is important to you?'

'Well, I don't want to get hurt and so on. But if we're talking religion and philosophy and all that meaning-of-life shit – Sorry.'

I don't want to give offence.

'No, please. You choose your words for a reason. That meaning-of-life shit. It makes you angry.'

'Not angry. I just can't see it.'

But he's right, it does make me angry. I hadn't spotted that before.

'You would say you live a happy life?'

'No. I wouldn't say that.'

'You would like to lead a happy life?'

'Sure. Who wouldn't?'

'So what stands in your way?'

'The real world.'

'The real world makes you unhappy?'

246

'It doesn't exactly make me unhappy. It just doesn't make me happy. I'm kind of neutral.'

'Neutral.' He lingers on the word, like he's feeling it for size. 'So. What is the happiest moment of your life so far?'

'The happiest moment of my life.' I have to search. I'm reaching back into my childhood, which is embarrassing. 'I'd have to go way back for that.'

'So go way back.'

It's still there. A fully intact memory of a woodland path, one spring day when I was maybe nine years old.

'I'd just learned to ride a bike. My dad and I went on this bike ride. We went down a lane and into a wood and back again. I really liked it. First he went in front, then I went in front. It was good, biking with my dad.'

'Do you know why it was good?'

'Not really. I suppose I was proud that I could keep up with him. And I liked having him all to myself.'

As I'm talking I find what I really liked about it, and it seems almost too simple.

'I liked us both doing it together.'

In my memory he keeps turning to see I'm okay, my father I mean, and every time he turns his bike gives a great wobble and we both laugh. I like the way his friendly face keeps turning back to see that I'm okay.

'But it's not like it gives my life meaning or anything.'

'No. I understand that.'

He says nothing more, which disappoints me. Our

247

conversation is turning out to be interesting. I'd like more. Then he starts up again.

'This meaning-of-life shit.' I can't help laughing, to hear the little old priest say that word. 'It's going to have to be very big shit indeed to do it for you, I think.'

'Well, life's a big thing. I mean, like, existence and everything. You can't make that meaningful with one bike ride.'

'I can,' he says. 'It's you who can't.'

'That's because you're the one who believes in God.'

'How do you know that?'

I'm about to say he's said so, but it strikes me that maybe he hasn't. So I point out the obvious fact here.

'You're a priest.'

'Can you imagine the possibility that there exists a priest who does not believe in God?'

This is even more interesting. I sit forward in my seat.

'Sure I can. Is that what's happened to you?'

'You want to know about me?'

'Yes. I do.'

'At last. We make progress.'

Now this annoys me. His tone of voice reminds me of poor Marker in the cab of his truck, telling me I'm not curious by nature. I don't like to be treated like some slow-witted student. So when he goes on to ask, 'What would you like to know?', I reply:

'What do priests do for sex?'

I say this to crumple his complacency. He takes it in his stride.

'Which priests? Priests in general?'

'Jesus! I don't know. There are no priests in general, right?'

'Just so. I can only answer for myself. You may be surprised to learn I was married once. My wife and I met at college. I was very shy. It was she who did the courting. We went on reading holidays together. We read each other books aloud, many of your English classics among them. She had a fine reading voice. And yes, there was love. I was a clumsy lover. We learned together. But perhaps I am telling you more than you wish to hear?'

All this comes out in an even ruminative tone.

'No. No.'

'She fell ill when she was just forty years old. And so she died. There it is. We loved each other. She died. I am alone.'

I am silenced.

'Does that answer your question?'

'Yes. Sorry.'

'Why are you sorry?'

'I was being childish. It's obvious when you say it. No one's born a priest.'

'Just so. We all lead many lives.'

'So your wife dying. Did that make you—?'

I stop, not wanting to produce another dumb question.

'Doubt the goodness of God?'

'Yes.'

'It did that, and a great deal more. I was very unhappy. Have you ever been deeply unhappy?'

This is a good question. But I don't want to talk about me, I want to talk about how he got out from under his unhappiness. If he did.

'What did you do?'

'I became very fond of wine.'

'You drowned your sorrows?'

'I learned to enjoy good wine.' He waves in the general direction of the back of the car. 'I have some bottles of Bulgarian Mavrud with me that are *vaut le detour*, as the guides say. Wine is like a cat, isn't it? You can't guarantee its behaviour. It lives its own life. I always feel it's something of a privilege when a good wine enters my glass and condescends to meet me. That is why I never complain when the odd bottle is corked. As wine lives, so it dies. What else is one to expect?'

Not this. I felt that for a moment we were trembling on the brink of something strong and true, something I would be glad to discover for myself. Instead, we have retreated into after-dinner prattle. My father goes in for this fine wine flim-flam. It's just another kind of train-spotting. I'm not saying I don't enjoy a glass of wine but spare me the reverence, it's not like it's the blood of Christ. Which reminds me of the time my friend Mac whose family is Irish Catholic stole a bottle of altar wine and we drank it and it was Z-class piss and Mac said he now knew the sacrament of transubstantiation was turning cheap wine into something you'd actually choose to drink. But I don't insult my friend the priest by repeating this anecdote.

We're slowing down. There's a road block ahead. I remember road blocks. My palms go wet and my mouth goes dry but Cello seems unconcerned. Two policemen sitting looking cold in their car pulled up across the road. They get out as we approach.

The priest lets the Renault roll to a stop apparently of its own accord, and reaches behind him into the disorderly mass of luggage. Out comes a bottle of wine. He has a corkscrew in his pocket, the basic model known as the Waiter's Friend, and with a couple of brisk shakes of the wrist he has drawn the cork. The man has done this before. Then he gets out to greet the policemen, and the next thing I know they're all standing in the slush taking pulls of wine from the bottle.

Cello beckons me out and offers me the bottle, so I too drink. It's rich stuff alright. I knock it back like it's beer in one great swallow and the tastes go on exploding inside me for about five minutes afterwards. The priest and the policemen are yammering away, not at all like a security check. Actually it's the policemen who do most of the talking while the priest tips his head on one side and listens and nods. Then the bottle is finished and Cello takes out a second bottle and gives it to them unopened, and the policemen get back in their car and we get back in our car and we drive on down the road.

'You liked the wine?'

'Yes. It was good.'

'Some think it rough. But I say, wait, wait for it, and you will find strength, maturity, character. You agree?'

'I guess so.'

What I really want to know is how come there were no awkward questions at the road block. I heard a deal of talking but none of it sounded like police stuff and no one seemed interested in me.

'Those policemen weren't bothered about me?'

'No, not at all. They have troubles of their own.' He throws me a smile, and the car weaves all over the road. I find myself hoping the Bulgarian wine of which he has consumed his full share is bigger on the maturity than on the strength. 'You want to know?'

Do I want to know the policemen's troubles? Not really.

'Yes. Okay.'

'The thin one with the big ears, he's going crazy because his wife won't sleep in the same bed with him, she sleeps with the children, she tells him the children have nightmares, but he knows it's because she doesn't want to make love with him any more, and what can he do?'

That's quite a road-block chat.

'What did you say?'

'I said maybe his wife has a pretty sister.'

252

'You didn't!'

'And you know what? She has. And my friend the policeman is working on her. And the sister is not unwilling. But here is the tragedy. With the sister, he can't do it. You understand?'

I do understand. My eyes are popping.

'So what did you say to that?'

'I gave him a bottle of the Mavrud and told him next time to drink two glasses of the wine, say three Hail Marys, and all will be well.'

'You are a bad priest.' I can't help laughing. 'You are a wicked priest. God will punish you.'

'But there is no God. Or so you tell me.'

'I have no God. But you have a God.'

'True enough. I stand corrected.'

This brings us back to our discussion on the existence of God. Now made more expansive by wine, we trade concepts of the divine as we rattle west towards our next contact with reality.

'My God who exists may not be the same as your God who does not exist,' he says. 'So maybe if you show me your God I will agree he doesn't exist, and if I show you my God you will agree he does exist. And so we will both have been right.'

'That would be cosy.'

'So you show me yours and I'll show you mine.'

'My god,' I offer, 'is like the Great Examiner, and the life he gives us is like one long exam.'

'Then I most decidedly do not believe in him.'

'So who's your God?'

'My God is you.'

'Me?'

'Yes.'

'So what does that mean? I created the universe? You worship me?'

'All that, and a great deal more. You see, my friend, your mistake if you will allow me to say so lies in thinking of God as an individual. A moment's reflection will tell you that can be no more than a picture for children. God in the image of the father. True divinity can't be limited in this way. In fact, true divinity can't be limited at all. God can be no less than everything that exists. Which includes you.'

'So I'm not really God at all. I'm just a tiny piece of God.'

'There! Again, the child's picture of God. You see an individual, an entity, shall we say, that possesses the attribute of size. Very big, no doubt, but limited and divisible. My God is not that kind of giant. Think instead of, say, fire. Suppose God is fire. And I am fire. And the road down which we go is a road of fire. And the clouds in the sky are clouds of fire. All things are made of fire. Now I say to you, You are fire. Do you reply, I'm not really fire at all, I'm just a tiny piece of fire?'

'But I'm not fire.'

'Not fire. But life.'

'I'm life?'

He nods, his eyes on the road ahead. 'You are life.'

'I am life.' This seems to me to be an odd formulation. 'Don't we usually say, I am alive?'

He shrugs, not interested in my semantics.

'You are life. You live. You contain all existence within yourself. You are God.'

'So if I'm God, I can have what I want.'

'Of course. If you know what you want.'

There's a question. I want the envy of men and the love of women, as they say. But it's not going to happen.

'I don't think so.'

'Why not? It's happened before.'

'When?'

'When you went on that bike ride with your father.'

This is something of a let-down after being told I'm God.

'Was that it?'

'Don't you see?' He bangs the steering wheel in his exasperation. 'Life! Joy! Adventures! Wonders! All to be found right where you live, among your family and friends!'

'The society of others.'

'Yes! YES!' He's going to snap the steering wheel right off if he hits it one more time. 'What is the Mass? It is a meal we share. It is our Last Supper. We celebrate the life that rises from the dead. Of course it rises from the dead! If we are all, each of us, life itself, then we are all living and dying, all the time. What then should we fear?'

'Next you'll be telling me we're all Jesus.'

'Of course! Every one of us! Ask yourself why the story of Jesus has such power. The baby in the manger. The dying figure on the cross. His birth is our birth, his death is our death – but he is also God. In theology, the word is "incarnation", the divine made flesh. *Et incarnatus est.* So we pray in the Credo. "And he was made flesh by the Holy Spirit of the Virgin Mary, and was made man."'

He fields my blank look.

'The words are unimportant. Think of the revelation! Look at Jesus Christ, God in man, and see yourself. See what you too can be. That is the power! That is the glory!'

He's getting quite excited.

'So we all get to be crucified?'

'How can it be otherwise? Now the vinegar, now the wine. The suffering is also the celebration.'

'I'd just as soon have the celebration without the suffering.'

'Ah. You are young. "Joys impregnate, sorrows bring forth." That is your own poet, William Blake.'

More poetry. You can't argue with it, so I say nothing.

'But you and I,' he says after a pause, 'we are at different stages of the journey. You at the beginning, I at the end.'

'The end? Are you planning on dying soon?'

I mean this lightly, but he nods his bald head.

'Yes. Very soon. This evening, I think.'

'What!'

'If I have understood correctly.'

'You're going to kill yourself?'

'No, no. But I think I will die even so.'

'Why? How?'

'Oh, that is all too difficult to explain.'

He seems almost uninterested in the prospect of his own death.

'Do you want to die?'

'Do I want to die?' He thinks about that. 'The answer must be no. But I miss my wife. I would like to be with her again.'

'And you think you will be, after death?'

'Let us say, I hope it. I look forward, with eager interest.'

As he says this I recall the poem I read to the old man in the little back room with Eckhard and the whores. Somehow I have retained whole lines in my memory. I recite them aloud.

> But hark! my pulse, like a soft drum
> Beats my approach, tells thee I come;
> And slow howe'er my marches be
> I shall at last sit down by thee.

The little priest starts to weep.

'Maybe you should stop the car.'

So he stops the car and sits there sobbing to himself

and I'm wishing I knew what to say or do to make him feel better.

'The mystery,' he says, snuffling into an old handkerchief. 'The mystery.'

'Right.'

I don't feel I should ask too many questions any more.

He turns and looks at me, blinking a little, smiling a little, but mainly just looking. I think I should say something but can't think what so I let him look, and after a while I find I'm looking back. This is quite an odd sensation because I've been looking back all along but now I'm seeing into him, and what I'm seeing is this deep well of kindness. This stranger really wants me to be happy. He wants to protect me from danger and soothe my fears and heal my pain. He really does. Naturally this makes me feel this wave of gratitude, which he sees rolling towards him, and he in turn is grateful. So altogether we have ourselves a little love-fest.

He doesn't look so much like a gnome any more. It's funny about people's faces. If you look at them for long enough they stop being beautiful or ugly and become just themselves. Then you see they couldn't be any other way because that person's life has formed his face, and if you love him you love his face the way it is. Cello has blotchy wrinkly skin and a bulging nose and grizzly eyebrows hiding little piggy eyes and no hair on top to speak of except the tufts coming out of his ears and nostrils, but what a lovely man he is, what a dear man. I'm so touched by his passionate generosity. My good wise loving Cello. I thank you for the ride. I thank you for showing me your God. Forgive me for being so earth-bound.

16

We reach the town in late afternoon, a little after darkness has fallen. As we pass through the streets, I feel again that I've been here before. As we enter the town centre, the feeling passes. It's an attractive old square, but unknown to me. Cello parks the car outside the steps to the church. There are people everywhere, and lights shining in all the cafés and shops and houses. Many passers-by carry musical instruments in cases. On the walls there are posters advertising musical performances, as I can tell from the names of the composers: Monteverdi, Haydn, Richard Strauss. The cafés are crowded, and the sounds of chattering voices and accordion music come spilling out into the square. There are policemen standing about, and some of them look at me, but they show no special interest in me.

Cello pats his round stomach and beams.

'The festival begins!'

To my astonishment I catch sight of Eckhard and Ilona sitting at a café table.

'I know those people!'

'Excellent! You must join them, and refresh yourself after our journey. I will meet you later.'

An irrational panic seizes me.

'Where are you going?'

'Not far. I have some calls to make.' He smiles to reassure me, and pats my arm. 'Don't worry. We'll meet again. I promise you.'

'But where will we meet?'

'At the concert this evening. At the castle.'

I have no idea when this concert is taking place, or where the castle is. How can he leave me like this? Doesn't he know he's my only guide in this alien land?

'I don't know the way to the castle.'

'Your friends will be going there. Everyone will be going there. Join them. All will be well.'

His words sound in my ears like a mocking echo of my night delusions. But he is determined to go, so we embrace and part. I watch the little priest go toddling off down a side street until he's out of sight. Then I go into the café. As I do so, I pass close by one of the policemen, and it seems to me that he follows me with his eyes. To check my paranoia, I tell myself his marriage is in trouble and he's sleeping with his wife's sister. He must be able to read my thoughts, because he blushes and looks away.

261

Eckhard is as surprised to see me as I am to see him. He jumps up with a cry of joy.

'You're safe! Thank God!'

'What are you doing here?' I ask him. 'You should be on your honeymoon.'

'Oh,' says Eckhard, waving away my question. 'Everyone comes for the festival. But you – you are not hurt? They let you go?'

I offer a short version of my experiences, leaving out the part about Marker's list, and my agreement to speak at the secret meeting. This leaves just the general notion that the authorities expect me, as a foreigner from a country with some similar experiences, to speak out against terrorism.

Eckhard is genuinely relieved.

'When they took you away – !' He rolls his eyes.

His friends find a chair for me, carrying it over the heads of the crowd of drinkers. They share their bread with me, and press a glass of wine into my hand.

'So. They know you are here.'

'No. I lost them.'

'That is not so easy.'

'Not so easy. But I did it. I was given a lift here by a priest.'

I turn to look out of the window at the crowded night square. Cello's car is no longer in front of the church.

'He's going to help me leave the country. I'm to meet him at the concert this evening.'

'At the castle?'

'Yes.'

Eckhard passes on what I've said to his companions. They talk about me with animation. Then Eckhard turns back to me.

'This priest. What is his name?'

'I don't know his name. I met him in the cathedral. He plays the cello in a string quartet.'

'You have a ticket to the concert?'

'No.'

'You must have a ticket. Without a ticket, you cannot go. But all the tickets have been sold, many weeks ago.'

My face falls. Why didn't the priest tell me this? Eckhard is in consultation with his friends.

'Don't worry. Stay with us. We will get you in.'

I feel cheated by Cello. Why arrange to meet me at a concert for which no tickets are available? I start to ask myself if there's any point in waiting to see the little priest again. Why not seek Eckhard's help here and now?

'I don't have to go to the concert,' I say. 'Are we far from the border?'

'Not so far. Maybe one hour's walk.'

'If you or one of your friends could direct me, I could go now.'

Eckhard shakes his head. 'In the dark you will not find your way. You must go with a guide.'

'Is there anyone who could guide me?'

'Yes, of course. But the concert begins soon. After the concert, I think.'

This concert is turning out to be too much of a big deal for my liking. I mean, here I am with my life in danger, and all they can think of is their musical soirée. The border is so near. Just an hour's walk away! For all that hour, and no doubt another hour too, I'll be sitting on a hard chair listening to choral Latin. I begin to feel sorry for myself. I drain my glass of wine in a brooding meaningful sort of way, but nobody notices.

Outside, the milling people are on the move. There's a more purposeful look on their faces and a brisker pace to their steps. Many tables in the café are emptying, as the drinkers reach down their coats off the wall-hooks and muffle up for the outside cold.

Our group also rises.

'We will go to the castle now,' says Eckhard.

I take the opportunity in the bustle of coats to return to my fears, speaking low to Eckhard alone.

'What if you can't get me into the concert?'

Eckhard frowns and wipes his misted glasses.

'One of us will give you his ticket. It is agreed.'

I'm touched, and a little ashamed of my earlier doubts. After all, helping me brings them no benefit. Rather the opposite.

So we go out into the square and follow the stream of people making their way on foot to the castle. One of the soprano soloists is a local star, and there's great excitement at the prospect of hearing her sing.

'The castle is very old,' Eckhard tells me. 'Six hundred years old. The town is here because of the castle. In the days when invaders came from the east, the people of the town took refuge in the castle. It is almost a small town in itself.' Then it strikes him that I don't know the most interesting fact of all. 'It was the home of the Vicino family.'

'Leon Vicino lives here?'

'Not any more. But he was born here. He spent his childhood here. The castle now belongs to the state. It's not possible in these days to maintain such a building as a private family home. But of course, for us the connection is a happy one.'

The road down which we are walking runs beside a river. The river is frozen, and many of the groups making their way to the concert clamber down and proceed on the ice. They run and slide and laugh as if it's a holiday. I watch a woman in a full red coat spin round and round on the ice, arms outstretched, skirts flying, while all round her the beams of torches sweep the riverbanks, the light tangling in the branches of leafless trees.

We round a bend in road and river, and the castle is before us. It's bigger than I had expected. Once more I get a shiver of familiarity. But I know I have never been here before. This is not the kind of place you visit and forget. It is constructed out of a cluster of circular towers, each one topped with battlements and conical pointed roofs. The towers are joined by massive vertical walls, pierced by high narrow windows through which light shines. Among the pointed roofs tall fragile chimneys reach up into the night sky, issuing plumes of smoke.

The entire structure stands on an island in the broad frozen river. A wooden bridge reaches from the bank along which we are walking, over the ice, to the castle entrance. It's a narrow walkway with timber hand-rails, carried on tall posts. The stream of concert-goers packs this bridge, moving slowly from the unlit road to the mouth of light that is the castle's arched doorway. The people who have come over the ice now scrabble back up the banks to rejoin the road. I look at the faces all round me, and everyone seems cheerful and unafraid. I feel like a fraud, because I alone am not eager to hear the Mozart Mass. This is nothing against Mozart, but I have other matters on my mind, such as what I will do if Eckhard and his friends fail to smuggle me past the ticket-checkers.

As we wait our turn to shuffle onto the narrow bridge I watch those ahead of us. They are all showing their tickets as they pass into the illuminated arch. Suddenly I see a figure I recognise. It's Petra. The same leather coat, the same unkempt beauty. She's with a group of men I don't know, speaking earnestly to one of them, an older man with a thick shock of grey hair. They too all have tickets. They go on into the building.

Now I'm confused. What is Petra doing at this music festival? I thought she was in hiding? I look round, and sure enough, there are uniformed police standing idly by the roadside, and here and there the black-jacketed men of the interior ministry. The police smile and nod as if to show they're only here to help on this festive public occasion. The men in black jackets keep back, watching the stream of concert-goers rather in the manner of customs officers at an airport. None of them have noticed Petra and her companions.

Now we in turn step onto the bridge, and my fears focus on the ticket check ahead. I see Eckhard and Ilona and their friends all taking their tickets out of their pockets and handbags, and holding them ready in their hands. At the point where the tickets are checked, the stream of people coming over the bridge narrows to single file. The official, a man in a black suit, glances briefly at each ticket in turn, and nods the holder through. As we approach, Eckhard arranges us in a new order, which is Ilona, himself, and then me.

He holds Ilona's arm. She moves slowly, exaggerating her pregnant condition. I begin to guess at their plan. As they approach the man in the suit, Eckhard speaks aloud to Ilona, clearly urging her to go slowly and to take care. Ilona pats her stomach and smiles at the man as he checks her ticket. Then, as she passes through, she stumbles and falls to her knees. Eckhard gives a cry of alarm and drops down to her side as does the man in the black suit. Together they help her up. Ilona straightens herself up and insists that she's alright. At the same time, I feel Eckhard's fist pushing at my hip. I take the concealed ticket he has just received from Ilona under cover of her fall, and he is nodded through. I hold up what is now my ticket, and I follow on behind, without any problem at all. I push the ticket into my pocket, irrationally nervous that it will be looked at too closely, and go with my friends into the entrance hall.

Eckhard turns to me with a smile.

'Well,' he says, 'I told you we would get you in.'

'You were brilliant.' I'm impressed. 'Ilona is alright?'

'Of course. Just our little game.'

All round us now there is a great crush of people, filling the air with bright chatter. For many, this is a reunion of old friends, and from all sides there come cries of greeting, outreached hands, sudden embraces. So we push on, into the Great Hall, where the concert is to take place.

It's an enormous room, bounded by high stone walls that rise the full height of two floors, with a handsome carved-wood gallery running round all four sides. The stone-flagged floor is filled with row upon row of cheap stacking chairs. Good-humoured scuffles are taking place as the concert-goers hurry to secure themselves and their friends the better seats. The chairs face right to left, and at the left end of the hall a tiered platform has been built out of scaffolding and planks, to hold the orchestra and the choir. Most of the orchestra are in place, tuning up. The members of the choir are scattered about, greeting their friends. A clumsy-looking scaffolding tower stands before the platform, a temporary pulpit for the conductor to command his musical forces.

We are among the last to enter. We take seats at the back, not far from the door. Eckhard is waving and calling to people he knows, so I stand by my chair and look over the crowd of faces, trying to locate the priest. Because I'm at the back, most of the people are facing away from me and it's impossible to make out individual faces, so after a while I stop looking and let my eyes drift. I realise I'm in a strange state. I'm alert, as if braced for danger, but for the next hour at least I have nothing more to fear than unfamiliar music.

My thoughts float free with my gaze. I wonder how I'll find Cello in this great crowd, and whether it matters very much if I don't. Eckhard has told me he and his friends can help me just as well as the priest. Should I ask them to take me to the border tonight, in the dark, or should we wait for morning? What will I do once I'm across the border? Truth to tell, I hardly care. All I want is to be out of this nightmare country. The rest of my journey home, though fuzzy in imagined detail, seems to me to be only a matter of endurance.

This was Leon Vicino's childhood home. Hard to imagine the child running about this Great Hall, with its heavy wooden gallery frowning down on the echoing stone space. No doubt there are smaller rooms elsewhere in the castle where he curled up in a window seat and gazed out over the river and dreamed his dreams.

As I think this, my wandering eyes find a small doorway half concealed by a curtain, and in the moment that I discover it I see a figure pushing past the curtain, out of sight. Only a glimpse, but I'm quite sure it is the little priest. I jump up from my seat and push down the row of people and hurry along the side aisle to the doorway. So many others are still moving about that no one remarks on my going.

The curtained doorway leads to a flight of stone spiral stairs. I climb the stairs and come out in the gallery above. No one else is there, but a further door, leading off the gallery, stands open. I go through it into a corridor lit by a fluorescent light. Here there are many doors, all closed. At the far end, in the chill glow, I see the banisters of a staircase, and I hear the click-click-click of descending footsteps.

'Wait!' I call out.

I run along the corridor and down the stairs. At the bottom there is a dark lobby, and another half-open door, through which falls a softer warmer light. I enter, and find myself in a small ornate chapel. A three-tiered rack of votive candles beside the altar has been recently filled with new candles, and all are lit. There, kneeling in the front pew, is my friend the priest, his head bowed in prayer.

I come to a standstill, in embarrassed silence. He can't have failed to hear me enter. Also he can't be so very deep in prayer, given that he was only just ahead of me coming here.

When at last he raises his head and turns to look at me I'm shocked to see the expression on his face. It's a look of anguish.

'I'm sorry,' I say, humbled. 'Would you like me to go?'

'No, no.' His voice seems to come from far away. He's struggling to return from whatever dread has seized him, to the recollection of who I am and what I want. 'You're here. That's good.'

'My friends can take care of me. If you'd prefer.'

'No, no,' he says. 'It's all arranged.'

I'm not at all sure what this means. But now he's getting up, and his former friendly manner is returning.

'How did you know where to find me?'

'I saw you leave the Great Hall. I followed you.'

'But I've been in this chapel for an hour or more,' he says, frowning.

'No. That's impossible. I saw you come in just a few minutes ago.'

He shrugs, and turns, and taking my arm, walks with me back out of the chapel.

'The concert will be starting. We must get back.'

'I'm not here for the concert,' I say. 'I'm here for you.'

'For me? No, no. I'm of no importance. But Mozart's great Mass, that is something wonderful!'

Why is everyone so besotted by this concert? He

walks me up the stairs, moving more slowly than I remember him doing.

'Are you in pain?'

'No, not pain. Nothing to be concerned about.'

'Where are we to meet after the concert?'

At least I've taken that much on board: the concert comes first.

'You will find me. It's all arranged.'

Again, he speaks as if this is the most marginal of concerns. So it may be for him. For me it's more along the lines of being the only thing I can think about. I don't like to sound self-obsessed, but this is my survival at stake.

Now we're heading back along the strip-lit corridor.

'I enjoyed our talk in the car,' says the priest.

'Me too. I learned a lot.'

'Oh, I have nothing to teach you. It's more a matter of throwing a little light on knowledge you already possess, don't you think? All of us have more rooms in our house than we inhabit.'

He waves at the closed doors on either side of us, as we make our way towards the gallery. From the Great Hall we hear a wave of applause.

'The soloists,' says Cello. 'We are just in time.'

'I shall look for you afterwards.'

'Yes, yes.' He holds out one small plump hand for me to shake. He looks into my eyes with a gaze suddenly full of unbearable sadness.

'Use your power gently,' he says.

Beyond the gallery door the audience in the Great Hall has fallen silent, and now we hear the music begin.

'Go.' He propels me through the door. I re-enter the high gallery just as the choir bursts out with the first great chant.

'*KYRIE!*'

The huge sound electrifies me. I hardly notice that the priest has not followed me into the gallery. I look down onto the heads of the crowd, trying to locate Eckhard and Ilona, or Petra and her group, all of whom are here somewhere, assembled in this hall as if for my benefit. But there are others too, many others. And there is the music. So for a short time my fear of the future gives way to the glory of the moment.

I abandon myself to the charging waves of sound, surrendering myself to Mozart, not trying to guess where he will take me, tumbling after him like a fish in a mountain stream. When the voice of the star soprano leaps up from the bed of the choir, hauntingly still, the long pure notes reaching ever further away — '*Christe!*' — I like everyone in the hall hold my breath and climb with her, until I seem to be higher even than this high gallery, high above my own life, looking down on it with affection but no great concern.

The music speaks to me, telling me: you are so little, you have nothing to fear. And yet I know now that I am at the very heart of all that is happening. I am both unimportant and entirely involved. My experiences have not after all been random. Just as these melting notes are finding their way back to the home key, so for me too there is a plan unfolding, and my task is to travel my road to the end. This sensation, which is one of meaning granted after all, has nothing to do with a greater mind controlling my life, neither God nor Mozart. It's the feeling that there is a natural and fitting path for me, in the way that a stone that is tumbling down a hill apparently at random is in fact following the only path possible to it, given its starting point. On this path there are obstacles, but these obstacles, into which I crash, off which I rebound, send me on my necessary way.

'Gloria in excelsis Deo!'

I too have longed for glory. I am the hero of an adventure story, but I am not the author. That necessary shaping work has been done by those who brought me into being, the little clan formed by accident that for so many years represented for me all the faces of mankind. Then as I grew my home began to dwindle, until it seemed too small to contain me, and I longed to set out on my own journey, to make my own way. My own way! What laughable folly! Who among us has his own way? The paths are too well trodden, the roads too heavy with traffic. And yet I went, without a backward look. Then little by little, day by day, the further down the road I have travelled, the more distinct has become the image of what I have left behind: like a range of mountains on whose lower slopes I was raised, but which I have never seen before whole and entire. So turning at last, weary, unsure of any safe haven ahead, I look back and am struck with wonder at the majesty of my own towering cloud-capped home. Astonished, I ask, have I come from this?

The great Mass marches on. Now the solo bass is booming out.

'*Credo in unum Deum!*'

The choir roars back its chant of triumphant faith.

'*Credo! Credo!*'

I think of the priest, who must say these words daily in the mass, and I wonder if he does believe in this one God, *patrem omnipotentem*, father almighty, *factorem caeli et terrae*, maker of heaven and earth, *visibilium omnium et invisibilium*, all things visible and invisible. If I'm God, as he tells me, I like to think I'm the maker of all things visible and invisible. Not souls or angels, but trust, friendliness, gratitude, love. These are my invisibles. Dimly, as I think these thoughts, I become aware that I am changing. That I have changed.

Now in the Great Hall of the castle, the orchestra and choir have fallen silent. Now, out of the silence, the violins and the flutes begin to play a gentle downward-spiralling tumble of melody that can only be the prelude to something big. Nobody moves: an intense stillness possesses us all. The soprano starts to sing.

As the haunting melody rises up from the platform I

follow it, tugged by the fragile skein of liquid sound, up into a high and far empyrean, where simple beauty floods my senses. The soprano sings exquisitely, with infinite lightness and infinite power. I'm ravished by the sound. Everyone in the Great Hall is ravished. While such beauty possesses us, nothing hurtful can come to pass.

Now I realise that the fine chain of melody is formed out of words, and that they are words I have heard before: *Et incarnatus est*. And he was made flesh. This is the sublime sound of God becoming man. Because my friend the priest spoke to me of the incarnation, and assured me that I am God, I choose to take this personally, and to hear in the soprano's voice the song of the spirit that is in me. And so I listen in a dual role, as a part of the audience, the receiver of this loveliness, and as God, its subject and source. The soprano sings to me and of me. I have entered the music.

As I listen and grow in power and lightness, as I expand to the size of clouds, to become as vast and empty as the sky, I see at last what has been happening to me in the course of my strange journey. There is a puzzle here, and a solution. *Et incarnatus est*: not merely the divine spirit made flesh, but my fears and longings, my memories, all the matter of my mind and the edifices of my dreams, all things visible and invisible, are taking on physical form. There are more rooms in my house than I inhabit.

I am awakening. I have more power than I ever knew.

The timeless solo ends and time returns. The choir rings out the victory.

'*Sanctus! Sanctus!*'

I hear the click of an opening door. I have been watching the singers on the platform below. Now I look up and see a second door has opened, at the far end of the gallery, and men in black bomber jackets are entering, carrying long guns. Three, four, five men: more and more. They pay me no attention. They have not come for me; but they are here on my behalf. They pad softly along the sides of the gallery and take up positions looking down on the audience below. More and more of them file quietly into place, unobserved by the rows of people listening to the final bars of the music. The last man to come through the door stays close to the wall, in the shadows. No light falls on him, and I have no face to recognise, but I can feel those dark eyes watching me, and I have no doubts that it is him.

Knowing now what I will find, I feel in my pocket for the printed card that was given me in an envelope as I left the television studio. I take out the card, and together with it the concert ticket slipped to me by Eckhard. I hold them side by side in my hands. They are identical. I had a ticket to the concert all the time. I have been expected. Even as I was running away from the man who hunts me, I was making my inevitable way towards him.

Applause erupts below. The performance has ended. The people stand, and hold their hands raised to clap high above their heads. Why don't they look up?

17

Nobody is leaving the Great Hall. The conductor descends from the scaffolding pulpit, and is replaced by another man, who speaks into a microphone. His amplified voice addresses the audience. They all sit. The speaker seems to be announcing the appearance of a notable figure, because I hear a buzz of excited surprise, and see heads turning.

This then is the secret meeting of the Society of Others. Except that it's not secret. The men of the interior ministry are watching, with machine guns cradled in their arms. I have been sent here by the authorities to influence the debate. I did not intend to come, but here I am. And here, I now see, down among the concert audience, is Magdalena. I scan the rows and find Petra. And near the back, Eckhard and Ilona. Everything is converging.

Will I speak? And if I do, what will I say? This isn't my war. I don't want to be here. This is my war. I am where I choose to be. Every turn I take brings me back to this hall, this evening, this decision.

Now there comes a surge of cheering from the audience, and they're back on their feet. Some even climb onto their chairs. They're cheering the entrance into the hall of the promised celebrity. He's passing down the centre aisle directly below me, but he's so crowded about by admirers that I can't get a clear sight of him. At last he reaches the foot of the scaffolding tower, which has been vacated by the previous speaker. There he turns, and stands bobbing his head in shy acknowledgement of the rapturous applause, and I see him clearly at last.

It is my friend Cello, the little priest. Except he no longer looks like a priest. He wears a pearl-grey shirt, open at the neck, and a light black overcoat. I hear voices calling out his name. Of course: how could I not have known?

'Vicino!' they cry. 'Leon Vicino!'

He climbs the scaffolding tower, and there, raising his hands, he pats the air before him to silence the crowd. So this is the old man, the irrelevance, the failed poet, the exile. Leon Vicino has returned, to play his necessary part in the convergence that is taking place this evening. I look up to see the man who waits for me, and I find that he too has looked up at the same moment, and it seems to me that out of the shadows our eyes meet.

The applause fades into an expectant silence. Vicino

takes a sheet of paper out of his pocket. He reads from it in English.

'I will not die for what I believe in, because what I believe in is life.'

So this is how it goes. My father wrote these words. I look down and see that Vicino is looking up at me, smiling up at me with a sad crinkly-eyed smile. It seems he expects me to speak. But what can I say? Am I responsible for what is about to happen? The burden is too great. I don't know what it is I must do. Others in the Great Hall, seeing where Vicino is looking, have turned and are craning their necks to see me.

I must speak.

Why don't they see the men with guns? Why aren't they afraid? Vicino goes on smiling up at me, his arms stretched out over the scaffold rails on either side of him, his hands gripping the rails.

I turn again to look at the man in the shadows. His unseen eyes seem to mock me with the question: Well? Will you speak? But how can I speak when I've not been given my lines? I see him shrug, and look away, and give a sign. All round the gallery the men with the guns bend to their business, preparing the guns with small movements and soft clicks. Why doesn't Vicino warn his people? Why don't they save themselves? Why does it have to be me?

I must call out to them. I must make them see the danger.

I shout, but the shout sticks in my throat and no

sound comes. My throat is stuffed with dry cloth. I shout again, and hear my own voice emerge, tiny and incomprehensible.

I am saying, 'Forgive me.'

You who have loved me, forgive me.

My eyes fill with tears, searching for faces that are far away. Where are you, my sister? Trotting after me all my remembered life, resented, familiar. Watch over me now.

(Click, click, go the guns.)

Where are you, my father? Your wistful smile tells me, I see it now, Believe in yourself, even if I have not entirely believed in myself.

(The guns are ready to fire.)

Where are you, my mother? You sit at your desk, glasses raised over your brow, and looking up, find me in the doorway. I ask for food, money, the use of the car. And you who gave me eyes to see the world, you who sang to me on the way to school, you go to the kitchen, put a pan on to boil, rummage in your bag for car keys.

(Petra draws a hand gun from beneath her coat. She thinks I am a traitor.)

I kneel at your feet. I kiss your hands. You who have loved me, forgive me.

(Petra aims her gun at me. Vicino smiles up at me. People stare at me from the crowd. Nobody moves.)

Am I to blame for what is about to happen?

(The bullet whines as it passes close by me. *Tikka-*

tikka-tikka, go the answering machine guns. The man in the shadows turns and leaves the gallery.)

I am to blame. I must go now.

(The people in the Great Hall begin to fall. They don't cry out or try to escape. They don't return violence for violence. They don't resist. They stand still, and then they fall. The only one that is hit but does not fall is Leon Vicino. He remains standing, locked to his scaffold, his eyes still open. He has become a living statue.)

I am on my own. I am responsible. All this is for my benefit. I must go now.

I am in control after all. My will works in ways both visible and invisible. Everything that is happening to me has been chosen by me. I am not the victim: that is no more than the fruit of my vanity. I am not the sacrifice. I am the God for whom others' lives are sacrificed. Even now as I sense the enormity of my own power I flinch from it, because I am not yet free from the source of my fear, from the pursuer who has hunted me all the days of my life, from the tormentor who drives me to hide in ever deeper burrows, in ever more desolate isolation. But I will be free. Soon now. This is what I have come to do.

I turn away from the rattle of guns. I walk past the men in black jackets, who make no attempt to stop me. I descend the stone staircase to the floor of the Great Hall. I pick my way between the dead and the dying towards the wide doors. Through the archway, onto the narrow bridge that leads to the road. Ahead, I hear the rear door of the grey Mercedes slam shut. Its engine grinds to life, its headlights blaze. The man who has hunted me is leaving. He flees me now. I have awoken. I am dangerous.

The grey car drives away into the bitter night. My boots ring on the wooden bridge as I cross to the river bank. I'm moving fast but I'm not running. I'm in no hurry.

Back along the bank of the frozen river, and into the town. The lights are all out now, the café windows all dark. I make no effort to find my way. Let my way find me.

Down a long dark street where I've been before, to a doorway I've seen before. The door stands open. Into an unlit lobby, across a cold marble floor to a closed inner door. I open this door, and close it behind me, and enter the room I have never forgotten.

Bookshelves on either wall. In the centre, a long table. An empty chair at the near end. A hand gun on the table's surface. The only light in the room falling faintly through the open door at the far end. I sit down and take the gun in my hand, and I wait.

He enters the room by the far door, partly closing it behind him. Moving slowly, he makes his way to the chair at the other end of the table, and sits down. He remains there in silence for a moment, with his head bowed. I watch him, and feel his anger and his loneliness. Then he looks up at me, and my eyes adjust to the faint light, and I see his face in full for the first time. No, not for the first time. This is the face I see at every window, the face I am compelled to look for everywhere I go, the face I dread to find: my own. Jealous as a lover, my hunter has stalked me all my life, has caused me to love him alone in all the world, has taught me there are no others in all the world. But he has deceived me. He has imprisoned me. Now I will kill him, this familiar jailer, this guardian self, in order that I may be free. What happens afterwards is my fault. Blame me.

No need to give him a name. If you want a name, use your own. As I will use mine.

He smiles at me. It hurts him to smile. I raise my gun. All that is left now is the act of will. He sees the gun pointing at him and makes no effort to save himself. He has no wish to live.

I fire once only.

Thob! The sound is not as loud as I had been expecting.

I open the door that was always open, into the long street that leads to my native land. I take the first step, and hear the tread of many feet. I draw the first breath, and hear the breathing of a multitude. I have become both one and many. I am walking a road that has been walked before, but to me it is new. It leads to the place

285

where I was born and raised, which soon now I will discover for the first time.

So begins the mystery and the adventure of going home.

THE END

New College Nottingham
Learning Centres

The narrator's journey in *The Society of Others* brings him into contact with thirteen paintings, all of which are in the National Gallery, London. Five are named in the text. A further eight are concealed, but identified by a trigger word.

The five named paintings are:

Giovanni Bellini, Portrait of Doge Leonardo Loredan
Salvator Rosa, Self Portrait
Antonella da Massina, St Jerome in his study
Andrea Mantegna, The virgin and child with the Magdalen and St John the Baptist
Diego Velasquez, The Rokeby Venus.

These eight concealed paintings, in order of appearance, are:

Pieter de Hooch, An interior with a woman drinking with two men
Philips Koninck, An extensive landscape with a road by a river
Jacob van Ruisdael, A landscape with a ruined castle and a church
Meindert Hobbema, The avenue at Middelharnis
Pieter de Hooch, The courtyard of a house in Delft
Nicolaes Maes, Interior with a Sleeping Maid and her mistress
Gerard ter Borch, A woman playing a theorbo to two men
Jan Beerstraten, The castle of Muiden in winter.

The Trial of True Love

In this gripping, searching novel of ideas, art and literature, William Nicholson weaves an intricate tale of suspense as he explores what it is men and women really want from each other.

Do people really fall in love at first sight? Bron is a writer who has been commissioned to research a book on the subject. He's also a commitment-phobe who doesn't believe it happens.

Then the chance combination of a misty morning, the dreamy setting of a woodland glade, and a glimpse of a beautiful stranger changes everything. Bron falls helplessly, hopelessly, head over heels in love – at first sight. He abandons his research and devotes himself to pursuing the enigmatic Flora and winning her heart. But each time he comes close to her, she slips out of reach again. Bron's pursuit of love leads him ever deeper into a maze where nothing is as it seems, until he finds himself having to defend the truth of his feelings in a 'trial of love'.

Now available as a Doubleday hardback

As a taster turn the page to read the first chapter. . .

Doubleday

1

Here where two rivers meet by an island, in the early morning, shortly after dawn, there is a mist along the valleys. The sun rises over the railway bridge, white as a moon, and everything is still. I stand before Taw pool, watching the water eddy round the island, my breath cloudy and my thoughts far away. I do not anticipate. And yet there is a moment before the moment, that is both a preparation and a culmination. What is about to happen to me is long longed-for, familiar, out of reach, needed, despaired of, completely imagined, but never known: so first, and memorably, comes the intimation that it is about to happen. The light falling from an opening door on to a winter's street. The silence before a phone begins to ring. Anticipation, in the razor-cut of time before it bursts into fulfilment.

The Barnstaple train, headlamp furry in the mist, booms suddenly over the bridge. Rooks rattle out of invisible trees, cawing up into the sky. The premonitory sounds disperse into the slow tumble of the rivers, into my own quiet breaths. The smell of soaked grass and the sharp white air that makes me shiver and the silence after the train.

And then I see her.

*

This is a story about falling in love. The time is 1977, a generation ago. I am twenty-nine years old, and waiting for my real life to begin. I am engaged in this waiting process in the very small second bedroom of a very small flat in Cross Street in north London, owned by my friend Anna.

She comes back earlier than usual and pours herself a glass of wine, which is not like her, not at five in the afternoon, and says we must talk. So I have a glass of wine too, and we talk.

'The thing is this.' She moves her hands carefully before her as if describing an invisible object about the size of a box-file. 'This is the thing. I have to think of myself. I have to think of the future. I'll be thirty in January. Which is meaningless, of course. But I would like, one day, to have children.'

Anna is home early because she's been visiting a friend who has recently had a baby.

'How was Polly's baby?'

'Like a baby. This isn't about that.'

'Yes, it is.'

'Alright, it is, then. The thing is this. For a baby, one needs a man. And one hasn't got one.'

She makes a comic-sad face as she says this, which makes me laugh. Also she's making me nervous.

'I don't know what to tell you, Anna. This is how it is these days. Everyone free to be with who they like, and everyone alone.'

'Well, I've decided to do something about it.'

Anna is small, slightly built, with a friendly, puzzled sort of face and short hair of that colour that has no name, between brown and blond. She's quick-thinking and funny and honest, and has no luck with men. There was a man called Rory who was part of her life for years and we all assumed they would get married, until he went to Johannesburg and married someone else. This in the apartheid era. Anna knew she was better off without him, but she still cried every night for weeks.

She calls me her walker. We have what is in some senses the perfect relationship, because the sex is behind us. There was a clumsy fumbling sort of affair at college, which went through what are for me the usual phases of eagerness, gratified vanity, claustrophobia, guilt, evasion and disappearance.

'Bron doesn't do break-ups,' Anna says. 'He does vanishings.'

She calls me a coward, but I've never pretended to be a war hero in the battle of the sexes. What am I to say, faced with the wounded eyes, the question why? Not the truth: that this can't be it, that this can't be enough, that there must be more. All love affairs are understood to be for ever, and the one who walks away a deserter from the human race.

In the case of Anna, time the great healer worked its magic, and there were other boyfriends who behaved yet more disgracefully, so by the time we met again I was received as an old comrade-in-arms. Since then I've seen her through the long lean years of the unspeakable Rory, and the short turbulent months of an affair with an artist called Jay Hermann. Anna deals in corporate art, which means she sources art works for hotel lobbies and company headquarters. This makes her a modern Robin Hood, who takes from the rich to give to the poor. Few of her artists are grateful. She tells them they are working in the tradition of the Florentine masters, all of whom painted to commission, but the model they identify with more readily is the Mexican artist Diego Rivera. Rivera, an ardent communist, accepted a well-paid commission from John D. Rockefeller to create a mural in the new Rockefeller Center in the 1930s. In order to prove that he hadn't sold out to the arch-capitalist of all time, he included in his mural a portrait of Lenin, hiding among many other figures. When Rockefeller found out and objected, Rivera hoisted the banner of politico-artistic integrity, and refused to paint Lenin out. Rockefeller paid him in full, and destroyed the entire vast mural.

Jay Hermann, a small aggressive sculptor, created large aggressive structures out of steel, which Anna sold to property developers. During their affair, he was remorselessly unfaithful to her, and on principle refused to conceal the fact. I had my own take on this.

'He's a prick.'

'It's his way of saying I haven't bought him. He minds terribly about his independence.'

'Tell him to fuck off.'

'I expect I will. But I do like him. And I don't want to have no one. And he's no different to other men. And at least he's honest.'

So like Anna. It may sound like masochism, but it isn't. Anna is a realist, and has long been in the habit of making the best of what's available to her.

So Anna has decided to do something about being alone.

'I'm not giving out the right signals. I'm like a taxi with the For Hire light turned off.'

'Are you? Why?'

'Because of you.'

This I have not seen coming.

'Me?'

'Think about it, Bron. You're a sweet, friendly man, you get my jokes, I don't have to pretend I'm someone else when I'm with you. You're really quite attractive, in your shabby way. And I'm living with you.'

'Yes, but we're not—'

'Sex isn't everything. Though it is a first step. If you want to have children.'

I feel bewildered.

'So what are you saying?'

'You're in my way. You've got to go.'

'But we're just friends.'

'No we're not. We're like an old married couple. It's disgusting.'

I'm tallish and darkish, with a mass of dark-brown hair and dark-brown eyes, thin and nervy, quick to smile, except I never see my own smiles. The self I see is grave, peers back at me in reflections without lightness or grace. I dress like a student: jeans, T-shirts, loose sweaters. I am a writer, none of whose writings have yet been published. However, I now have a commission, a real contract with a real publisher naming real sums of money, to write a real book. This book will not be one of my three completed novels, all of which lie in a cardboard box alongside letters ending 'but I would be interested to see your next work'. It will be a work of non-fiction. I call it, for the present, The Book of True Love. It deals with the phenomenon of love at first sight. For this, a publisher is paying me £2,500, half on signature, meaning £1,250: enough to keep me alive for maybe six months. I am therefore very poor.

'You could always get a job,' says Anna the brutal.

'Of course I could get a job,' I reply. 'But in return for the money I'd have to do the work, yes? Nine to five, yes? Leaving me knackered, yes? So when do I write?'

I have chosen to be time-rich and cash-poor. This has a romantic air about it in a student or a very young man. But soon now I will be thirty years old, and my lifestyle will begin to look sad. So I am in a hurry.

As for The Book of True Love: the subject has not been chosen at random. Love at first sight fascinates me. In my own love life I appear to suffer from the standard-issue male malady called commitment phobia. It has never presented itself to me as a phobia. Far from hating and fearing commitment, I long for it. But it doesn't happen. Each love affair begins with a flurry of enthusiasm, but soon dwindles into the so-so, the acceptable, the could-be-worse. The prospect of promoting such half-measures into marriage and children appals me. There must be more.

This pickiness baffles Anna.

'What exactly is it you're looking for, Bron?'

'I don't know. I truly don't know.'

I don't know. So I conclude that I am fated to repeat the familiar cycle until some outside force stronger than my power to resist blasts me out of my bunker. I conclude that I need to fall in love.

People use a conventional metaphor for falling in love at first sight. They say, 'I was struck by lightning.' I am in the position of a man who wishes to be struck by lightning and so walks about hatless in storms.

Freddy Christiansen, of whom more later, is vastly amused that I was compiling a book on love at first sight at the time that I myself fell in love. He teases me in Latin, calling me *praeceptor amoris*, the teacher of love, after Ovid, and *exclusus amator*, the lover shut out. But of course he too knows that it is no coincidence. In Devon, that October of 1977, my mind was crammed with true-life love stories, to which I was more than ready to add my own.

I pour myself another glass of wine. So does Anna.

'Look here, Anna. This is all wrong. Why do I have to go? Why can't men and women be friends?'

'I don't know, Bron. I think maybe it's because of sex.'

'That's a terrible admission of defeat.'

'Yes, it is rather.'

'So don't give in.'

'No. I've thought about it very carefully, and I'm sure I'm right. You have to go.'

'Thanks a lot.'

I feel ill-used.

'Now you're cross.'

'I just don't think me being your friend has anything to do with this other thing. It would be a sad world if we were only allowed to be friends with one other person all our lives.'

'You're cross because you don't know where you'll go to live. I've thought about that. You can go to Bernard's place, in Devon.'

'You're tidying me up.'

'You could do your book just as well in Devon as here. Probably better.'

'That's all sorted then, isn't it?'

More wine.

'Oh, Bron. You know I don't want you to go. Don't be mean to me about it.'

Her hand on mine.

'Oh, hell.'

'You do understand really.'

'Yes. I suppose I do.'

Oh yes, I understand. If I loved her more, I would be the man she's looking for: the husband, the father of her children. So why don't I? Because I'm not in love with Anna. There it is again. The mystery ingredient.

'You'd be a lousy provider, anyway.'

'You don't know that. I'm just a late developer, financially speaking.'

'Actually I don't mind about that. I meet enough rich men in my work.'

'Have one of them.'

'They're all dull and old. Even the young ones. Oh Bron, wish me luck. It's so fucking hard.'

'Good luck, Anna.'

I raise my glass and she raises hers and we drink and refill.

'So you will go?'

'Alright, alright, I'll go. You want me to go right now?'

'No. Not right now.'

'Do you realise we've drunk a bottle of wine in a quarter of an hour?'

'It's because I'm tense.'

'So I must be tense too.'

'Are you still tense?'

'No. Now I'm drunk.'

'Me too.'

We look at each other and grin like fools.

'Anna, if I'm going to fuck off out of your life for ever—'

'I didn't say that.'

'I'll re-phrase. If I'm to go—'

'No. I do want you to fuck off out of my life. Just not for ever.'

'Until you're hitched up.'

'Exactly.'

'After which I take it the occasional friendly intimate moment will be out of the question.'

'Entirely off the menu.'

'So this is our last chance.'

'Don't even ask.'

She opens a second bottle of wine, unoffended.

'Just a thought.'

'I do have some pride. I don't want to be the easy fall-back option. The one who'll do when there's nothing better around.'

'No,' I protest, gallantly and also truthfully. 'You're the best. A man can dream.'

'Quite a small dream, Bron. A dream of short duration.'

'Only because we're friends. Or not-friends. Or whatever it is we are.'

'Only because you're not in love with me.'

No answer. Pour the wine. But Anna drunk can be very direct.

'And by the way, why not? Why aren't you in love with me?'

'Oh God. I don't know.'

'You look so moronic when you say that.'

'I feel moronic. I'm not doing this deliberately. I'd be in love with you if I could. And anyway, you're not in love with me.'

'That's because I don't want to do it on my own. It's too fucking miserable, being in love on your own. I've been there.'

'So have I.'

'Liar.'

'I have. When I was younger.'

'Oh, sure. For ten minutes.'

'So anyway. I'll call Bernard.'

'I already called him. He said you could have the gate-lodge. He sounded pleased.'

'Well, fuck you.'

But she doesn't. So we eat takeaway pizza and watch *Goodbye, Mr Chips* on television and cry at the end. The next morning I move out.

READ THE COMPLETE BOOK

AVAILABLE NOW FROM DOUBLEDAY

CASE HISTORIES
Kate Atkinson

'HER BEST BOOK YET . . . A TRAGI-COMEDY FOR OUR TIMES' *Sunday Telegraph*

Investigating other people's tragedies and cock-ups and misfortunes was all he knew. He was used to being a voyeur, the outsider looking in, and nothing, that anyone did surprised him any more. Yet despite everything he'd seen and done, inside Jackson there remained a belief – a small, battered and bruised belief – that his job was to help people be good rather than punish them for being bad.

Cambridge is sweltering, during an unusually hot summer. To Jackson Brodie, former police inspector turned private investigator, the world consists of one accounting sheet – Lost on the left, Found on the right – and the two never seem to balance.

Jackson has never felt at home in Cambridge, and has a failed marriage to prove it. Surrounded by death, intrigue and misfortune, his own life haunted by a family tragedy, he attempts to unravel three disparate case histories and begins to realise that in spite of apparent diversity, everything is connected . . .

'HER BEST BOOK YET, AN ASTONISHINGLY COMPLEX AND MOVING LITERARY DETECTIVE STORY THAT MADE ME SOB BUT ALSO SNORT WITH LAUGHTER. THE SORT OF NOVEL YOU HAVE TO START REREADING THE MINUTE YOU'VE FINISHED IT' *Guardian*

'SHARP HUMOUR, TOGETHER WITH A NUMBER OF UNEXPECTED TWISTS . . . A PACEY AND INTELLIGENT READ' *Daily Mail*

'A GREEDY FEAST OF A STORY BY A MASTERFUL AUTHOR . . . A PROFOUND, EXCITING AND LINGERING READ' *Daily Express*

0 552 77243 7

— **BLACK SWAN** —

PAST MORTEM
Ben Elton

'A WRITER WHO PROVOKES ALMOST AS MUCH
AS HE ENTERTAINS' *Daily Mail*

With old friends like these, who needs enemies?

It's a question mild mannered detective Edward Newson is
forced to ask himself when, in romantic desperation, he
logs on to the Friends Reunited website in search of the
girlfriends of his youth. Newson is not the only member of
the Class of '88 who has been raking over the ashes of the
past. As his old class begins to reassemble in cyberspace,
the years slip away and old feuds and passions burn hot
once more.

Meanwhile, back in the present, Newson's life is no less
complicated. He is secretly in love with Natasha, his lovely
but very attached sergeant, and failing comprehensively to
solve a series of baffling and peculiarly gruesome murders.
A school reunion is planned and as history begins to repeat
itself, the past crashes headlong into the present. Neither
will ever be the same again.

In *Past Mortem*, Ben Elton – previous winner of The
Crime Writers' Association Gold Dagger Award for
Popcorn – delivers both a heart-stopping thriller and a
killer comic romance.

0 552 77123 6

BLACK SWAN

A SELECTED LIST OF FINE WRITING
AVAILABLE FROM BLACK SWAN

77115 5	BRICK LANE	Monica Ali	£7.99
99313 1	OF LOVE AND SHADOWS	Isabel Allende	£7.99
77243 7	CASE HISTORIES	Kate Atkinson	£6.99
99860 5	IDIOGLOSSIA	Eleanor Bailey	£6.99
77131 7	MAKING LOVE: A CONSPIRACY OF THE HEART	Marius Brill	£6.99
99979 2	GATES OF EDEN	Ethan Coen	£7.99
99686 6	BEACH MUSIC	Pat Conroy	£8.99
99767 6	SISTER OF MY HEART	Chitra Banerjee Divakaruni	£6.99
99836 2	A HEART OF STONE	Renate Dorrestein	£6.99
99985 7	DANCING WITH MINNIE THE TWIG	Mogue Doyle	£6.99
77123 6	PAST MORTEM	Ben Elton	£6.99
77206 2	PEACETIME	Robert Edric	£6.99
99935 0	PEACE LIKE A RIVER	Leif Enger	£6.99
99954 7	SWIFT AS DESIRE	Laura Esquivel	£6.99
77078 7	THE VILLAGE OF WIDOWS	Ravi Shankar Etteth	£6.99
99656 4	THE TEN O'CLOCK HORSES	Laurie Graham	£5.99
77178 3	SLEEP, PALE SISTER	Joanne Harris	£6.99
77082 5	THE WISDOM OF CROCODILES	Paul Hoffman	£7.99
77109 0	THE FOURTH HAND	John Irving	£6.99
77005 1	IN THE KINGDOM OF MISTS	Jane Jakeman	£6.99
99807 9	MONTENEGRO	Starling Lawrence	£6.99
99580 0	CAIRO TRILOGY 1: PALACE WALK	Naguib Mahfouz	£9.99
77200 3	NO WONDER I TAKE A DRINK	Laura Marney	£6.99
77095 7	LONDON IRISH	Zane Radcliffe	£6.99
99645 9	THE WRONG BOY	Willy Russell	£6.99
77204 6	SAINT VALENTINE	Nick Tomlinson	£6.99
99864 8	A DESERT IN BOHEMIA	Jill Paton Walsh	£6.99